How I Survived
A Nightmare

Vance Albright

Other works by Vance Albright

Depths of Paradise

Cover Designer: Brandi Doane McCann. https://www.ebook-coverdesigns.com

Developmental Editor: Savannah Gilbo. https://www.savannahgilbo.com

Spelling and Grammar Editor: Sara Kelly. https://reedsy.com/sara-kelly

E-book 978-1-7340628-3-0

Paperback 978-1-7340628-1-6

Website https: https://lightanddarknovelizations.com

Facebook page: https://www.facebook.com/lightanddarknovelizations

Business E-mail: lightanddarknovelizations@gmail.com

Chapter 1

Tara Cymric awoke to the sound of loud beeping. She groggily reached out to turn off the alarm clock. She stretched with a yawn and threw the covers off her body. Before she got out of bed, the bedroom door opened. Her boyfriend Brandon Aiden was holding a breakfast tray. A vase with a purple rose adorned the tray. A plate with a strawberry crepe and maple-roasted bacon was placed in the center, and a cup of chocolate mocha sat next to them.

"Aww, Brandon, what's this for? When did you have time to make this?" she asked, staring at her handsome boyfriend as the pleasant aroma filled her nose, fully awakening her.

"Hey, I'm a master chef," he replied, sitting the tray on the nightstand next to her.

Tara looked at him skeptically.

"Okay, I went down to Breakfast World and ordered it for you."

"Still sweet of you." Touching his clean-shaven face, Tara replied before eating a piece of bacon. "Seriously, what's the occasion?" They had been together a little over a year, during which time she had learned Brandon only did stuff like this for special occasions.

"We're celebrating your new modeling job." Brandon paused, realizing he may have hit a nerve. A look of bitterness formed on Tara's face.

"We shouldn't need to celebrate my new job. I should have never lost my old one," Tara said, shoving the pillow off the bed in frustration. Her light blue eyes met Brandon's brown eyes. "I mean, I was only the hottest model Summer to Winter Fashion had, so what if I didn't always show up on time?"

"Everyone makes mistakes and letting you go was sure a big one," Brandon replied, stroking her shoulder length light blue hair.

"At least you found me a new one quickly. I still can't believe you managed to negotiate that deal," Tara said, impressed.

"I'm glad you think so. I thought Dimitri low balled me."

"Five hundred dollars for a few hours of work is not low balling," Tara replied, looking at him with starry eyes, grateful Brandon had found her a new job just when she had nearly given up looking.

"If you say so. I just wish the job site weren't so far away. If something happens it will take me a while to come save you."

Tara shook her head and laughed a little. "My knight in shining armor," she said, rubbing his blond hair. "Waterford is only an hour and a half away. I've driven longer than that for a photo shoot. By the way, how did you meet Dimitri anyway?" Tara asked for her own curiosity.

"He's a friend of mine from college. After college he started his fitness company and I became a boring bank manager at New Castle Bank."

"Nothing to be ashamed of," Tara replied. After finishing her breakfast, Tara got out of bed and showered. She changed into her photo shoot gear: a purple sports bra and purple exercise pants. She looked in the mirror, admiring her healthy slim build. Her attention soon turned to her hair, noticing the pink tips were starting to fade. *I'll have to get Romy to re-dye these,* she thought. She exited the bathroom and went to the kitchen. Brandon was sitting at the kitchen table with his work laptop, finishing his own breakfast of sunny-side-up eggs and toast. Being a bank manager, he had the luxury of working from home several days each week. She noticed Brandon looking closely at her outfit.

"You're planning on wearing that tonight, right?" Brandon asked in a lustful voice.

"Maybe," Tara replied, using her index finger to gently tap him on the nose. She sat down next to him and played on her phone, occasionally talking to him while he worked.

At nine-fifteen, Brandon, pointing to the clock, said, "Tara."

She glanced at the clock. "Aww, shoot!" she said, getting up. After taking several minutes to find her keys, which were in the right pocket of the pants she had worn the previous night, she returned to the kitchen and kissed Brandon on the cheek.

"I'm meeting Romy for dinner, so I won't be home until around ten."

"It's okay; I'll order out." They kissed again, then Tara headed for the door. She abruptly stopped and moon walked back to Brandon with a look of forgetfulness on her face.

"Do you happen to know where the contract Dimitri sent over is?"

"I believe it's on top of the dresser," he replied. "You should have gotten organized last night instead of playing on your phone and watching TV."

"That's what my hero's for," Tara answered, returning from the bedroom holding the contract. "Found it. Emergency avoided," she said, intentionally being overdramatic.

"Have fun at the shoot. I'm sure it's an experience you'll never forget." The two shared a kiss, then Tara left her apartment. It was a pleasant seventy-five-degree spring day in New Castle, Pennsylvania. The leaves had returned to the trees and the grass was nearly long enough for the first cut of the season. Tara took a moment to admire the flowers that were beginning to bloom around the apartment complex. She thought years ahead to when she and Brandon would have enough money to purchase a home of their own.

The first landscaping project on her list was a koi pond surrounded by tiger lilies. The thoughts brought her feelings of joy and excitement for the future.

Tara's thoughts returned to the present when she heard the landscaper say,

"Good morning." Tara politely smiled and waved back. *Creep. You're not even near my league,* she thought as she approached her car. She got in, typed the job address into her phone, and put on some pop music.

Chapter 2

After driving for about half an hour, Tara hit the favorite contacts button on the car's home screen and clicked "your sister."

After several rings she heard, "Hi, Tara."

"Hey," she said happily.

"Tara, turn the music down, I can barely hear you," Romy Cymric said.

Tara turned the radio off. "Happy?" she replied in a loud playful voice.

"Yes," Romy answered. Tara snickered, knowing her sister was rolling her eyes. "You're talking on Bluetooth, right?" Romy asked.

"No, I'm holding my phone going around eighty on the highway," Tara said seriously.

"Not funny, Tara," Romy replied.

"I have some fantastic news to tell you," Tara said in a giddy voice. "By the way, you're not with a client, right?"

"No, I'm in my office. What's this fantastic news?" Romy asked with interest.

"I got a new modeling job! On my way to a shoot now!" Tara answered with a happy yell.

"That's great news," Romy replied in a happy, surprised voice. "Where are you modeling at?"

"Some type of fitness company one of Brandon's college friends started in Waterford, Pennsylvania."

"That's like an hour away, right?" Romy asked.

"Three hours for the entire trip, not that bad. I should be back between three and four. I might hit the tanning salon before I drop by your house—getting kind of pale."

"Does five-thirty for dinner still work for you?"

"Sure," Tara confirmed.

"When did you get the job?" Romy asked, hearing about it for the first time.

"I found out yesterday at dinner. Sorry I didn't get around to telling you until now."

"You have a contract, right?" Romy asked.

A feeling of irritation came over Tara. She hated when her sister's business side came out. "Yes, Mom, I was sent a contract, not going to get screwed over."

"Sorry for watching out for my younger sister. Are you modeling for the gym equipment or clothing?" Romy inquired.

"I have no idea. I'll find out once I get there."

"Wait, you don't even know what you're modeling for?" Romy asked, slightly concerned. "What's the company's name?"

Tara thought for a moment, then said, "Dimitri's Gym Wears. Brandon said they don't have an official office building yet, so they're currently working out of Dimitri's apartment." Tara replied without a sign of worry in her voice.

"Wait, you're going to someone's apartment?" Romy asked, her concern growing.

Tara rolled her eyes. "Yes, Brandon knows the guy and researched the company, so everything is fine."

"Tara, I really don't like this; maybe you should cancel it," Romy suggested in a worried tone. Deep down Tara knew her sister was right. She should have researched the company and people herself. Normally, she would have before agreeing to model for them. However, since Brandon claimed to have known these people and she was desperate for work, she skipped that step.

"Look, Romy, I appreciate your concern, but everything will be fine. You need to loosen up a bit," Tara suggested. "Get out of your hair salon. Find a boyfriend, go have fun." Romy didn't reply right away. Worried she had upset her, Tara added, "Romy, don't worry, Brandon vouched for Dimitri. If someone tries anything, I'll let them know I have a brother in the Pittsburgh SWAT team, and if that doesn't work, I've taken a self-defense class and I always have my pepper blaster." The voice of the GPS caught Tara's attention. "Hey, Romy, the GPS has me doing about five turns coming up. I'll call you when I'm done with the shoot to let you know I'm alive."

"Not funny, be careful," Romy emphasized.

"I will. See you tonight." The two sisters said bye before Tara hung up.

◆　◆　◆

An hour later, Tara entered the parking lot of a small rundown motel. She parked near room number eight. The motel had sixteen rooms, eight on the ground floor and eight on the top floor. Two flights of stairs were located on each end of the building. *This looks real inviting.* She double checked the address on her phone. It matched the address showing on the GPS. Romy's warnings started to fill her head. Her internal radar was going off, telling her not to go in, drive off, and forget you were ever here.

"Like Brandon said, just a small startup business, **that's all,**" she said to herself, trying to ease her concerns. Tara looked in the car mirror, fixing her hair a final time. She glanced at the car clock, which read nearly ten minutes past eleven. Tara leaned back in her seat, frustrated she was ten minutes late. *I hope they have a grace period,* she thought.

She got out of the car and looked for room sixteen, soon spotting it on the upper level. She approached the staircase on the left only to be greeted by a pile of wet trash. Cockroaches and flies crawled over portions of decomposing food. A disgusted look formed on Tara's face. "Brandon, you're going to hear all about this when I get home." She walked over to the second set of stairs, which to her delight was clean. She walked up to room sixteen and knocked. A few seconds later the door opened.

"Hi, Tara?" the man asked.

"That's me," Tara said in a bubbly voice. Her voice gained an apologetic tone when she said, "I'm so sorry I'm late. The traffic was horrible."

"That's perfectly fine. Please come in; my name's Peter Jacobs," he said, extending his hand. Tara shook it, trying not to snicker at the man's nerdy look. *Virgin boy who dreams of getting with the models,* Tara thought. He was a thin built man with short brown hair. A pair of computer glasses sat on his clean-shaven face. Peter stepped aside so Tara could enter. She was pleased to see the room was pleasantly clean compared to the outside. A white studio backdrop was draped to the back wall. Two men sat on a couch, and another man sat at a folding table with a laptop. "Okay, Tara, let me introduce you to the team." Before he could continue, Tara's phone pinged. On instinct she looked at it.

"Sorry," she said, embarrassed, putting it back.

Peter continued. "The big guy on the couch is Ivan, and the man next to him is Miguel." Both men waved. Ivan was a bulky man with a stubby beard and shaved head. Miguel was Hispanic. He had an average build but was jacked. He had semi long black curly hair. Tattoos covered the length of both his arms. Both men looked to be around 6'1" and 6'3. "The man sitting at the table is Dimitri, our company's data collector and website manager." Dimitri was a thin built man with fair skin and brown hair. His handlebar mustache and goatee beard, along with the black suit, made him look like he was born one hundred years too late.

"Hello, Tara. You are as pretty as Brandon described you. Looking forward to working with you," Dimitri said, getting up to shake her hand.

"Thank you," Tara replied with a wide smile. *Wait, I thought Dimitri was the owner of the company? Why would Brandon be college friends with someone who looks at least twenty years older than him?* Tara thought.

"You're a friend of my boyfriend's, correct?" Tara asked, followed by her phone pinging. "Sorry," Tara said, noticing the look of annoyance on Dimitri.

She switched the phone to vibrate as Dimitri said, "Brandon was a bright student of mine I got along with well; if that qualifies, then yes, we were friends."

"So you were his teacher?" Tara confirmed, wondering why Brandon never mentioned that.

"Yes. I teach financial accounting part time, and work on growing my business full-time." Tara chose not to focus on the differences between his and Brandon's stories. She figured there was an explanation for them, plus she needed the money. She had been unemployed for a little over a month. Her living arrangement was Brandon paid the rent and she paid for food, utilities, and her car payment. Her savings were running low and she had too much pride to let him cover everything.

"Really nice setup you got here," Tara complimented. "Did the motel let you remove the beds?" she asked, noticing they were missing.

"The bed and bathroom is behind that door," Peter said, taking over the conversation. "I know the setup's not much at the moment, but we're a growing company and will soon have an actual office." The vibrating sound of Tara's phone filled the room.

"I'm sure you will. Now what would you like me to do?" Tara asked, anxious to start her new job. *I'm going to get fired before we begin,* she thought nervously.

"This is kind of embarrassing to ask, but would you mind placing your phone in the locker behind you?" Peter asked. Tara turned around to face the five foot metal locker behind her.

"Um, okay. Why do you want me to put my phone in there?" Tara replied, not feeling entirely comfortable with the idea. Peter noticed and gave a slightly embarrassed laugh.

"In the past we have had major problems with models and cell phones. Phones have gone off during shoots, like yours," Peter hinted. "Or a model would stop to text. It's really distracting, so our company policy is every phone goes in here during work hours." He opened four of the nine lockers. "See, even our phones are in here." Tara shrugged her shoulders.

"Okay, that makes sense." She turned her phone off and placed it in the locker.

"My baby's safely tucked away," Tara said with a sad face. "Now what would you like me to do?"

"Believe it or not, you're going to have a pretty easy day," Peter said.

"That's always good to hear," Tara replied.

"We already got the paperwork you signed online—any questions related to it?" Peter asked as he walked over to the studio backdrop and grabbed a sign lying next to it. Tara shook her head no. Peter handed her the sign. "For now all you need to do is hold this sign in front of the white backdrop." Tara looked at the white sign with the Chinese symbols 妓女 on it.

"If I have to read this, I have no idea what it says," Tara admitted.

"I didn't think you would. It's our company's name, which translates to Jìnǚ," Peter replied.

"Won't your customers need it in English to read?" Tara asked.

"It's for our Chinese customers," Peter replied. His voice was pleasant enough but Tara could tell the question annoyed him. Out of the corner of her eye she caught Miguel give her a momentary glare. Her internal radar started to go off again. Something about him and Ivan made her uneasy. *Why were they even here? And if it's a startup company, how did they have customers in China?* she thought. Once again she tuned the warnings out and tried to rationalize them. *Brandon knows these people. Ivan and Miguel are probably just the people who move the equipment around.* Tara wanted to ask more questions but soon decided against it. *You need this job and, more importantly, good references, so don't mess this up,* she thought. She thought about the past two jobs she had been let go from, and knowing she was gaining a bad reputation in the modeling field. Tara walked over to the table where Dimitri was sitting.

"Okay if I sit my purse down here?"

"Of course. Please," Dimitri replied. Tara set her purse down as Peter readied the camera sitting on a tripod. When he was ready, she walked in front of the backdrop. Having the camera in front of her brought her back to her element. She focused on it, removing the negative thoughts from her mind.

"Alright, Tara, give us a big smile," Peter said. Tara held the sign up and gave a happy smile. "Beautiful, now turn to the right, then the left." Tara changed to an open mouth and seductive smile on the two poses. "Those will do," Peter said in a natural voice. He took down the camera and handed it to Dimitri. "Okay, we're done."

"Wait, that's it? We're completely done?" Tara asked, surprised. The entire shoot had taken less than ten minutes. Now she was getting nervous; five hundred dollars for three photos did not make any sense.

"What did I just say?" Peter replied, this time not hiding the rudeness in his voice. Tara stood, still confused. Had she done something wrong? She saw Ivan and Miguel walk over to Dimitri. They began speaking in a language she did not recognize. The feeling of nervousness began turning to fear. The short photo shoot, and now she couldn't understand what the large men in the room were saying. At this point she didn't care about the money she was owed; she just wanted to go home. She waited until Ivan and Miguel moved from the table. To her relief, Ivan walked out the door.

Acting bubbly and unaware, she walked over to her purse and started digging in it. She had intentionally gone to the side of the table the laptop screen was facing, wanting to get a look at what Dimitri was up to. She pulled out some lip gloss and a travel mirror. She turned her back to Dimitri and started putting her lip gloss on while at the same time looking at Dimitri's computer screen though the mirror reflection. It was a trick her brother had taught her. She saw multiple copies of the photo set she had just done, only the language on the sign was different on each photo set. Spotting the set in English, she focused in on it. A stiff feeling of fear filled her entire body, and she could feel it beginning to tremble. Sweat started forming on her face and hands when she read the word prostitute.

She closed her mirror, shut her eyes, and breathed in heavily. *What do I do? What do I do?* she mentally said, nearly ready to panic. *Stay calm. Freaking out will only alert them that you know something's wrong,* her inner thoughts suggested. She walked back over to her purse and placed the mirror and lip gloss inside. *Okay, think, Tara, think,* she said to herself. *People know where you are. That's a start. Now how do you get out of here?* She knew her phone was out of reach. Now it made sense why they wanted it in the locker. *Okay, plan A. Grab your purse and start walking for the door, see if anyone takes notice.* She doubted it would work but it was worth a shot. Tara put the purse sling around her shoulder and started casually walking towards the door. Tara gave a slight gasp and her feeling of terror increased when she noticed the dead bolt and door handle were locked.

"Hey, where are you going?" Miguel asked.

"The photo shoot is over so I'm heading out," Tara replied, still walking at a slower pace to avoid suspicion.

"Why leave so soon; do you have somewhere to be?" Miguel replied.

"Actually yes, I'm heading to my next modeling job, and after that I have a dinner date with my sister and possibly my brother if nothing happens that needs a SWAT team." Tara hoped the mention of her brother being in the SWAT team would scare them off.

"No, no, we're not done yet. We have a lot more stuff to do," Miguel insisted in a tone that said *listen or else*. Tara noticed mentioning the SWAT team didn't faze any of them.

Putting on an act, Tara said with a bubbly smile, "Well, if you want to take more photos, I'm game." She turned her back to Miguel. *This is not good, this is not good.* Out of the corner of her eye she noticed Dimitri moving nearer to the door. She swallowed hard, knowing she was going to have to fight her way out. She had taken a self-defense class with her brother. One on one, she thought she could knock down Peter and Dimitri long enough to escape, but there was no way she could win against someone Miguel's size. *Okay, you can't win in a straight-up fight, but you might be able to outsmart them.* Tara set her purse back down and reached into it. Inside she was still trembling but managed to keep a calm appearance on the outside.

"What are you doing?" Miguel asked, walking over to her.

"Bubble gum break," Tara replied, talking out a roll of it. She put some in her mouth and offered some to Miguel; he refused. "You two want some?" She offered Peter and Dimitri, but both men ignored her. Tara looked at

Miguel and seductively blew a bubble. She put the gum back in her purse while staring at him with interested eyes. With his focus on her, she grabbed her pepper blaster. Keeping it out of eyesight, she hid it between her pants and hand. She walked in front of Miguel, putting herself between him and the door.

"Ugh, my shoulders are stiff," she said, moving them. Thinking he got the hint, Miguel walked over to her and started rubbing them. "That feels much better." She sighed happily. She smiled slightly because he was right where she wanted him. With all her might and flexibility, Tara kicked her leg backward, hitting Miguel between the legs. He fell over screaming in pain.

One down, Tara thought as she bolted for the door. Now it was time to deal with Dimitri, who was strategically positioned between her and the door. She pulled out her pepper blaster and fired. She hit her target dead on.

Dimitri knelt down, howling in pain as the liquid spray dripped down into his eyes. *Only one left.* As she grabbed the door handle with her left hand, Peter grabbed her left shoulder, trying to slam her to the ground. With her left hand keeping her upright, she and Peter's eyes locked.

"Try using your little toy on me," he dared.

A confused look formed on Peter's face as he looked into Tara's confident grin. Since he was wearing glasses, she fired at his forehead. The spray flowed down into his eyes. Just like Dimitri, he fell to the ground.

Tara pulled the door open, turning her head to make sure Miguel was still on the ground. She ran outside, feeling the pleasant spring air right before a large arm clotheslined her. The next thing she knew she was looking up at the motel's outdoor celling. Her vision was blurred, a loud ringing sound filling her ears. She could taste blood in her mouth. She reached for her nose and felt a steady stream of blood coming from it. *What happened, where am I?* she thought, disoriented by the blow. She felt a hand clamp around her leg and everything came back to her. She looked up to see Ivan dragging her back inside the motel room. She used her free leg to kick him in the stomach, causing him to lose his grip. Tara spun herself on her stomach and started crawling. Seconds later, she felt hands around her legs again.

"Help!" she screamed as loud as she could. "Somebody help me!" A hand covered her mouth before she could let out a third scream. Her mind was in survival mode, knowing she had to escape before she was taken back inside. Tara opened her mouth, causing her lower jaw to slip under Ivan's hand. She bit down, hoping to force him to release his grip.

"Miguel, help me get this stupid bitch inside!" Ivan yelled. Recovered, Miguel grabbed both her legs. The two stronger men easily started pulling her back. Tara grabbed on to the door frame in an attempt to prevent herself from getting pulled back inside. Miguel released a leg and used his free hand to slam the door against her fingers. The pain caused her to release her hold. With a hand still covering her mouth, Ivan lifted her up and slammed her back against the floor. The impact knocked the wind out of Tara. She tried to breathe, but Ivan's hand around her mouth and nose was nearly suffocating her. "Miguel, grab the drug!" Ivan ordered.

"I'll do more than that," he said, lifting his leg for a kick. Tara winced.

"No, grab the drug!" Ivan reinforced. Miguel noticed Dimitri and Peter were still on the ground, so he did as Ivan asked. Tara tilted her head to see Miguel reaching into the locker. "That's right, you lose," Miguel taunted. In a last ditch effort, Tara moved both hands to Ivan's face, hoping to stab him in the eye, still clinging to the hope of escaping, but the fighting and damage her body had sustained had drained most of her strength. As a result, her arms did not move nearly as quickly as she planned. Ivan caught both her arms with his free hand, and then he moved his knee onto her throat, slamming

Tara's arms to the floor, his vice-like grip making it impossible to move. Miguel knelt down next to her with a medical syringe in his hand.

"No, no, please!" Tara begged. Her words fell on deaf ears. Miguel rammed the needle into her arm. Tara felt lightheaded, and then everything went black.

Chapter 3

Tara Cymric let out a moan as she slowly awoke.

"Where am I?" she asked, looking around the small room she was lying in. She licked her lips, tasting the dried blood from her nose. She touched her forehead, feeling a slight bump. She had no idea where she was or how long she had been unconscious. Suddenly the memories of what had occurred came flooding back to her. She quickly got to her feet. The effects of the drug made her feel dizzy, and the room was slightly spinning. She used the wall for balance as she walked towards the room's bay window. The moment she reached it, she saw the steel mesh covering it. *Please, God, no!* she said silently. Having a good idea what her kidnapers wanted from her, her first urge was to start screaming for help, but she knew that would only alert them to the fact she had woken up. *The door's a better option,* she thought. She quietly walked over to the door and turned the knob, and to her surprise the door started to open. She opened it enough to peek her head out. Any hope of escape faded when she saw Miguel and Peter standing in the hallway. They spotted her immediately. Tara tried to slam the door shut. Miguel placed his boot in the door frame and tore it open, knocking Tara to the ground.

"Enjoy your nap?" Peter asked in a casual voice. "My eyes are fine, by the way."

"Don't worry, we're under strict orders not to harm you. Unless, of course, you do something stupid," Miguel said.

"So please do something stupid," Peter added.

"Now get up. Time to meet your new employer," Miguel ordered, showing a hostile pistol. Knowing she had no choice, Tara reluctantly exited the room. A hallway went in both directions. They began walking to the right,

Miguel in front, Peter behind her. At first Tara needed to hug the wall for balance, but the more she walked, the less vertigo she felt. After several yards, the hallway took another right turn. After walking several more yards, Tara saw a room on her left; from her momentary glance, she thought it could have been a medical room. A yard or so ahead, Miguel turned to his left and knocked on a closed door with an eye in the center. The sclera was black, the iris was bright blue, and the pupil was green, making it slightly resemble a picture of the world taken from space. He opened it, then motioned for Tara to go through.

When she walked in, she stood on a red velvet carpet. The room had a matching red velvet antique Victorian-era sofa and four antique Victorian-era chairs. Red velvet curtains hung on the sides of the room's large bay window.

"What is this place?" Tara asked out loud, taken back by the sudden change in scenery.

"Ah, Tara. Welcome to Heartwood Manor. Please sit down," a women said in a thick Eastern European accent. Tara's head turned to a woman wearing grey business attire sitting in one of the chairs. She appeared to be in her late thirties. She had light skin, a thin build, brown eyes, and blond hair kept in a neat bun. Tara's eyes scanned the room, searching for an exit. She grunted when Peter's hand smacked the back of her head.

"Move!" he commanded. Slowly, Tara moved to the seat across from the woman. She didn't feel any better about the situation, but at least she might get some answers. She sat down on the couch across from her, while Miguel and Peter sat in two of the chairs.

"Who are you? Where am I?" Tara asked in a soft yet demanding voice. She was hoping acting confident would help hide the fact that inside she was trembling. Her brother Ryan had told her bad guys like the scared girls that would beg for mercy.

"My name is Nora Peters, your momentary employer, and you're in Heartwood Manor, every girl's dream," she replied smugly as she took a puff from her cigarette.

Okay, she told me the name of the location I'm in, Tara noticed.

"Where's Heartwood Manor? Why did you kidnap me?" Tara asked, hoping Nora would reveal something.

"Heartwood Manor is your new home," Nora replied. "You're going to be spending the rest of your life with us." Despite her best efforts, Tara felt a look of fear form on her face. Noticing it, Nora added, "Don't worry, the life of a prostitute can be glamorous. You might even learn to like it." Hearing that sent Tara into full blown panic mode. She remembered the sign she was holding said prostitute, so this women was not lying. On instinct, she resorted to her favorite threat.

"You really think you'll get away with this?" Tara said in a tough voice, trying to keep up her confident act. "I have a brother in the…"

Before she could finish, Nora spoke up. "In the Pittsburgh SWAT Team. Lieutenant Ryan Cymric, who is married to Krista Cymric. They have a six-month-old child named Ryan Jr." The look of confidence Tara had turned to a look of surprised shock. "You also have a sister Romy Cymric who owns a hair salon in Ellwood City, Pennsylvania. Both your parents died in a car accident when you were sixteen." Nora shrugged, then said in the same smug tone she used when they first met, "See, we know all about you." Tara felt her mouth go dry. *How did she know all this?*

Like she had read her mind, Nora asked, "You're wondering how I know all this?"

Tara did not reply. The shock and fear had paralyzed her vocal cords. She felt sweat forming on her forehead.

"Your boyfriend Brandon told me everything. In fact, he sold you to us." *No, that couldn't be true; it has to be a lie,* Tara thought. She tried to suppress it, but in the back of her mind it was starting to make sense. Brandon was the one who told her about the job and assured her the company was owned by a friend of his. Tara lowered her head, feeling her eyes watering up. She had tried to stay strong, but this new revelation was too much.

Tara heard a snapping sound inches from her face. She looked up to see Nora's hand in front of her.

Nora snapped her finger again. "Now that that is out of the way, I will explain your expected duties." Tara looked at her with a frightened expression. "You will provide sexual activities as requested for clients." Tara felt her breathing increase. She started shaking her head no from shock. "Blowjobs are one-fifty per session, sex is three hundred per hour." Tara felt tears starting to fall; this woman could not be serious. "Pony play is four-fifty per hour-long session and bondage is one thousand per hour-long session." Tara's face had turned pale, and her skin broke into a cold sweat. *No, this is not happening,* Tara thought, desperately trying to force herself to wake up.

"What's the matter, Tara? Aren't you going to try something sneaky?" Peter taunted.

"Please just let me go," Tara begged out of pure desperation.

"You seem frightened," Nora said, pretending to notice for the first time. "Don't worry. Now I'm going to explain some pleasant news." Tara gave a brief confused look. "You will keep fifty percent of your earnings. After your orientation period, if you are behaving, you will be free to walk to the dining and recreation area on your own." Nora's voice got stern. "All other parts of the facility are off limits. Under supervision you can use your money to buy

food, clothes, and any furniture you desire." Nora sat back down. "Now, as unpleasant as this is for me, I will now explain to you what will happen if you become a problem." Nora's tone became more menacing when she said, "If you refuse to preform, you will be punished. If your own pain is not enough motivation, we will harm a member of your family. We have creative ways of doing that." Tara swallowed in fear as thoughts of the different ways these people might harm her or her family filled her head. "I'm sure escaping has crossed your mind, so I'm giving you a warning before you try it. The organization I work for is Omnipotent. Meaning we see everything, and have the power to do anything." Nora pointed to the door. "The eye symbols on the doors act as a consent reminder that we are always watching. If you do manage to escape, you will not get far, and as punishment, someone you love will die." Nora got up again and walked up to Tara. Now standing inches from her, she said, "In front of you." The reality she may never get out of this situation broke through; even if she did escape, these people would find out where she was and recapture her.

That was too much for Tara to handle, and she felt herself beginning to hyperventilate. In a panic, she started crying and begging. "Please let me go, I'll pay you whatever you want, I'll give you whatever you want."

"Now, now, don't cry," Nora said, gently slapping her to bring her attention towards her. "We want our employees to be happy here." She motioned for Miguel and Peter to come over. "Please take Miss Tara back to her room; we want to give her time to adjust to her new surroundings." Still in shock, Tara started to go with them without speaking or putting up a fight. As they approached the door, Tara turned to Nora. She needed a question answered. With heartbroken eyes, she asked, "How much?" She stopped as she began to choke on her words. "How much did Brandon get for me?"

Sitting back down, Nora gave a brief smug laugh. "He originally wanted one hundred thousand, but we talked him down to fifty. We'll make our

money back in no time, I'm sure." Tears started rolling down Tara's face. *That's all I was worth to you, Brandon?* She still did not understand how any human could sell someone they loved, someone they spend days of their life with for money.

Getting impatient, Miguel shoved her forward. Moments later, Miguel opened the door to Tara's room. Tara walked in almost in a trance state. *This couldn't really be happening, could it?*

"See you in a week," Miguel said before shutting and locking the door. Tara slowly walked to the bay window. She could see a grass lawn dotted with different types of trees. Several acres of land separated the building from what looked to be a ten foot wall that seemed to stretch around the compound. Not seeing anything of interest, she turned her attention to the room. The only thing in the room was a toilet in the corner farthest from the room door, and she also noticed another door that was located directly across from the room door. Tara approached it, thinking it might lead to a neighboring room where another victim was being held. As much as the thought sickened her, she hoped someone else was behind the door so that she wouldn't have to suffer alone.

Tara held her ear against the door and lightly tapped on it. Hearing nothing on the other side, she turned the knob. The door opened to a small empty closet. Tara slammed the door in frustration, then put her back to the wall and slowly fell down. When she felt her body stop, she stared straight ahead, an occasional tear running down her cheek. *How could this have happened?* she thought. She had heard about human trafficking and sex slaves on TV, but she never dreamed it would happen to her. More tears formed as she thought of Romy and Ryan. *Will I ever see them again?*

Chapter 4

Romy Cymric held her phone tightly to her ear as she nervously paced in her living room. Again Tara's phone went straight to voicemail. Tara was now three hours late. Romy knew Tara was irresponsible, but she had never been this late without at least a text. Plus, she knew Tara could not go two seconds without her phone. Romy dialed another number, hoping Tara had just had a terrible day and decided to blow off their dinner plans without telling her.

"Hello," she heard Brandon's voice say.

"Hey, Brandon, it's Romy. Did Tara come home or call you?"

"No, I thought she was with you," Brandon said, puzzled. Now Romy was really worried.

"Tara's not with me!" Romy said in a worried tone. "I have not heard from her since this morning."

"Maybe the photo shoot's taking longer than expected," Brandon suggested. "I mean, we both know how irresponsible she can be."

"No, that's not it. If she were having fun, she would have called to cancel our dinner plans, and if she were miserable, she would have left and then called to complain."

"Good point," Brandon replied, now sounding worried himself. Romy nervously ran her fingers through her black hair; then she remembered something Tara had said.

"Wait. Tara said you knew the owner of the company she's doing the photo shoot for. Do you have his number?" Romy asked hopefully.

"Unfortunately, the only communication I had with the company was over email. I gave Tara the lead, and she handled the rest." *That's not what Tara told me,* Romy thought, confused by the differences in Brandon's and Tara's accounts.

"This morning Tara told me you knew the owner," Romy said seriously.

"Dimitri was an old college professor of mine, but we have not talked in years. We're not even friends on social media. I explained all that to her when I gave her the website link and email address."

"Well, that's just great!" Romy replied. The concern for Tara she was feeling caused her tone to be more vicious then she intended.

"Look, I don't know what I did wrong?" Brandon asked.

"Maybe you shouldn't have let Tara go model for a place neither of you knew anything about!" Romy snapped.

"Romy, yes, I should have looked into the company more, but since I knew the owner of the company, the thought of the modeling job being dangerous honestly never crossed my mind," Brandon replied in a pleasant tone but one that also showed he did not appreciate Romy's hostility towards him.

"Sorry, Brandon," Romy apologized. "I'm really worried about Tara. Aren't you?"

Brandon laughed a little. "Honestly, I think she made some new girlfriends at the modeling job and is having fun and lost track of time," Brandon said seriously. "If you recall, she has disappeared for a few hours before." Romy remembered the several occasions when Tara had gone out partying and did not answer her phone or come home until well after midnight.

"I hope you're right," Romy replied with worry still in her voice. Brandon's calm demeanor made her wonder if she was overreacting.

Brandon's calm tone continued when he assured, "If we don't hear from her by tomorrow, I'll have a missing persons poster on every billboard and utility pole in the state."

"A lot can happen between now and tomorrow," Romy countered.

"If you're that concerned about her, why don't you call your brother, Ryan?"

Romy closed her eyes and thought for a moment, then replied, "No, you're right, it's probably Tara being Tara." Romy tried to convince herself he was right. "Please, let me know if you hear from her, and when you do, give her a lecture about calling people to let them know you're okay!"

"You'll be my first call, and I'll scold her for not inviting me to her night out," Brandon replied in a charming voice.

"Scold her for missing her dinner plans with her sister!" Romy replied in a slightly happier tone.

"I will. Talk to you later, Romy."

"Talk to you later. Hopefully we hear from her soon," Romy said and ended the call.

◆　◆　◆

Romy sat in front of her computer, listening to the eleven o'clock news. While listening, she searched the internet for any accidents or hospital admissions along Tara's travel area. Romy heard her phone buzzing and picked it up. She looked at the caller id, which read Brandon Aiden.

"Hello," she answered, hoping he had good news.

Brandon's voice was full of concern when he said, "Romy, Tara still hasn't come home yet. Please tell me you heard from her."

"No, I haven't." She breathed heavily. "Something's wrong. I'm calling Ryan." She regretted not calling him sooner. "How soon can you be at my house?"

"I'll leave as soon as I get off the phone with you. I might still have Dimitri's phone number. I'll bring it along if I find it."

"That would be great," Romy replied. She said bye, hung up, and dialed Ryan's number. *I should have done this earlier this morning,* Romy thought, regretting her decision to let Tara go to a job she thought was sketchy.

"Hey, Romy. You alright?" he asked, knowing Romy normally was in bed by eleven-thirty.

"No, Ryan. Something's wrong. Tara, she's…" Romy paused to hold back tears. "She's missing. Neither Brandon nor I have heard from her since this morning. She's not replying to texts and when I try to call, her phone goes straight to voicemail."

"Romy, how long has she been gone and does anyone know where she went?" Ryan asked in a serious tone. Romy quickly explained the conversation her and Tara had that morning. "Romy, you should have called me as soon as you thought something was wrong. Time is essential in a possible kidnapping." Romy choked up as a few tears ran down her cheek, knowing she might have been able to prevent it.

"I know I should have. I wanted to believe nothing was wrong so I kept telling myself Tara had a bad day and went to a bar or something to blow off steam."

"Is Brandon with you?"

"Brandon's heading over here as we speak. I really need you here."

"I'll be there in about an hour," Ryan replied. "I'm going to start a missing persons report and I need you and Brandon to give me the following information. Do you have a pen handy?"

"Notepad's opened on my phone," Romy replied, fighting through her tears, knowing helping Ryan would do more for Tara then regretting her past mistakes.

"I need a description of the clothes she was wearing when she left, a list of possessions she had on her—jewelry, wallet that kind of stuff—a list of places Tara normally goes to, and a written account of where she went and what she was doing. I also need a list of Tara's credit cards so we can monitor them for use."

"Got it. I'll get this to you soon. Need anything else?"

"When he gets there, see if Brandon knows Tara's social media passwords." *I'm not sure he'll know it,* Romy thought, knowing Tara never gave her passwords to anyone.

"Okay, see you soon," Romy said and hung up.

An hour later, Romy and Brandon sat around Romy's kitchen table. Two cups of coffee sat in front of them. Brandon was on a laptop trying to figure out Tara's social media passwords. Romy sent out emails and texts to her two employees, explaining the situation and that she was going to be away for a few days. A knock at the door sent Romy bolting towards it. She opened it and immediately fell into her brother's arms.

"I'm glad you're here," she said, releasing the hug. "Have you found anything?"

He placed a gentle arm on the back of her neck. "Let's sit down so we can begin planning our next moves." Ryan Cymric was in his early thirties with a slim muscular build and short black hair. "Brandon, you doing okay?" he asked, offering his hand before he sat down.

Brandon shook it and said, "I'm trying to keep my mind off how much I miss Tara so I can focus on finding her."

"I wish I could do that. I don't know how you can be so calm?" Romy added, annoyed that Brandon still felt Tara was just fooling around. Romy handed Ryan a cup of coffee before sitting down. "Did you file the missing persons report?"

"Yes, I've filed a missing persons report, issued an APB on Tara, and contacted the National Missing and Unidentified Persons System, so they will be keeping an eye out for her. I also checked the state databases. No one matching Tara's description has been discovered dead or has been admitted to the hospital."

"I thought we had to wait twenty-four hours to file a missing persons report?" Brandon commented. Romy looked at Ryan, believing the same thing herself.

"Only in Hollywood. In reality you should contact police the moment you suspect a family member or friend is missing," Ryan replied. Romy felt a look of guilt and regret form on her face, envying her siblings for having significant others. Having someone to vent their feels to or cry in their arms.

"Any luck getting into Tara's social media accounts?" Ryan continued.

"So far, no. The good news is I know she uses the same passwords for everything. I sent Dimitri's business website to you, and I sent an email to him explaining the situation; unfortunately, I don't have his personal number anymore." *Why would you explain the situation to him if he's involved?* Romy wondered, thinking Brandon had made a mistake, but then she realized something. In an excited voice, she said, "Wait! Tara told me the modeling job was at this Dimitri guy's apartment. We know where he lives!"

"That's not what I told her," Brandon said, looking like he was annoyed by Tara was twisting people's words again.

"Wait, what?" Romy asked, surprised.

"I said she would be working out of an apartment. If you look on the company's website…" Romy slammed the table in frustration, cutting him off. *Tara, you idiot.*

"You have got to be kidding me," Romy said, tearing up.

"Romy, calm down; let's look over the website and see what we can learn," Ryan suggested. Knowing her brother was right and appreciating him being the voice of reason despite missing and worrying about Tara himself, she nodded an apology to Brandon and lay back in her chair. "Brandon, can I see the laptop please?" Brandon slid the laptop over to him.

"I'm already on Dimitri's website. Dimitri's Gym Wears." The website's main page had ten different male and female gym and workout clothes with a banner above it, saying "Dimitri's gym wears." Other than the shopping cart and checkout page, the site had two other links: the "about" section and "model for us." Ryan skimmed over the gym clothes, but none of the models were Tara.

"He might not have put the photos up yet?" Brandon suggested.

"Or she never made it to the photo shoot," Ryan said, thinking out loud.

"If that were the case, don't you think Dimitri would have called to complain?" Brandon asked.

"Not if he only had Tara's cell phone number," Ryan pointed out. Ryan clicked the "model for us" link. The text read:

"We are currently traveling the East Coast to advertise our product. In each new city, we are looking for one or more models to wear our product or promote our brand. If interested, fill out the information below."

Ryan looked over the requested information and saw nothing unusual. He then clicked on the "about" page. It was a photo of Dimitri and gave details about the business. Below it was a link that gave a list of cities on their upcoming tour. Ryan clicked it, and Romy gasped when she saw three pictures of Tara holding signs that said State College, Pennsylvania, Bel Air, Maryland, and Lynchburg, Virginia. The background was the centerpiece of each city.

"Well, we know she made it to the photo shoot. What's our next move?" Brandon asked.

Ryan thought for a moment and said, "You go home and get some sleep. In the morning, see if you can find anything that will help you get into Tara's social media accounts, and write down anything you can remember about your old professor. Meet us back here at eight."

"I can do that," Brandon replied. He shook Ryan's hand and shared a brief hug with Romy. As they embraced, she again found herself wishing she had a boyfriend or husband to share her feelings with.

"I'm going to start printing out missing persons photos," Romy said, sitting in front of her laptop.

"Romy, that can wait. We should get some sleep too; we're going to have a big day tomorrow." Romy gave him a shocked look. "How can you even think about sleeping when our little sister is missing?"

"Romy, we have done all we can tonight; right now the best thing we can do for Tara is get some sleep so we're well rested and able to think clearly tomorrow." Ryan placed both his hands on her shoulders and said in soft voice, "Now go get ready for bed." Hearing her older brother tell her to get ready for bed made her feel like she was a child, but she knew he was right.

"Ryan, can you stay here tonight? I would feel a lot better if you're here."

"Okay, I'll call my wife and take the guest bedroom."

Romy smiled, then went into the bathroom to get ready for bed. While she was brushing her teeth, she could hear Ryan talking to Krista. She dropped her toothbrush and listened more intently when she heard Ryan say,

"I'm really concerned about Tara. If I'm right, she's in a very bad situation."

Romy exited the bathroom while Ryan and Krista were making small talk. As she grabbed a pillow and two blankets, she wondered if she should ask Ryan about his comment about Tara. She walked over to Ryan just as he was ending the call.

"Sheets are already on the bed, Ryan," she said, handing him the pillow and blankets. She briefly placed both hands over her face and asked, "Why did you say you think Tara's in a bad situation?"

Ryan sighed and said in a slightly frustrated tone, "I wish you didn't hear that."

"Well, I did. Ryan, please tell me what you think happened."

Knowing he had no choice, he replied, "There's no easy way to say this, Romy. It's looking more and more like Tara was kidnapped by human traffickers." Romy placed a hand over her mouth and gasped. Images of Tara locked in a cage in the back of truck began filling her head.

"God, please, no," Romy said as several tears rolled down her cheek. Ryan placed the pillow and blanket on the floor.

"Come here," Ryan said, hugging her, which helped calm her down a little.

After they released, Romy said in a reassuring voice, "We don't know for sure if she was kidnapped. If she was, the situation's not as bad as it could be. We have a pretty good idea where Tara went missing, and we have the name of a possible suspect."

"Tara freaks out when she sees a spider and can barely handle it when she can't get cell service. I can't imagine how frightened she must be if she's been kidnapped."

"She might surprise you," Ryan replied.

"How?" Romy asked, confused.

"Remember the few times I managed to get her to play chess with me?"

"Ya, you won every game," Romy answered, having no idea where he was going with this.

"I did, but it wasn't as easy as when I played against you or anyone else."

Romy huffed in frustration. It was late, and she was worried and tired. "Ryan, why are you even bringing this up?"

"Tara was playing with no motivation, and she always managed to make me seriously think out every move." Romy gave him a look that said *get to the point*. "My point is Tara has a hidden talent as a natural strategist. If she's able to keep her head, I'd bet she will find a way to escape."

"I hope you're right," Romy said, still not sure if she believed him. After that, the siblings said goodnight and turned in for the night, knowing they had a long unpleasant day ahead of them.

Chapter 5

The next morning, the ringing of her phone woke Romy. Romy tiredly rubbed her eyes, thinking it was someone from work calling out. When she saw the caller id, she quickly grabbed it and asked, "Hey, Brandon, did you find anything?"

"I'm on my way over with good news."

"We could use some. What is it?" Deep down she knew it was false hope, but she was hoping he was going to say Tara came home last night.

"I hit the jackpot. Last night I found the password to Tara's social media accounts. I'll text it to you as soon as I end the call."

"Has she used them?" Romy asked, hoping they would have some clues.

"Not since yesterday morning. She posted about driving to the modeling job, mostly complaining about traffic." That made Romy grin—typical Tara.

"Well, it's something," Romy replied.

"I'm not done yet," Brandon continued. "I was digging through some of my old stuff from college and managed to find Dimitri's number."

"Brandon, that's great! You're like my hero right now!" *We're on the right track, and we're going to find Tara today,* Romy thought.

"Thought I always was," Brandon replied in a cocky voice. The comment made Romy's eyes move up, and then she said happily, "I'll tell Ryan the good news. See you soon."

Romy put the phone down and started walking down her small hallway. She noticed the guest bedroom door was open. *Ryan must be up already,* she thought. She made a detour to the bathroom, then walked to the end of the hall that opened to a living room connected to a small kitchen. She was pleased to see Ryan was already hard at work. She was not pleased that the clock read seven-thirty.

"How long have you been up?" she asked, noticing the plate full of pancakes.

"Since six," he replied. "Not much of a cook, but I made pancakes for everyone."

"Wish you would have woken me up," Romy stated, more than a little annoyed as she poured herself some coffee. *Thanks for making me feel more useless,* she thought, knowing Brandon and Ryan had both found useful information, while she slept in.

"I wanted to let you sleep. I've been doing police stuff, so you really didn't miss much."

"Brandon's on his way." Romy sat down and explained everything Brandon had told her.

"That's great. I'll call Dimitri around nine."

Why not now? Romy wondered. Instead of asking that she said, "Have you found anything?" Ryan gave her a look that told her the news was not good. Romy closed her eyes, preparing herself for the coming mental blow.

"I was able to trace Tara's cell phone. The signal was coming from a garbage dump near Waterford."

Romy put her head down and said, "Noo," softly, knowing Ryan was right about the human traffickers. After a few moments, she regained her composure and asked, "What can I do to help?"

"Create a missing persons poster and send it to Brandon. Have him get about two hundred created at a printing shop. While he's doing that, start calling or messaging all of Tara's contacts."

Romy picked up her phone. When Brandon picked up, she said, "Hey, how close are you?" Romy asked while she opened a Photoshop program on her laptop.

"About fifteen minutes."

"I need you to do me a favor?"

"What do you need?" he replied.

"In about ten minutes I'll be sending you a missing persons photo I need you to stop by Ken's Printing & Marketing Services to get two hundred missing persons flyers made, and I will reimburse you."

"Romy, Tara's missing; don't worry about it."

"Thank you, Brandon. Hopefully we get some good news today." After creating the poster, Romy brought up four web tabs, each with a different social media site. She typed in Tara's password, which was HottiewithBluehair223. She started messaging Tara's friends and contacts, hoping one of them had heard from her. While she worked on Tara's contacts, Ryan made arrangements with the local news and radio stations to broadcast Tara's story. It was around eight-thirty when Romy was halfway through Tara's listed friends and contacts.

"Do you want to give Dimitri a call?" Romy asked. She'd been wanting Ryan do it since she got up but understood why he wanted to wait. A person angry about getting called so early would be no help at all.

Ryan, who was looking up information on the Old Time Waterford Motel, looked at the clock. "It's late enough. I'll call him."

"Can you put the call on speaker?" Romy asked with a smile, wanting to hear the conversation.

"Get me a pair of headphones."

Romy reached into her purse and handed him a pair of green headphones. Ryan opened an app that allowed him to record the call.

"Is that legal?" Romy asked.

"Unfortunately, Pennsylvania is a two party consent state, so I need to tell Mr. Dimitri he's talking on a recorded line."

"So, if he says no, you will have to turn it off."

Ryan shrugged his shoulders. "I'll tell him I did."

Romy's mouth dropped slightly, not believing her strict law-following brother had said that. *Ryan, you're willing to go that far for Tara?* Romy thought, knowing doing that would be risking his career.

Ryan handed an ear bud to her and hit call. Anticipation filled Romy's body, hoping Ryan could get a lead.

"Hello, Dimitri speaking," a voice said moments later. Romy gasped when she heard him.

"Hello, this is First Lieutenant Ryan Cymric with Pittsburgh SWAT speaking to you on a recorded line. How are you today?"

"Doing fine, sir. May I ask what this call is about?"

"I understand that yesterday, you conducted a photo shoot with a women named Tara Cymric."

"Yes, officer, that is correct." Dimitri paused for a moment, then said, "Wait, you're Tara's brother? Tara's check should have cleared, but I'll be happy to clear up any misunderstanding with her."

Ryan laughed a little. "That's not what I'm calling about. I wanted to ask you a few questions about the photo shoot."

"Should I be looking into hiring a lawyer?" Dimitri asked seriously.

"No, you're not under suspicion. I just have some questions. Tara never returned home last night and I was hoping to get some information from you."

"Sorry to hear that. I'm afraid due to company policy, I cannot send you any of the photos we took or share any information about our employees or the photo shoot itself."

"I don't need any corporate information. I just have a few questions about Tara."

"I'll answer what I can," Dimitri replied.

"What time did Tara leave, and did she seem to be in distress? Like worrying about someone following her?"

"If I recall." The line was silent for a moment. *Did he hang up?* Romy wondered. "She left around one o'clock. We wrapped up the photo shoot around noon, she stayed for lunch, then left."

"What did you have for lunch?" A confused looked formed on Romy's face.

"Um, pizza. Why is that a relevant question?" Dimitri asked, unsure.

"I was just curious," Ryan replied. "Funny thing is Tara does not eat pizza." He winked at Romy when he said that. Romy smiled back, understanding what he was doing.

"Well, she ate it with us," Dimitri replied without any sign of nervousness or hesitation. "She had one piece of Hawaiian pizza and a small diet soda." If Dimitri was guilty, Ryan was hoping to trap him, but his story seemed true. The one unhealthy food Tara would eat was Hawaiian pizza.

"That makes sense; she does like Hawaiian pizza," Ryan confirmed.

"Did I pass your test?" Dimitri asked, showing he knew what Ryan was doing. "Do you need anything else?"

"I'll let you go in a moment. Can you give me the location of the photo shoot and copies of your company's records?" Ryan asked, wanting to see if Dimitri would give him the photo shoot location's address.

"I can give you the photo shoot location, but as I explained before, any company records are private; if you get a search warrant, I will gladly hand them over."

"I understand you concerns. Again, you're not under suspicion. I'm only trying to locate information that will help find my sister. I'm ready for the address now." Romy could hear Dimitri shuffling through some papers. She didn't know what to think about him. Was he guilty and good at lying or an honest business man who had nothing to do with Tara's disappearance?

"I admit I don't have the full address in front of me. The location is the Old Time Waterford Motel. It's an old beat-up motel located on PA 97 just outside the city of Waterford." Both siblings had looks of disappointments, realizing this was a dead end.

"That's all I needed. Thank you for your time," Ryan said.

"No problem, officer. I hope you find your sister, and tell Brandon I said hello and hope he is doing well."

Romy tapped Ryan on the shoulder. "How does he know you knew Brandon?" Romy whispered.

"He knows I'm Tara's brother, but I'll ask him," Ryan whispered back.

"I will. Just curious, how did you know I knew Brandon?"

"I put two and two together. You're Tara's brother and Tara's dating Brandon."

"Thank you again for your help, Dimitri."

"No problem. Goodbye," Dimitri said.

Great, now what do we do? Romy thought. A knock on the door caught her attention.

"Come in." Brandon opened the door to Romy's apartment holding an arm full of flyers under one arm.

"Sorry it took me so long. The printer was surprisingly slow." He set the flyers down on the circular wooden table. "How are things going here?" Brandon asked, sitting down.

"I'm messaging all of Tara's friends about the situation, asking for any information they have. Some have already responded wanting to help." Romy moved the laptop so he could see the event she created. "At noon a group of us our going to meet at your apartment complex. Everyone is going to take a stack of flyers and hang them between there and Waterford."

"While you guys do that, I'm heading up to Waterford to speak with the model staff to see if they know anything," Ryan added. "I can take some posters along and hang them around the area." Romy picked up a poster of Tara. *You'll be home soon,* she thought, looking at the picture of Tara smiling.

◆ ◆ ◆

After Ryan hung up, Nora Peters, who was listening in on the conversation, asked, "Do you think he'll become a problem?"

"I expect he'll do some digging, maybe call again."

"Should he be taken care of?" Nora asked, not wanting Tara's siblings to cause unwanted problems.

"I don't think that will be necessary," Dimitri replied. "I have no doubt Tara's siblings will continue to search for her, but they will be focusing on our decoy company, which is why we have it."

"Speaking of Tara's siblings, I heard Tara's sister Romy is not bad-looking herself?" Nora inquired.

"As you know, looks are one of many things that make a good product. We must also consider health, temperament, and age. From the photos, Romy is as pretty as Tara but she is also much more cautious," Dimitri pointed out.

"Once corporate finds us a new facility, we can find prettier girls that will be much easier to break."

"I agree completely with your assessment. Wonderful work as always," Nora complimented. Joseph Jackson sat across from Nora and Dimitri, shaking his head in disagreement. Joseph Jackson was a thin built man in his mid-thirties with short brown hair.

"Don't be so sure they won't figure it out," Joseph added. His body showed clear signs of stress. Signs that had become the norm since Nora and Dimitri arrived. "In case you've forgotten, due to carelessness from your people, the East Coast training brothel was raided two weeks ago." Nora lit a cigarette as he continued. "Cost the organization two hundred and forty-seven thousand dollars, which my golden goose made back in less than a week." Joseph got up to open a window to let out the smoke.

"I assure you Tara will remain undiscovered here. Soon she will be making money for Omnipotent," Nora assured.

"Your over-confidence is what concerns me. You should have never brought that girl here." Joseph sat down quickly, showing clear signs of frustration.

"Arrangements with clients were already made before the incident occurred. We also have a waiting list of customers that the main office wants fulfilled," Nora shot back, now also showing signs of frustration.

Joseph pulled three shot glasses and a bottle of scotch whiskey from a drawer in his desk. As he poured, he said, "This facility brings in over a billion dollars a year and is a major supplier for East Coast operations. Does our head office want to risk that just to keep a few horny guys happy?"

"Mr. Jackson, if those horny guys get angry, they may talk, which means we will need to kill them and anyone they had contact with. That would be a wildfire that would get out of control quickly," Dimitri said, taking his drink.

"You read the email like we did. No new facilities are to open until corporate find the leaks and handles the loose ends."

"Until then, Tara stays here and performs," Nora added before gulping down her whiskey.

"I want Tara's siblings and boyfriend monitored. If they get too close, I want them taken out, understood?" Joseph said in a voice showing he meant it. Nora relaxed in her chair.

"We're already monitoring them. If they get too close to the truth, our informant will take care of them."

Chapter 6

Tara Cymric held her arms close to her shivering body as she lay on the cold floor. Her head was pressed up against the wall, acting as an uncomfortable makeshift pillow. She had no idea what time it was; she only knew the sun had risen and set twice since they had locked her in here. During that time, the only human contact she had was from Miguel, who had come in due to her constant pounding on the door. She was hoping to get some food and water, but all she got was shoved to the ground and a few kicks to the ribs and stomach.

The sun was about to set for a third time. She watched as the lines of sunlight on the floor got smaller and smaller. Her stomach growled from hunger, and her lips were dry and starting to crack. She used her remaining salvia to ease the burning feeling of thirst inside her mouth. *Do they want me to die in here?* Tara thought. *No, that couldn't be it. Nora had already said what they were going to do with me. Ivan had said "see you in a week."* She remembered learning from a survival TV show that people could go three to four days without water. *They have to know I won't last a week without water.* As she continued her thought, a sudden horror dawned upon her: she did have a water source. Feeling goosebumps rise on her skin, she stared at the toilet in disguise. Unfortunately, the situation started to make sense. Forcing her to drink from the toilet was designed to break and humiliate her.

"No, I won't do it. I won't let them break me," Tara said out loud. She closed her eyes. For comfort, she tried to think of home, though this only managed to bring tears to her eyes. "You're so stupid, Tara, you should have noticed all the warning signs, but no, you had to be gullible and full of yourself," Tara said in a soft teary voice. Then through her saddening thoughts, another came to her, which was a beam of light breaking up the dark thoughts in her mind. She remembered her last conversation with Romy. *You told Romy you were going to a modeling job and you told her Brandon knew the guy who owned the business.* A glimmer of hope formed on Tara's face. *There's no way Brandon will be able to show any of Dimitri's contact information. Ryan will see right through his lies and excuses, his story will fall apart, Ryan will learn the truth, and Brandon will crack under the pressure.* "Unless." Tara felt herself relax. *What if Nora made up the story about Brandon to make me lose hope? Dimitri was acting on his own. Brandon still loves me and is looking for me right now.* Thinking about that eased Tara's mind. She closed her eyes and drifted off to sleep, thinking about the weasels that kidnapped her being hauled off to jail in the back of a police car.

◆　　◆　　◆

Tara woke up, starting to become uncomfortably familiar with her surroundings. It was now day three of her nightmarish situation. She looked out the west-facing window, and she could not see the sun, so it was sometime before noon. She sat on the window seat and stared out the window, dreaming of freedom. Thinking about the smell of coffee in the morning, thinking about the fun she had at the bars and clubs with her friends, thinking of Brandon's warm embrace when she was upset. By midday she was dizzy, irritable, and confusion was starting to set in. She was having trouble thinking and would occasionally forget where she was, though she wished that would remain. She tried to swallow salvia to quench the burning in her throat, but her salvia reserves were gone. "I'm thirsty," she said, falling to one knee. "So thirsty."

She stared at the toilet, which was looking more and more like a desert oasis. Not caring about her pride anymore, she walked over to it and lifted the lid. After flushing several times, she made a cup with her hands. She brought the water inches from her mouth and dropped it back into the toilet. *You need to Tara, you need to get water,* she told herself. She closed her eyes and pictured a moving stream with crystal clear cold water. "Ouch," she said when her dry tongue bumped her dry lips. She cupped her again hands. *A clean crystal clear stream,* Tara thought. She took a drink. The relief on her burning throat was instant, and before she knew it she had taken several more. She stopped drinking when she started to feel sick. She opened her eyes and looked at the toilet. She hit it in frustration and burst into tears.

"AHH! What have I done? What have I done?"

◆　◆　◆

The next four days were a mix of rage, tears, and looking out the window hoping to see a rescue team coming for her. Tara sat on her knees, staring out the window. The sun had risen for the seventh time. She was constantly cold, lightheaded, and tired from the lack of food. Knowing she needed to keep what little strength she had left, she went through the unpleasant task of drinking water once a day. A task she hated. What hurt her worse than the pain brought by the ravishing hunger was the fact that help had not come yet. She was sure Ryan would have figured out what had happened by the third day and come to rescue her by the sixth day at the latest. *Come on, Ryan, your sister needs you.* She grunted in frustration.

"Just hurry up and come **save me!**" she yelled. She placed her hands on her head, trying to think; of course, anytime she tried, her only thoughts were on food. Suddenly a concerned look formed on her face as a horrible thought entered her head. *If Brandon is working with these people, what if he killed them? No, Tara! No! Don't even think that! It didn't happen, so get it out of your head!* The sound of the door unlocking caught her attention. Nora Peters and a new man entered.

"Hi, I'm Devin," he said. Tara's eyes moved to what he was holding, a paper plate with a turkey sandwich, apple, and bottle of water on it. *Is that for me?* Tara thought hopefully. Like he had read her thoughts, he walked over and handed it down to her. She slowly reached out to take it, expecting it to be taken away from her. To her delight, it wasn't. She placed it in front of her, keeping an untrusting eye on her capturers. Devin left the room, leaving her alone with Nora. The smell of the bread and apple caused her stomach to growl. The possibility the food may be poison entered her mind. *No, they want me alive; they won't poison me.* She grabbed the sandwich and felt drool drop from the roof of her mouth as her body awaited the food it had been craving for days. The sight of Nora's finger approaching her face caused her to drop the sandwich. Nora gently struck her on the head.

"Ah, ah, ah. What do we say?" *I don't understand what you want,* Tara thought, confused. *What do we say?* Then she understood what Nora wanted. She played along, knowing this was not the time to fight. If she showed any signs of disobedience, the only thing her stomach would get was the leather of someone's boots.

"Thank you," she replied in a neutral voice, hoping it was the right answer.

"Very good. You may eat," Nora confirmed. At first, Tara ate the sandwich and drank the water faster than she thought was possible, but the sick feeling in her stomach soon forced her to slow down. "While you eat, I thought you might enjoying listening to your brother's voice on audio recording." Tara was half-finished with the apple when her appetite left her. Nora opened a file on her phone, and the conversation between Dimitri and Ryan began playing. Tara tried to hold back tears as she listened to Dimitri calmly give the information she thought for sure would lead to her freedom to Ryan. The hope she had been clinging to left her, but strangely she didn't care. In fact she was feeling happy without a care in the world. *What's going on? Why do I feel like this?* Tara thought.

"Tara, now that you're done eating, it's time to get down to business. Your first customer will be here shortly." *Customer? I have a customer?*

"You will shower and then you will be provided with the outfit and makeup the client requested."

"I get to take a shower?" Tara asked, jumping up excitedly.

"Yes, dear." Nora pointed to the bottle of water. "The water contained a large dose of anti-anxiety drugs to make you more cooperative." Tara didn't respond to the comment; she was too busy examining her nails. "I know you're not planning to give us any trouble," Nora said.

Tara shook her head no. "I'm still hungry," she said in a dazed childlike voice.

"You can eat again when you're done," Nora replied, pleased she was cooperating so well. Tara exited the room to see Miguel and Peter waiting outside. She smiled and waved. Nora told her to make a left.

"Where are we going?" Tara asked.

"To your dressing room," Nora replied.

"I have my own dressing room. This place is great!" Tara said in a bubbly voice. After a short walk, they made a left and stopped at the first door in the hallway. A small black sign with white letters said "dressing room."

Nora opened the door and said, "Welcome to your dressing room," acting like Tara was some type of movie star. Tara's eyes glimmered, her insides filled with joy. *I have my own dressing room!*

Tara, Nora, and Peter walked in. The small room had two racks of clothing and a makeup stand at the back of the room. "That door behind the makeup stand is the bathroom," Nora pointed out. "You have ten minutes to shower; if you try anything, there will be consequences."

"What would I try?" Tara asked, rolling her eyes. Nora's face showed an annoyed look. "Ten minutes. Got it," Tara continued, giving her a thumbs up. The idea of a shower felt like heaven to her. She skipped towards the bathroom.

"Tara, wait a moment," Nora said. She stopped and sat on the makeup stand.

Miguel entered the room and said suspiciously, "I don't like this."

"Relax, it's the effect of the drug," Nora assured as she walked over to a cabinet and opened it. Miguel kept a close eye on Tara.

"Are you my bodyguard?" Tara asked. Nora handed Tara a bottle of strawberry scented shampoo. "The client requested this type of shampoo. So use it." Tara took it, shook her head she understood, and walked into the bathroom. She undressed and got in the shower. The pleasant feeling brought by the stream of hot water made her smile. She was back home enjoying a shower, washing and shampooing her matted hair. Fierce pounding on the door broke the illusion.

"Tara, you have three minutes," Miguel shouted.

"Be right out!" Tara replied, slightly frightened. *Why am I scared?* she thought. She turned off the water, dressed, and came out.

Nora handed her a piece of paper. "Here is the outfit and hairstyle the client requested. You have five minutes to dress and fifteen in the makeup station. If you look acceptable, you'll get dinner tonight."

The mention of more food made her stomach growl. Tara gave a happy jump. "Lobster, champagne. By the way, where's my boyfriend?"

"I love this drug," Peter said, mocking Tara's childish behavior. "Hey, Miguel, remember the one girl who kept singing loudly?"

"Had to break her jaw," Miguel commented. Satisfied she was under control, Nora and her henchmen left the room. Tara looked at the piece of paper. It read: "The client has requested a school girl outfit; hair style is ponytail."

Tara followed the instructions. She was using the makeup station when Nora opened the door and said excitedly, "Ready for your grand entrance, Tara?"

"In a minute," she replied, adding the finishing touches to her makeup. After she finished, she followed Nora to the room with the red velvet carpet. Tara stopped, remembering she had been in this room before. *This place is beautiful, so why is it making me so uneasy?*

"Tara?" Nora said, opening a door to a connecting room. Tara approached the room and saw a king-sized bed with red velvet sheets. Light pink curtains hung from a canopy. White string lights hung from the top of the bed canopy. Tara jumped on the bed, ecstatic.

"This is my room!" In the back of her mind, a voice yelled, *You're in danger, Tara. Find a way out, fight your way out!* With the voice came feelings of pain and fear. Tara rubbed her head, trying to figure out why she was thinking that.

"Make yourself comfortable," Nora ordered. Tara heard the door close behind her. She laid her head down on the bed and hugged a pillow. *She said get comfortable,* she thought, and that was what she was going to do. She had not felt this good since she could remember, but the screaming voice inside her was becoming clearer. She could feel anxiety start to overtake her warm feelings. *I have a nice bed, and those people will bring me dinner in a few hours,* Tara thought, trying to suppress her unpleasant feelings. The sound of the door opening made Tara look up. An overweight man with a small messy beard and thinning hairline walked in.

"Hello, I'm Anthony," he said. "You're Tara, right?"

"Never seen you before; are you room service?" Tara replied in a spaced out voice.

Anthony gave a nervous laugh. "I have to admit, this is going to be my first time, so you're going to have to walk me through this."

Tara gave a confused look. *What do you mean, first time?*

Anthony sat on the bed. Seeing him taking off his pants helped her break free of the drug's grip. Tara felt the fog around her mind start to clear. "No, no, this is not happening!" she said to herself in panic, now fully understanding what was going on. She hit herself in the face twice, trying to bring her senses back.

Anthony laid his pants down and looked over at her. "I love your outfit. You're even prettier than I imagined. I guess my shirt needs to come off next." Tara backed up to the wall with a look of horror on her face. *This can't be happening,* she thought, watching Anthony remove his shirt. Turning to her, he said, "Well, I'm ready. Let's get started."

"Don't touch me. Stay away from me," Tara replied, frightened.

Anthony's face showed a noticeable look of irritation. "What! My mom paid good money for me to have this experience, so I expect you to deliver on your end."

"I'm not giving you anything, leave me alone!" Tara yelled in the most menacing voice she could form. Undeterred by her warning, Anthony grabbed her left arm.

"I said come here!" he shouted.

"No!" Tara screamed. She thrust her right leg forward, kicking him in the face. Anthony hit the floor, screaming in pain. Tara leaped off the bed, landing next to him. Anthony was holding his nose, a visible stream of blood coming between his fingers. A crazed look formed on Tara's face. "You sick freak!" Letting out all her anger and frustrations, Tara unleashed kick after kick across his body. Anthony screamed in agony. Seconds later the door burst open, and Nora, Joseph Jackson, and a massively overweight woman came rushing in. The woman screamed when she saw what was happening.

"She should have been drugged for hours!" Nora said, stunned. "Do something!" she screamed at Joseph in a panic. Knowing he had to fix Nora's mess, Joseph grabbed Tara around the waist, taking her to the ground. The overweight woman got in Nora's face, who was yelling for help.

"Look at my Anthony!" the woman yelled, pointing to him moaning in pain. "You said this was a professional establishment!"

"I'm so sorry for this. We will give you a full refund," Nora quickly replied. Joseph was still wrestling with Tara, who was hitting him with every elbow or knee strike she could get in. She briefly turned her head, stopping Nora and the open door. *If I can get away from this guy, I know I can get past Nora, then I can make it out of the pleasure room and escape through the entrance the client used.* Tara stopped moving, wanting Joseph to think she had given up, and she felt Joseph's body relax. She thrust her knee between his legs. Joseph let out a cry of pain, releasing her. Tara rolled away from him and got to her feet. *Oh no,* she thought, seeing Miguel and Peter enter the room. Anthony had just gotten to his feet, blocking Miguel's path to Tara. Miguel charged at Tara, shoving him into a wall. The mother screamed as his face slammed into it. With one arm, Miguel picked Tara up by the back of the shirt. Tara started begging for mercy right before Miguel delivered a punch to her stomach. She gasped from the shot, and her body collapsed onto the bed.

Struggling to catch her breath, Tara watched Peter help Anthony up while Nora tried to calm his hysteric mother down. Joseph got up, having a few bruises and scratch marks himself. He clenched his fists, ready to return the favor.

"Joseph, not now, help the client!" Nora ordered.

I have to get up, need to run. Tara slowly started to crawl, willing her aching body to move.

"You don't give me orders!" he snapped back, striking Tara in the ribs. She yelled in pain, rolling onto her back.

"I think my nose is broken," Anthony mumbled weakly. Reluctantly, Joseph walked over to Anthony, figuring it would be better if he handled the situation.

"Don't worry, we have a good doctor on staff. Dr. Bodkin will see you right away," Joseph assured, helping Anthony out of the room. His mother followed, shouting profanity at Joseph. Nora angrily turned to Miguel and Peter.

"Take as long as you want. Don't hurt her face." Hearing that gave Tara a second wind. She started kicking and punching at Miguel, who had briefly taken his eyes off her. Miguel picked her up like a rag doll and slammed her to the ground. Tara felt a sudden sharp pain go through her back. Miguel picked her up. Peter punched her in the stomach twice before Miguel tossed her back on the bed.

"Hold on to her. I'll go first," Miguel said. Peter put both knees on Tara's arms, preventing them from moving. Tara tried to move, tried to fight, but the men's grip was too much. *No, this can't be happening.* Tara looked up at him with a look of frightened desperation as she heard Miguel removing his belt.

"Please, no," she said in a soft frightened voice. Peter didn't reply. He looked down at her and smiled.

◆　◆　◆

Sometime later, Tara lay in the shower. A small stream of red water flowed from between her legs into the drain. The mid-section of her stomach was light and dark purple. Her eyes were wide with shock, her body felt numb, her mind was completely blank. The water was a pleasant temperature, but her body was still shaking. She didn't know how long she had been lying there; all she knew was Miguel and Peter had taken turns with her multiple times. What scared her the most was this was not going to end anytime soon.

Chapter 7

Romy Cymric sat on her living room couch, twirling her phone around in circles. A half-eaten Hot Pocket sat on a plate next to her. Tara had now been missing a little over a week. On the first day of the search, they had around three hundred volunteers helping them, consisting of family, friends, and strangers who were kind enough to give up their day to help with the search efforts. Some volunteers handed out or hung missing persons posters, while others searched the patches of woods along designated search grids. Ryan had coordinated the search groups, focusing most of their efforts in the area between Waterford and New Castle. Simultaneously, he worked with police and news stations to get Tara's story national attention, widening the search to a national level. He also questioned people working at the businesses Tara frequented. Everyone pretty much said the same thing. The last time they remembered seeing Tara, she was acting normal and didn't notice anything out of the ordinary the day she was there. Despite all this, they had found next to nothing.

The only breakthrough occurred the first day of the search when Ryan received a call from the Waterford police informing him Tara's car had been found in the Old Time Waterford Motel's parking lot. He and a K-9 unit from Pittsburgh SWAT joined the local police in the investigation. A search of Tara's car and the motel room Dimitri had rented found nothing of interest. The search dog confirmed Tara had entered the motel room before losing the scent. When questioned, the motel owner, an overweight old man in his late sixties, spent ten minutes complaining about how bad business was. Once his rambling was finished, he claimed a man fitting Dimitri's description had rented room sixteen for two days and left it in good condition, and during that time no one had seen or heard anything suspicious. Ryan believed his story because judging by the condition of the motel, he doubted anyone was around to hear anything. To be safe, he checked the motel's records, which matched the old man's story. Only two other people had rented rooms during the time Dimitri had rented his. Both people checked in at night and left the next morning. When the question about what to do with Tara's car came up, Romy and Ryan agreed it should be taken back to her apartment.

Romy lay back, tired and discouraged. The first two search days, she and Ryan had pulled two all-nighters, only stopping at fast food drive-thrus for on-the-go meals. The rest of the week they had been lucky to get three to four hours of sleep. Romy closed her eyes and thought, *Get some sleep; tomorrow's going to be the day you find her.* She had told herself that same thing every day since Tara went missing, and every day ended in disappointment. She couldn't believe after all the work they had done to cover Tara's disappearance, nothing had surfaced. Despite being exhausted, Romy could not bring herself to go to sleep. She picked up her phone and started scrolling through her photos, searching for ones of Tara. The first photo she found was from a birthday shopping spree the two of them had gone on a few months ago. Tara's arms were stretched out with two bags of clothes on each, and she was smiling a guilty smile. She scrolled through a few more modern pictures, then opened an album of pictures from their childhood. The first photo was from Halloween. Ryan was a futuristic solider, she was a zombie, and Tara was a princess with the words "I'm a star" printed on the dress.

After looking through the photos, Romy put her phone down and thought about the last time she spoke to Tara. *I should have pushed harder for you not to go. If I had called Ryan right when I thought something was wrong, would you be back home?* she thought, blaming herself. Deep down she knew Tara's disappearance was not her fault, but the questions from her previous thoughts would haunt her until Tara was safely home. *Maybe I should call*

Brandon to see how he's doing? During the search, Brandon Aiden took charge of placing missing persons posters around New Castle. He went home often, to check Tara's social media accounts and take time to clear his head. On the third day, he had broken down, claiming he missed Tara and needed some time to mourn in his own way. Romy looked at the clock. It was a little past eight-thirty. She then picked up her phone, went into contacts, and called Brandon.

"Hey, Romy," he replied in a neutral voice.

"Hi, Brandon. I just wanted to see how you were holding up?"

"As well as can be expected. I just…" Sadness and regret filled his voice. "I just wish I never got Tara that job. She would still be with us if I didn't."

"I feel the same way. Somehow I knew something was wrong and didn't act soon enough."

"The apartment is so empty without her. I've been putting on her favorite music to pretend she still here."

"We'll find her soon, Brandon. Ryan's working nonstop, and millions of people know about her disappearance. It's only a matter of time before we find her." *Now you believe what you just said,* Romy thought.

"Thanks, Romy," Brandon said, a little happier. "Tara will be back and then we can take that vacation we talked about this summer."

"I admit I'm jealous of you two. I always wanted to go on a cruise," Romy replied.

"You can come along," Brandon offered. "Australia and New Zealand is big enough for the three of us."

"It's okay. Tara will want it to be just the two of you," Romy replied, knowing she would be a third wheel.

"I can smuggle you aboard in a shipping crate," Brandon joked. An image flashed in Romy's head of Tara bound and gagged, locked in a shipping crate bound for another country.

"Oh, God," Romy said out loud.

"What?" Brandon asked.

"Nothing," Romy replied, regaining her composure. "I was just thinking about how scared Tara must be."

"Like you said, Tara's disappearance has national attention, thanks to Ryan. Soon someone will call with information about Tara." Hearing that brought a smile to Romy's face.

"I hope you're right," Romy replied, feeling herself getting emotional. "What time do you want to start searching tomorrow?"

She heard Brandon make an upset moan. "Sorry, Romy, I have several meetings at the bank that are going to take up most of my day." Romy huffed in frustration. "Romy, don't worry. I'm going to monitor Tara's social media accounts and the website we made for her."

"I guess I don't understand how you can be going back to work when Tara, your girlfriend, is missing," Romy said, confronting him on his decision.

There was a pause before Brandon replied, "Romy, I love Tara and will do anything to find her, but the sad truth is I have to go back work or else Tara won't have a home to come back to. You should do the same. It's healthy to get your mind off what's happening."

How can you even suggest I take my mind off Tara? Romy thought, then lashed out.

"What are you saying, we should give up and go back to our normal lives!"

"All I'm saying is we need to slowly get back to our normal jobs and routines. That is what Tara would want." Romy didn't provide a counter-argument, so he continued, "Of course, like you, I will never stop searching, but we can't spend the rest of our lives searching the woods. We need to think about our needs. You have a business to run. It will do your mind good to focus on that." Romy thought about her business, how she had not been there in person since Tara's disappearance.

"I know where you're coming from," Romy admitted. "Sorry I lashed out."

"I understand your feelings completely. I'm sorry if I'm coming off as uncaring," Brandon said in an apologetic voice. "Let's spend the next few days creating a search plan and we can go looking on the weekend."

"That's a really good idea," Romy replied.

"Between the three of us, we'll come up with something," Brandon assured. "Alright, I have to prepare for tomorrow's meeting. I'll talk to you tomorrow."

"Sounds good. Bye," Romy said and hung up. She lay back on the couch, looking through pictures of Tara. The more she looked, the more her feeling of sadness and emptiness increased. She closed her photos, scrolled down her contacts, and called Ryan.

"Hey, Romy. Do you mind if I call you back in five minutes? I need to finish putting little Ryan to bed."

"Sure, that's fine." Romy nibbled on her Hot Pocket until Ryan called back.

"Hey, Romy. What's going on?" he asked.

"Just missing Tara. Wanted someone to talk to."

"We are all," Ryan agreed. "Romy, I can tell by your voice something else is bothering you." The emotions Romy was keeping inside came to the surface.

"Since Tara went missing I have all this sorrow and anger inside and no one to vent my feelings to," Romy said in a fast, upset voice. She stopped for a moment to calm herself. "I mean, Ryan, you have Krista and little Ryan to comfort you. I don't have anyone. I just need someone to vent my feelings to." It was times like these Romy regretted her life choices. Choosing to focus her time and energy on starting and running her business over romance and friendship. Ryan, not being the best at dealing with emotionally hurting people, tried his best to comfort his sister.

"Romy, I know I'm not the same as a boyfriend but you can always talk to me about anything. If you need girl talk, you know Krista loves you and is always willing to talk."

"Thanks, I know that," Romy said, feeling a little better. "Ryan, I'm so frustrated right now, and honestly out of ideas. What else can we do to find Tara?"

He didn't answer right away. That told Romy he was out of ideas or was about to give some bad news. His voice had a defeated sound to it when he replied.

"Honestly, Romy, there's nothing more we can do. Right now all we can do is wait, hope, and pray someone finds a lead and contacts us." Romy felt a tear roll down her cheek.

"Ryan, I know I may not like the answer, but I need to hear it. What are the odds of finding Tara alive?"

Sounding like he was about to tear up himself, Ryan replied, "Romy, I'm not going to lie to you. The odds of finding Tara alive are decreasing daily. We've already passed the investigation critical timeframe." He went on to explain the seventy-two-hour rule to her. How those hours were critical in locating a missing person, and after that the odds of finding Tara alive went down every day. If she was alive, she'd most likely be in another country. Ryan's words confirmed what Romy was already suspecting.

"I wish Tara would walk through that door or someone would find her dead in a ditch. Not knowing whether she's alive or dead is killing me," Romy said softly, then started speaking in a quick, teary voice. "What should we do? Do we have a funeral for her? When do you or I start clearing out her things?"

"Romy, we're not going to do either of those things. There is no evidence she's dead. I know it seems like it's been forever, but in reality she's only been gone a week. Something will turn up. It always does," Ryan said in a positive-sounding voice.

"You're contradicting yourself," Romy replied, remembering he had just said the odds of finding her were not good.

"I'm trying to remain positive," Ryan countered. He started to speak again, then stopped. Romy could tell he was trying to tell her something, and she could tell she wasn't going to like it.

"Ryan, what is it?" Now his voice sounded upset.

"I hate to tell you this, but I only have a few vacation days left. I'm returning to my unit the day after tomorrow."

Romy gasped in surprise. "So, you're siding with Brandon and leaving me to search for our sister alone?"

"Romy, I'm going to keep searching, but like we talked about earlier, right now the only thing we can do is wait. We're going to need to get back to our lives eventually."

"Fine," Romy said, sounding betrayed. "I'll keep printing flyers and handing them out myself."

"Romy, I know it's going to be hard, but we need to try to get back into our daily routines. If you keep searching nonstop, you're going to burn yourself out both physically and financially. When was the last time you did anything at or thought about your business?" Ryan asked seriously. Romy cursed under her breath. Brandon had asked her the same thing, and deep down she knew they were right. She couldn't spend her entire life searching every corner of the earth for Tara.

"Did Brandon call you and give you a script to read?" Romy asked, lighthearted.

"No, why?" Ryan asked.

"He told me the same thing you did."

"That's good advice. As hard as it's going to be, we need to slowly start getting back to our normal routines."

"Are you truly going to do that?" Romy asked, knowing this was the perfect example of "do as I say, not as I do."

"In truth, I'm going to return to work, think about how to find Tara several hours a day, and possibly execute those ideas on the weekend." Both siblings giggled in the phone.

"I'll do the same." Romy approved, then explained Brandon's plan, which Ryan approved of. Her voice gained a happier tone when she said, "Ryan, thanks for talking with me. It really helped."

"What are big brothers for? Try to get some sleep, okay."

"I will. Goodnight," Romy said, feeling much better then she had.

Chapter 8

The sound of her door bursting open woke Tara. She opened her eyes to see Miguel and Peter storming in. Tara let out a frightened yelp. Her stomach and ribs burned as she ran for the farthest corner of the room and crouched into a ball.

"Boss wants to see you. Now!" Miguel shouted in an angry voice. Tara did not respond. She remained in the corner, trembling. "If you refuse to come, we have orders to repeat last night's events."

Tara felt her breath leave her. *No, I can't go through that again.* She tried to stand, but her body would not move.

"Get up!" Miguel screamed, losing patience. Tara closed her eyes and concentrated on something she loved, a warm summer day on the beach. *Get up. Tara, go for a walk on the beach.* Tara slowly got to her feet and opened her eyes. She could feel her body shaking as she reluctantly followed them. As they walked, Peter placed an arm around her. Tara felt her skin crawl; she wanted to push his hand off but knew if she did, things would only get worse.

"You know, Tara, I really did enjoy myself last night," Peter said smugly. She didn't reply to his comment, just looked away from him. For the first time she noticed that there was another door a few yards from her room. This door had a keypad lock and an area for a security card. *That's odd,* she thought, not remembering seeing keypads on other doors. When they passed the room she suspected was a doctor's office, she focused her attention on the door. It had a deadbolt but no high-tech security. They entered the room with the velvet carpet, which was a client meeting and waiting room. To Tara's relief Peter took his arm off her shoulder. She cringed in alarm when she saw the door that led to the client's pleasure room. Miguel headed for a door on the opposite side of the room, which was Nora and Joseph's office area.

Miguel knocked before they entered. Tara looked at the door knob and noticed the same type of security as the mystery door. As soon as they entered, Nora got up from her desk and slapped Tara across the face. Tara shrugged the shot off. A week ago a slap would have brought her to tears, but compared to what she had gone through, the pain was bearable. Nora looked at her furiously for a moment, then started shouting in an angered voice.

"What you did last night was unacceptable!" Joseph, who was sitting at a large desk working on a computer, hardly noticed. "I should let Miguel and the other nineteen men here have their way with you for a week." A frightened expression formed on Tara's face. "You look frightened. You should be," Nora said, pleased. "Sit," she ordered, pointing to the chair facing her equally large desk.

Tara sat down. Nora told Miguel and Peter they could go and sat down at her large office chair. She lit a cigarette, trying to calm herself. "Now what do you have to say for your actions last night?" Tara wanted to say she was proud of what she did, that she would kick that sick pervert again if she could, along with Miguel and the rest of them. *Be smart*, she reminded herself. She thought over her options for a moment. She knew saying "I'm sorry it won't happen again" would only make Nora angry, because she would know it was a bogus apology. Tara thought of a different approach and hoped it was the right one.

"You kidnapped me and were trying to force me to have sex against my will. Of course I reacted violently." Nora glared at her, but before she could speak, Tara continued. "Last night's lesson,"—Tara cringed, trying to block out painful memories—"taught me I have no choice but to follow your orders." Nora's glare turned to a look of pleasure.

"It appears you're a smart girl after all." Inside Tara sighed with relief. "Regardless of what you have learned, you still cost the company a client and the three hundred dollars the client paid for the session. For that you will receive no income from your next two sessions to pay back your debt." Tara felt a rage building inside her. She couldn't stand how this woman was treating her like she was an employee at a normal everyday job. "I also understand you probably are sore after last night, so I will be generous and give you four days to recover."

Instead of saying what she wanted, Tara replied, "I understand, thank you. Do you need anything else from me?"

"No, I believe you learned your lesson, but before returning to your room, I want you to go to visit our onsite physician Dr. Heinrich Bodkin. His office is down the hall. I'll walk you to it."

"I didn't know you cared," Tara commented, knowing the risk, but she couldn't hold her frustration in anymore. Nora only smiled.

"You are an investment, so you will be taken care of," Nora replied, getting up. "I want to be sure any injuries you sustained last night will not impact your work." She walked over to the office door and motioned for Tara to follow her. Tara did. The thought of attacking Nora, of slamming her head into the wall over and over, crossed her mind. It brought a slight smile to her face as they walked. *One day very soon.* Moments later Nora and Tara entered the room Tara had suspected was a doctor's office.

"Dr. Bodkin appears to be out. Have a seat and he will be right with you." Tara sat on the examination table, which was located against the left wall.

Before leaving, Nora turned back to Tara and said, "Friendly warning, if the events from last night ever happens again, you will lose your brother, your sister-in-law, and your nephew." Tara's face briefly showed a look of concern. She soon hid it, then shook her head to indicate she understood.

Nora exited the room, leaving the door open. Seeing the open door with no one around, **Tara's** first instinct was to rush out of the room and find a way to escape. *No, Tara, that's what they are expecting. Just stay put, Tara. It's the best thing you can do,* her inner voice warned. Even if she could get out of the room without being seen, she had no idea where the exit was, and it was more than likely guarded. She looked around the office. It was filled with normal examination room equipment: an exam light, diagnostic equipment, and a vital signs monitor surrounded her. Several X-rays hung on the walls. Directly opposite from the room entrance were cabinets surrounded by a large work station. A laptop, centrifuges, autoclaves, and microscope sat on it. Tara's full focus went to the laptop. She checked to see if anyone was coming, then rushed over to it. She clicked the keyboard once. The laptop woke up, showing a password screen.

"Of course," Tara said, irritated, though really not surprised. She opened the cabinet drawers, hoping to find a surgical knife or something sharp to use as a weapon when she did create an escape plan. After searching several drawers, she found nothing but useless medical supplies. She reached above her, opening a larger cabinet with twin doors. A look of horror and disgust formed on her face. "What da hell!" she said out loud. Inside was a human-shaped statue that looked to be made from infant skeletons. Two humerus bones were attached on each arm, making the arms unusually long. Patches of animal fur covered the skeleton, acting as an odd form of clothing. The rib cage's sternum and costal cartilage was missing, leaving the sharp pointed rib bones surrounding an empty crevasse. Filling the hole where the stomach should have been were tiny hand bones and several heads of small animals and birds. The head of the statue was a deer skull carved from human bones. Four sharp points sat on each antler. Inside the eyes sockets, two miniature candles burned. The statue's elbow touched the ribs, the arms stretched out, demanding sacrifices. Two jars with baby skeletons were placed on both sides of the demonic statue. Tara wanted to look away, but it was like the faint orange glow from the eye sockets had hypnotized her. In her mind she started hearing voices in a language she couldn't understand. Tara quickly turned away and gasped. A man that looked to be in his late fifties with short grey hair stood in front of her.

"Looking for something?" he asked in a cold German accent. His face showed no sign of anger, just a hateful scowl, looking at her with revulsion. Tara tried to form words but couldn't. She briefly turned back to the statue. "Sent to me by friends, unwanted accidents," Dr. Bodkin said in disgust as he slammed the door shut. Tara felt her body beginning to tremble. She couldn't explain why, but this man frightened her more than Nora, or even Miguel. She could feel the hatred and contempt for human life in him.

"Take a seat," he ordered. Tara sat down, wanting to get out of here as soon as she could. As Dr. Bodkin started getting the examination equipment ready, Tara focused in on the X-rays, a decision she instantly regretted. One X-ray was a deformed-looking skull, while another was the left side of a human body with a membrane of skin attached to the arm and hip. Bat-like wing bones ran through the membranes. Several other X-rays were human skeletons with bones coming out of the arm, elbows, and back. Two X-rays were separate from the others. One looked to be six human torsos fused together with the arms still attached. The second looked like a baboon's head on a muscular human body. *What are these things?* Tara wondered.

Her thoughts ended when she heard Dr. Bodkin say, "I'm ready to begin."

"What's that for?" Tara asked nervously, noticing the shot in his hand.

"A test for STDs," he said. Tara clenched her teeth and cringed when she felt the needle enter her skin. She was waiting for the doctor to break the needle inside her skin just for the enjoyment of causing her pain. She let out a breath of relief when he pulled the needle out.

"Needles make you nervous?" he asked, amused. Tara shook her head yes. Dr. Bodkin put the needle down and asked, "Are you experiencing any pain?" He said it in a neutral voice, not overly concerned if she was. *Emotional or physical?* Tara thought. She wanted to say it out loud, but after seeing that statue, she was too afraid to make a sarcastic comment.

"My stomach and ribs hurt when I move." Thinking about getting hit in the stomach made her tense.

"Anything else?" he asked. The tense feeling turned to alarm. The incident was still fresh in her mind, and it was taking everything she had not to focus on it.

She shouted out quickly, "After the incident, I bled and I'm really sore." She closed her eyes, trying to move the traumatic memories to the back of her mind.

"What incident?" Dr. Bodkin asked. Tara's dread-filled eyes opened. Her anxiety levels began to rise. She was sure he knew what she was taking about.

"You know," Tara said softy. *Please, please don't make me explain it.*

"No, I don't know why you would be experiencing pain," Dr. Bodkin replied. Tara was sure she saw him grin when he said that. She felt her body beginning to tremble. Her breathing increased. Tears started to roll down her face.

"Just answer my question!" he screamed, slamming his palm down near her. Now Tara broke into a full-blown panic attack. She felt her body break out in sweat, as a sudden feeling of nausea hit her. She felt bile move up her throat into her mouth. She turned over the side of the table and started vomiting bile and what little food was left in her stomach onto the grey marble floor. Dr. Bodkin threw his arms up in frustration. He opened a medicine cabinet, pulled out a medical vial, and jammed a shot into it. Tara pulled her head back up, her feeling of nausea replaced with lightheadedness and chills. Tara became alert when she saw the good doctor had a second shot.

"Wait! What are you doing?" Tara asked, terrified as he approached her.

"This will calm you," he said. Moments later the anti-anxiety drug took effect. She wasn't completely out of it this time but calm enough to explain what had occurred. Dr. Bodkin did a full examination and found Tara's bodily injuries were mainly severe bruising on her stomach and ribs. Her female area had several small open wounds, which were treated with antibiotic cream. While he worked, he showed no sign of remorse for Tara's injuries; in fact, he actually seemed to enjoy seeing them.

"We're done here," Dr. Bodkin said, tossing his gloves into the trash. Not needing to be told twice, Tara got up. "Here," Dr. Bodkin said, throwing a towel at her. "Clean up your mess." He pointed to the drying vomit on the floor. Tara did what he said without giving a smug look or arguing. She was sure this man would love nothing more than to torture her to death or use her for some twisted medical experiment. *Is that what's going to happen to me if I cause too much trouble?* she thought. After cleaning the vomit, she held the towel in front of her.

"Dispose of it, and leave," he said as he removed the plastic from a large shot. Tara tossed the towel in the trash can, turned, and rushed out the door. When she left his office, the feeling of evil and danger left her. *What do I do now? What do I do now?* Tara thought. Looking down the empty halls, she started stressing out. *If I stay here, will I get in trouble? If I go back to my room, will I get in trouble? How do I get back to my room?* Wanting to create some distance between her and Dr. Bodkin, she started walking down the hall in the direction of her room. Before she got there, the door opened. Two men and a woman came through, having a conversation she couldn't make out.

They had the same type of clothes Miguel and Peter wore, and she could tell they were not friendly.

"Who are you?" the girl asked in a Russian accent. She was a few inches taller than Tara with light skin, brown eyes, and light brown hair.

"I know who she is. She's the cotton candy-haired girl Miguel told us about," one of the men said in a ghetto accent. He was around six feet with dark skin, brown eyes, and short black hair braided into dreadlocks. The man next to him stood a least half a foot taller than his comrades. He had a muscular build, green eyes, and a buzz cut.

I need to get back to my room. I need to get away from these people.

"Why are you alone standing in the middle of the hall?" the girl asked. Tara wanted to run; she was beginning to feel herself stressing out again.

"I'm, I'm trying to get back to my room," she said nervously.

"Do Nora and Joseph know this?" the tall man asked.

"Nora said to go back to my room when I was done getting checked by the doctor," Tara replied, hoping that would satisfy them.

"I'll go ask," the tall man said. For several minutes, Tara stood in the hallway. The girl had leaned up against the wall, using a small knife to remove dirt from her fingernails. The remaining guy looked up and down her body, checking her out.

"Yes, yes, fine body," she heard him say under his breath. Tara wanted to go smack him but knew she couldn't. Instead she just stared out the window.

"She's telling the truth," Tara heard the tall man's deep voice say behind her. He looked down at her and said, "Keep walking until you get to the second door on the left." Tara shook her head she understood and started to walk. She felt his large hand wrap around her arm, and her body tensed in panic.

"What did I do?" she asked in a stressed voice, expecting to get hit. The man's face showed no remorse. "When you get to your hall, don't go near the first door," he said seriously.

"There are cameras in the hallway; we'll know if you do anything you're not supposed to," the girl added.

"I'll go straight to my room," Tara reassured.

"I heard what you did to that client. If you ever want to go a few rounds with me, let me know," the man with the ghetto accent said, smacking her behind. Frightened, Tara burst into a sprint, wanting to get away from everything. She could hear laughter and insults as she ran around the corner. *Will this ever end? Every time one sicko gets done tormenting me, another shows up.* She went straight for her room, too stressed and upset to think about using the time to explore or try to find a way to escape. She rushed into her room and slammed the door. She immediately fell on the floor. The drug, panic attack, and stress had taken their toll. She closed her eyes and passed out.

◆　◆　◆

When Tara awoke, the room was completely dark. *How long was I out?* she wondered. Not knowing the time was driving her crazy. She got up and looked out the window. A half-moon and the stars occasionally came out between clouds. "God, what did I do to deserve this?" she said out loud. Her eyes became wet with tears. "I'm not getting out of this, am I? I'm going to be shipped off to another country and spend the rest of my life as a sex slave for god knows who." *No, you can't think like that,* her inner voice said. She ignored it. She wanted to believe help was coming, but deep down she knew it wasn't. She had no doubt Ryan, Brandon, and Romy were doing everything they could to find her, but they had nothing to go on. This organization had covered their tracks too well, and they seemed to be well funded and established. She had no doubt about that. Images of what Miguel and Peter had done to her started flashing in her mind, and her feeling of sorrow turned to anger as she punched the front wall in frustration. The way the punch sounded caused her to pause, feelings of curiosity overtaking her anger and sorrow. She pressed her ear against the wall and tapped it again. It sounded like there was empty space behind the drywall—it sounded hollow. *Wonder how big the hollow space is? If it's large enough, I could move through the walls and possibly escape.*

Tara wiped the tears from her eyes, sat down, and placed her hands on her cheek as she stared at the floor. She did this when she was trying to concentrate or think of a solution to a difficult problem. *You have to accept the fact that help is probably not coming and you need to get out of here on your own. You also need to accept the fact that you're going to be here for a while, and are going to have to perform.* The thought of having to perform for clients made her sick. *Break a hole in the wall, climb inside, and then smash your way to the outside.* Tara thought quickly. Thinking of herself smashing through walls to freedom like some kind of superhero made her grin. Logic soon poked holes in her plan. *Even if you could manage to get outside, you still have to get over the wall. You know the gate will be guarded, and if by some miracle you do escape, you have no idea what state or country you're in.* She hated it but she knew her analysis of the situation was correct.

She closed her eyes and tried to think harder. She drifted into deep thought, which had a calming effect. *Now that I laid out my situation, I need to create an escape plan.* Tara thought long and hard, running through lists of escape scenarios. *Even if I escape, these people know where I live and who my family and friends are. I need to come up with something that would get rid of all of them at once. That would ensure that I and my family are safe.* "To do this, what do I need?" she asked out loud in a soft voice. "And when did you become a problem solver?" she continued almost in a mocking tone, surprised herself at how she was handling the situation. *Okay, before I do anything, I need to find out what state and city I'm in.* "Good luck getting anyone to tell you that," she said to herself. Tara continued to think for a several minutes, and then an idea came to her. She thought about it over and over. Yes, it would work; in fact, it was perfect. It would trick her captors into thinking she was broken and beginning to accept her new lifestyle. At the same time it would mentally help her get through her unpleasant duties by using them to work towards her ultimate goal of escaping. "Okay, you worked out the first step," Tara said, finding herself getting excited. *Okay, once I figure out where I'm at, how do I call for help?* Tara laughed. *You just answered your own question. Find a phone.* Tara thought of possible locations a phone might be in, then began to realize she didn't know the building layout. *I'll need to figure that out.* Tara reentered her world of thought, and soon a memory from that morning came back to her.

"Stay away from the door," the tall man had said. *The door with the security locks. What's behind there?* She tried to focus, but she couldn't remember any details other than the lock was different from the others she had seen. She cursed herself for not thinking clearly when she passed it. Although unpleasant, she thought long and hard about her morning walk. The only other security locks she remembered seeing were on Nora and Joseph's office. *Something important is behind that door, but what?* She started to form a mental list. *I know where Nora or Joseph's office is. Guns maybe, another girl? No, I would have seen or heard about her, plus my door doesn't have a security lock.* Another train of thought interrupted her. *Speaking of other girls, why am I the only girl here? If this is a training center for girls to be broken and then sent off to other countries, there should be a couple dozen at least.* The possibility that they were in part of the compound she had not seen crossed her mind. *If that's true, why am I separated?* Another question entered her mind. *Why is Dr. Bodkin here?* She thought of the sickening statue, X-rays, and large needle he had right before she left. *Is he some sick doctor that enjoys conducting grotesque medical experiments on people? Maybe, but if he was, Nora would have threatened me with it... no, he has to be here for another reason.* Tara shook her head in frustration. *Maybe you're overthinking it. Maybe he's the facilities medical doctor. After all, it would take a sick man to want to work in a place like this.*

Tara slightly pounded her head. *One thing at a time, Tara, get back to focusing on the door.* She remembered hearing about other locations, which meant there were probably other people who outranked Nora and Joseph. *That might be it.* She opened her eyes in excitement. *It's some type of VIP office area and bedroom. That's it! That has to be it! An office area with a computer and a phone.* She found herself smiling as she hastily started creating a plan. *My room and the office room are on the same side of the building. The side with the hollow wall.* A feeling of hope started to form inside her. *I can crawl inside the wall and enter the office room. All I need to do is cut a hole in the wall. Assuming the hollow part of the wall is large enough for you to fix through,* the voice of self-doubt said. Tara didn't let it bring her down; instead, she jumped to her feet. Without thinking it through, she crouched to a lower portion of wall and made a fist. With all her might, she slammed it into the drywall. She felt a wave of pain travel though her hand and wrist.

"Oww! Darn it! Stupid idea!" she said in pain. The wall had a small dent in it but was mostly undamaged. The sound of approaching steps and voices caught her attention. She lay back down, pretending to be asleep. She waited for the door to burst open, for someone to start screaming about the noise. To her relief, the people walked by. Tara's body relaxed as she continued to think. *I'm going to need some type of cutting tool, and a way to muffle the sound.* She felt a jolt of pain in her back from lying on the hard floor. *And a bed.* The thought of sleeping on a soft mattress covered by a warm blanket felt like heaven. She was getting tired of waking up with sore muscles. A growl from her stomach reminded her she had not eaten since yesterday. She remembered Nora telling her she could buy her own food. *Does that mean they feed me and I can buy my own snacks, or does that mean I have to buy everything? Who do I tell what I want? Am I even allowed to leave the room?* She recalled Nora mentioning after her orientation period she would be free to walk around the facility. *When does the orientation period end?* She guessed the orientation period was the first week and ended with her first client. That made the most sense, but if that were the case, she failed. Tara palmed her head in frustration. There were too many questions about this place she needed answered.

She got back up and turned the door knob, and to her surprise, it turned and began to open. Fearing someone had seen it, she gasped and closed it. She put her ear up to the door, listening for voices or footsteps. When she heard nothing, she opened the door halfway and looked down both halls for people and cameras. Seeing nothing, she slowly and cautiously walked into the hallway. The chance of getting a better look at that mystery door overcame her fear of punishment. Her senses were on high alert as she walked towards the mystery door, her legs ready to run back to her room at the slightest sound.

After what she guessed was a little less than thirty seconds of walking, she saw the door, and she also noticed a camera on the opposite wall. Tara watched the camera, seeing if it would turn, but after several minutes she was satisfied it was stationary. She hugged the wall the camera was on, stopping when she was directly under the forward-facing camera. Down the hall she could see the turn in the hallway that led to Nora's and Peter's office. What worried her was if someone came around the corner, she wouldn't notice until it was too late. *Make it quick, Tara,* she ordered herself. The door looked to be made of strong solid wood. The knob was a grey level handle, which she found odd because all the other doors had round knobs. She focused on the security lock, noticing the red neon keypad. Above the keypad was a square green area. *Is that something to scan fingerprints with?* Tara wondered. *Wish Ryan were here.* She focused on the facts in front of her. *The door had a keypad and possibly a fingerprint lock. Something important is in there.* Suddenly what sounded like a tarp blowing in the wind caught her ear. She quickly turned her head, thinking the sound was coming from the turn in the hallway. *Screw this, I'm out of here,* she thought as her anxiety of getting caught built.

Once inside her room, she lay down and thought excitedly, *It's a VIP lounge with a phone that confirms it! Jumping to early conclusions, are we? It could also be an armory,* the voice of doubt said. Tara tried not to dwell on that thought, despite knowing there was no way she could confirm it was a VIP room, but it was the only hope she had and she was keeping hold of it. She lay down and thought about home until she fell asleep.

Chapter 9

When Tara awoke the next morning, she used the bathroom, then stared outside, dreaming of freedom. Looking at the trees and grass created the illusion she was somewhere else. After staring out the window for what she guessed was several hours, she became convinced no one was coming to bring her food. *Okay, I need to talk to Nora,* Tara thought with a nervous swallow. She felt her hand slightly tremble as she got off her knees and started walking towards her room door, intent on visiting Nora and Joseph. That was the last thing she wanted to do, but she needed answers, and food on a consistent basis. She breathed in and out a few times, mustering the courage to face her captors.

She opened her room door, checked to see if anyone was around, and when she saw no one, she started walking at a casual pace, figuring it would look suspicious if the camera saw her running. She blocked out her fear by focusing her mind on noticing any details she may have missed during her other excursions down the hall. She passed the strange door without giving it any notice. She wanted to know what was behind there and didn't want to give the man or woman watching the camera any reason to suspect her. When she reached the turn in the hallway, doubt started creeping into her. *What if I'm not supposed to do this? What if they get mad and have someone hurt me?* Tara closed her eyes and started to walk forward. When she rounded the corner, she opened them. She yelped when she saw Ivan standing a few feet from her.

"Going somewhere?" he asked in a calm, neutral voice. Tara's heart was pounding. *At least he doesn't sound angry*, she thought with relief. She had no doubt Ivan was just as cruel as the others, but to this point he had not hurt her, so in a way she was happy she was dealing with him.

"Um." Tara swallowed as she tried to form words. "Can I see Nora? I need to ask her something."

"Come with me," he ordered. *Where's he taking me?* Tara thought as she nervously followed. As they walked, for the first time, Tara took notice of the fact the hall layout went from horizontal to vertical. She thought back and remembered when she was taken to the dressing room. *The hallway went to the right. Is this building square-shaped?* When they reached the door to the client waiting room, Tara noticed a camera sitting above it facing down the hallway. *Two cameras so far, both near room entrances,* Tara mentally noted. When they entered the client waiting room, Ivan ordered Tara to wait, while he entered the office. While she was alone, Tara noticed two cameras in the client waiting room. She looked at the security lock on the office door. It was one of those locks common in office building, not nearly as advanced as the one on the mystery door. Inside Tara could hear the three of them speaking. She tried to eavesdrop but couldn't make anything out. Moments later Ivan, exiting the office, said, "They will see you." Tara wanted to ask if they were upset but knew better. She squeezed her hands together nervously as she walked in.

"Have a seat, Tara," Joseph said, not looking up from his computer. The office area was around the size of an average conference room, with the same type of décor an average business room would have. Tara sat down in the chair facing Nora's desk.

Nora closed her laptop, looked at Tara, then asked in a neutral voice, "What do you want, Tara?"

Stay calm, don't freak out. Tara kept eye contact with Nora and said, "I had a few questions I was hoping you could answer."

"Go on, say them," Nora replied, lighting a cigarette.

"I was wondering, when are you going to give me food and water? As you know, I have not eaten or had anything to drink in nearly two days." Tara readied herself, thinking she was about to get cigarette smoke blown in her face. Nora took the cigarette out of her mouth and blew the smoke to the side.

"You should have thought of that before you acted up." Nora's face showed no size of remorse when she said, "Anything else you need?" *So, you're going to let me starve for who knows how long,* Tara thought. Her emotions ran between wanting to start screaming in rage and breaking down into tears and begging her for something to eat. *No, don't do either. Be smart.* An idea started to come to her, knowing she didn't have time to think it through. Her inner voice said, *Start talking and add to the idea as you go.*

"We both know I need food and water to live. If I don't get the daily amount I need, I'm going to get sick, possibly even die. If I get sick, I can't perform, and if I die, your investment was wasted." A look of interest formed on Nora's face; she glanced over at Joseph, who had stopped his typing and was also listening. *Yes, it's working. Keep going.* "I know you said I'm not getting money until—" Tara made air quotes in her mind. *My debt for my actions is paid off.* Tara paused for a moment to think, then said, "Since I need food, couldn't you open a line of credit for me?" *Let that convince them, please God, let that convince them.* Nora looked over at Joseph, and both laughed a little.

"Worked on that speech last night?" Joseph asked.

"Yes," Tara lied. "Did I say anything that was not true?"

"She's your girl, Nora. What do you think?" Joseph stated.

"The girl's got brains. I'll give her that," Nora replied. "Smartest I've seen in a while." Nora looked back at Tara and said, "Okay, Tara, you've convinced me. I will allow you two hundred dollars' worth of credit."

"That's more than fair. Thank you," Tara replied, playing nice. Inside she was ecstatic. *Yes, yes. You did it, you won against these people.* "If you don't mind me asking, when and how do I get food?"

"When Joseph is finished, you may use his computer to purchase the items you want," Nora replied, getting back to work on her laptop. "You may sit here until he's finished." Joseph shot her a look that Tara read as *I never agreed to that.* A look Nora ignored. For around half an hour, Tara remained still and quiet. She looked at the walls, which were bare, except two cameras that appeared to cover the entire room.

"Tara, ready when you are," Joseph said, not sounding thrilled. Tara got up and started to walk over to him. "Bring your chair unless you want to stand." Tara fake smiled and grabbed it. When she looked at the screen, The Monopoly Superstore's website was up. The Monopoly Superstore was the largest superstore in the country.

"Tara," Nora said. Tara turned to her. "Joseph and I are both watching. Try anything and there will be consequences."

"I've learned that already," Tara answered quickly, trying to bury the incident in the back of her mind. "Do I need to get my own water?" she asked. Knowing these people, she expected to have to pay for it. "No, we provide water from the kitchen at no charge," Nora replied. Two other things came to Tara's mind.

"Can I get items that need to be cooked or refrigerated, and do I need to order glasses and bowls?"

"We have an oven and microwave to cook food and a freezer-refrigerator, where you can store your food items. If you wish, you may purchase paper or plastic dining ware," Nora replied. Tara gave another fake smile and began her shopping list. She filled the cart with a forty-eight-box pack of fifty-one-ounce breakfast cereals, two weeks' worth of healthy eating TV dinners, an assortment of fruit, a few snacks, plastic dining ware, and a gallon water jug. She looked at her total, which was just under one hundred dollars.

"You finished?" Joseph asked, sounding like he could not wait for her to be done. Tara knew it was risky but decided to push her luck a bit further.

"I still have one hundred dollars left. I was hoping to get an air mattress and a few other items to help me sleep." Joseph and Nora showed no signs of objecting, so she continued. She added an air mattress, blanket, toothbrush and toothpaste, table fan, flash light, digital clock, a pack of double A batteries, and a makeup kit. When she finished, her total came out to one hundred and ninety three dollars. Joseph told Tara to get up and step away from the screen.

"Why do you need a fan?" Joseph asked, looking at her suspiciously.

"I fall asleep better with the sound of a fan. It's to remind me of home," Tara replied. *Please let me have that. I need it for the escape plan.*

"Sorry, Tara. I don't like the idea of someone with your track record having a battery powered fan," Joseph commented.

"What could I do with a fan?"

Joseph deleted it from the list and replied, "Ram the spinning blade into someone's face." Inside, Tara was becoming tense. This was probably her only chance to buy stuff for a while. She needed a noise reducer. She had one last trick, and if that didn't work, she would need to forget about. Causing too much of a fuss would confirm his suspicions that she was up to something.

"Could I have a normal fan that plugs into the wall?" Before Joseph could speak, Tara continued, "Here's why you should let me get one: if I have a comfortable place to sleep, I'll be better rested. A better rested girl is a better preforming girl, which means happier clients."

"Tara dear. Did you ever have a career in sales?" Nora asked.

"No, never," Tara replied, hoping she had again convinced Nora.

"You would have been good at it. Joseph, let her have her fan; it's not like she can do any harm with it." Showing clear annoyance, Joseph typed "electronic fan" in the search bar and picked the first fan on the list. He looked up at Tara as if daring her to complain. She remained silent, and several minutes later, Tara's order was placed.

Seeing Joseph was agitated, Tara turned to Nora and asked, "If you don't mind me asking, how is my stuff getting here?"

"Someone will go pick it up for you later today and bring it to your room."

"I've never been to the kitchen. Could you tell me where it is?"

"The person bringing your items will show you." Nora snuffed out her second cigarette. "Is that all you needed?"

"One last thing."

"What now?" Joseph cut in. Tara put on her acting face and formed a look that said she was about to say something she didn't want. "Sorry for asking so many questions. As much as I don't want to accept it, I know I'm stuck here and want to know the rules so I don't get punished again." Joseph's look did not change but Nora appeared pleased.

"That's what I like to hear," Nora complimented. "You may ask your question."

"Am I free to leave my room to go to the kitchen or do I need to wait for someone to escort me?"

"As long as you behave, you're free to come and go from your room as you please." Nora laughed a little. "It's not like you can escape."

"You're free to go to and from the kitchen and shower area as you please," Joseph added.

"Okay, thank you," Tara said. "If it's okay with you, I'll return to my room."

"Ivan," Joseph yelled. Ivan entered the room a few moments later. "Escort Tara back to her room."

◆ ◆ ◆

When Tara left, Joseph turned to Nora and said in a serious voice, "What the hell was that? Saying she can walk around the facility as she pleases?"

Nora scoffed at him. "At my facility, once they are broken, the girls are allowed to roam as they please. Makes them easier to control if their minds are occupied."

"Need I remind you, your facility was raided by police, maybe due to policies like that?" Joseph countered.

Unfazed by the comment, Nora continued, "You have no experience breaking girls, dear Joseph. You have to understand breaking someone is a balance of cruelty and kindness. You have to teach them that you are in control. When they disobey, they will be punished, and when they obey, they get rewarded. That is how you get a girl to perform."

"You seriously think that girl's broken?" Joseph asked. Nora lit another cigarette. Joseph made an irritated expression. Her chain smoking habit was becoming aggravating that and her lackluster attitude towards the situation.

"The lesson Miguel and Peter provided was enough. Did you notice the look in her eyes when she thought of it? You're correct she's not fully broken yet, but she'll break, just like all the other girls do."

Joseph shook his head in disagreement. "In case you forgot. This is the same one-hundred-pound girl that nearly escaped four grown men. The entire time she was here I could tell something was going on inside that head of hers," Joseph replied, visible signs of anger starting to show. "We should have never let her have that fan, on the principle that we're in charge."

"You give her too much credit, Joseph. She was hungry and desperate. Are you concerned she'll cause trouble for her next client?"

"With her, who knows. I don't like that girl; she's too clever," Joseph replied. "Remember what she did at the hotel?" Joseph stood up to open the window. "I should have never agreed to help you get her. I'll be happy when she's gone, let someone else deal with her."

"Then why did you allow Ivan to go with Peter and Miguel?"

"To make sure everything went according to plan. I don't know or trust those goons of yours. For all I know one of them could be the leak."

"Miguel and Peter are both loyal men, more loyal than any of yours," Nora countered.

Joseph turned and walked in front of Nora's desk and said in a serious voice, "I'm in charge here, and as long as she's here, I want her locked in her room."

"No. She's my girl and she can walk around the facility freely," Nora answered, flexing her political muscles. Joseph slammed the desk. The sudden motion caused Nora to jump slightly, but soon a feeling of pleasure came over her. She had pushed the right buttons.

"She might be your girl, but this is my facility." Joseph was sure to emphasize the words "my facility." "You and I may hold the same rank, but in case you've forgotten, you're a guest here."

"You're afraid one frightened girl who doesn't know where she is can escape?" Nora added. Hoping to push his buttons a little further, she said, "Once my new facility" she emphasized the words just as Joseph had—"is finished, Tara will be out of your hair if she is not shipped off to another country sooner."

Joseph turned, made a fist, brought it up to his face, and blew into it. He turned around and said, "We're used to holding, transporting, and smuggling guns, drugs, and the occasional whore of yours to different locations. We're not equipped to holding someone for long periods or operate as a pleasure house."

"That is why you have me."

Joseph ignored the smart comment and continued, "We also hold Dr. Bodkin's special project that brings the organization over a billion dollars yearly, and that's not even counting the possible new medical breakthroughs we could discover."

"Harvesting human organs can be done anywhere," Nora said, grabbing another cigarette.

"That's not what I was taking about," Joseph replied, his voice becoming slightly tense.

"What?" Nora asked, taken back by the answer. "Next to Tara's room is where the bodies are held for organ harvesting?"

"No, that's not what's in there, that thing is," Joseph said, this time with a hint of fear in his voice.

"What do you mean 'that thing'?" Nora asked. Concern grew in her own voice now. Joseph didn't reply right away as if thinking about what he should say.

"The only people who know about this are my most trusted men, and a select few high-ranking Omnipotent leaders. So, what I'm about to tell you never leaves this room." Joseph leaned in closer to her to show his seriousness. "Understand?" Nora shook her head yes. She would have assumed this was a joke, but the seriousness and hint of fear in his voice proved otherwise.

"Dr. Bodkin keeps something in there. I don't know if he created it in a lab or found it in some forsaken part of the earth." Joseph stared down at the desk, his breathing rate increasing. "Every other week he takes it to his office."

"You mean the one down the hall?" Nora asked, shocked. "You can't be serious. I would have noticed something."

"You've only been here a little under a month. I made sure you weren't around when it happened." For the first time, Nora was thinking about bunking down at a local hotel over her private suite.

"Have you seen it?"

"Once and I never care to again." He pulled away from the desk and started to pace nervously. "Only a select few of the staff are allowed to walk him to Doctor Bodkin. Other than that we keep him locked up and forgotten about."

"You said him. Is this a man or beast we're talking about?" Nora inquired. The idea was frightening but she had an urge to see this thing for herself.

"Both, neither, I don't know." Joseph locked eyes with her again. His eyes were wide, a serious death stare on his face.

"This facility cannot be found." Joseph pointed towards the hallway. "What's behind that door can never see the outside world." He slammed Nora's desk. "That is why we cannot have a whore running around the facility freely."

"Very well. I will only allow Tara to go to the kitchen several times a day and under guard." Content with her words, Joseph returned to his desk. Nora tapped her fingers against the table, thinking about Tara. "Perhaps you are right—maybe she does believe she can manipulate us. But I have an idea of my own before her next session." She leaned back and smiled. "I have a little surprise for our dear Tara."

Chapter 10

For several hours Tara sat in her room. She was famished, but at least she would be getting some food soon. An excited look formed on her face when she heard someone outside the door. Devin walked in pushing a wire cart.

"Here's your stuff," he said in a neutral voice. Tara got to her feet and rushed over to the cart. She quickly opened a bag of fruit and grabbed a banana.

"Hungry?" Devin asked, watching the banana rapidly disappear. *What gave you that idea?* Tara thought. The ravishing hunger she felt made her want to eat everything in sight. It was hard but she managed to restrain herself, knowing this was the only food she would be getting for a while.

"Here, this is on the house," Devin said, handing her two bag with three changes of clothes in them.

"Thanks," she replied. She tossed the bags towards the closet, then started going through her food bags. She laid the frozen food, half the fruit, and snacks in a pile, then placed the cereal boxes and remaining fruit in a room corner.

"You know it was a pain to get, and bring you these things," Devin said. "I think I should get something for this," he continued in a charming voice, puckering his lips. Tara rolled her eyes. She knew what he wanted and was not about to give it to him. She didn't want to start a fight either, not with the possibility of losing her food.

"Hold on," she said, thinking of a solution. She reached into a bag, opened a box of chocolate chip cookies, and handed him one. "There you go," she said with a sarcastic smile, then placed the box next to her pile in the corner.

He scowled in disappointment, then said, "If you're hungry, I'll take you to the dining hall now."

"Just give me directions. I can go myself," Tara replied, wanting him to leave.

"Ms. Peters told me you were not allowed to walk around by yourself. Which means you're stuck with me."

"What! She told me this afternoon I could come and go as I pleased!" Tara replied, shocked.

"Plans changed, I guess." He shrugged. "Now do you want to go to the kitchen or not?"

"Next you going to tell me a guard is going to be posted outside my door?" Tara asked in sarcasm, but also to get information. If a guard was going to be standing outside her room, it would make conducting her escape plan next to impossible.

"I have no idea. Now can we get going? I have things I want to do." Devin's attitude pleased her. Despite his earlier unwanted gesture, he seemed to be the type of guy who was more interested in video games and streaming movies than tormenting her.

"Hold on," she said, opening her clock. "What time is it?"

"Fifteen minutes to six," Devan replied. Tara set her clock and grabbed five bags of food. Devin didn't offer to help her carry them, but fortunately years of shopping sprees had made her an expert at carrying lots of bags. Upon exiting the room, Tara scanned the ceiling to see if someone had installed a new camera. She was relieved to see nothing, but the idea of having to be escorted when she was told she could roam freely worried her. *Are they suspecting I'm up to something, and if so, how much do they suspect?* As she thought, the hallway took a sharp right. A few yards from the makeup room the hall opened up into a recreation room and dining hall.

Two pool tables were in the center of the recreation room. Various arcade games hugged the right wall. A full bar covered half the left wall with a lounge area occupying the other half. Two large TVs hung on the right and left sides of the wall.

Next to the recreation room was the dining hall. Four large benches covered most of the room. A stove, microwave, and sink were placed at the middle of the left wall with a refrigerator and freezer at the left end. Storage cabinets were placed above them. Between the benches and appliances was a large counter used for preparing food. Fourteen men and four women were eating, or enjoying themselves in the recreation room.

Feeling uneasy, Tara quickly searched for Miguel, wanting to be as far away from him as possible. She spotted the guy with the ghetto accent playing pool with two other people. "You going to go in or what?" Devin asked. *Okay, I'm going,* Tara thought, annoyed, as she started walking towards the dining hall. It was hard, but she managed to walk like she belonged, figuring she would draw more attention if she were acting frightened, which is what she was feeling inside. She approached the refrigerator, placing her fruit inside. She pulled out a sesame chicken TV dinner and placed it in the microwave before putting her frozen food in the freezer. "You planning on eating here?" Devin asked. *Ya, like I'm really going to eat here,* Tara thought, looking again to make sure no one was coming to torment her.

"No, I'm going to go back to my room as soon as this cooks. Where do I put this stuff?" she asked, holding up her bag of snacks.

Devin pointed to the upper cabinets. "It can go there." He grabbed a sharpie from on top of the refrigerator. "Use this to put you name on your items. Trust me, someone will eat it otherwise."

"You know what, I'll take this stuff back to my room," she said, knowing people would not hesitate to steal her things. "I'm going to mark my frozen stuff, then head back." She hated leaving it but knew she had no choice.

"Okay," Devin replied. He pointed over to a nearby bench. "I'm going over to talk to those guys. Just come over when you're ready." Tara laid her bag down on the counter and started labeling her frozen food. The thought crossed her mind to label everything Nora Peters. That would deter any would be thieves. In the end she decided it was not worth the risk.

Tara heard someone approaching. Thinking it was Devin, she said, "I'm nearly done. I still have to label my fruit." She heard the rustling of her bag. Tara turned around and let out a frightened gasp. Peter was casually going through her snack bag. He opened a box of strawberry wafers and started shoving them into his mouth.

He looked over at her and said, "Very good." Inside Tara was trembling. She wanted to run out of the room, and the way Peter was looking at her, that's exactly what he expected her to do. Tara briefly looked down at the floor. She knew running was easiest but would never help her get over her fear. Even a minor victory over one of the men who had violated her would do wonders for her mental state. Tara looked Peter right in the eye with a confident look.

"Give me that," she said in an equally confident voice. For a moment Peter's face had a surprised look.

"Come and take it, tough girl." Like a high school bully, Peter held the box above her head. Inside Tara cringed he had called her bluff, and now she needed to back it up. The first thought that came to her was punching him in the stomach. A pleasant one, but she couldn't find the courage to go through with it. Instead, she jumped up, trying to reach the wafers.

Peter laughed. "Come on, is that all you got?" he asked, smacking her on the head.

That's it. You're not pushing me around anymore. Tara raised her fist and lunged forward. Peter causally stepped to the side, causing Tara's punch to completely miss. Her momentum sent her flying forward right into Miguel, who was sitting at the closest table, enjoying Peter's tormenting. Tara slammed into him. *No!* she thought, feeling his whiskey spill all over her.

"You stupid whore!" he screamed. With one arm, he shoved Tara forward. Her back slammed into the oven. She hit the ground moaning in pain, holding her back.

"Come on, guys, if she gets hurt, I'll get blamed," Devin said, not bothering to get up. People started to circle around, wanting to see what would happen next. Others did not care and went about their business. When Tara regained her senses, she saw Miguel and Peter standing over her grinning.

"Please! Please don't hurt me!" she begged, curling up into a defense ball.

"You really are pathetic," Peter said. He bent down and gave her two taunting slaps to the face and head. Tara covered up the best she could, hoping that was the worst he did. "What happened to that tough attitude?" A ding from the microwave caught Peter's attention. He opened it and pulled out the TV dinner.

"Here's your dinner," he said, dumping the tray on top of her. Tara let out a whimper as the heated sauce burned her skin. Miguel tapped Peter on the shoulder.

"We have work to do. Let's get on with it." *What does he mean by that?* Tara thought, petrified.

"I'm not done having fun with Tara," Peter replied.

"There will be plenty of time for that later," Miguel answered. Tara felt herself calming down when she heard them walk away. She got on her hands and knees. She looked around the room, hoping someone would have the heart to at least help her up.

Only Devin stood beside her. His only words were, "Tara, come on, quit fooling around. I have stuff I need to do." Tara shot him an upset look. *Excuse me, I was just beaten and humiliated.* She managed to hold back any tears as she scooped the chicken and noodles back on the tray. She got up, grabbed her bag of snacks, and started filling her water jug. When she looked into the sink, she noticed someone had left a serrated steak knife in it. She wanted to grab it, chase down Miguel and Peter, and stab them to death. *That will only get you killed or worse. Could be useful for later on, though.* Tara laid her filled jug on the counter and internally tilted her bag over the sink so the snacks would fall out.

Tara put on her acting voice and said, "Why can't I get a break?" She was already upset so it was easy to sound convincing. She moved what was left of the pack of wafers over the knife, then picked them up along with it. She placed the rest of the spilled items in the bag, then ran out of the dining hall back to her room.

"Tara, hold up. Wait," Devin yelled as he chased after her.

"I'm in eyesight, aren't I?" she replied, too upset to think through what her defiance might cost her. When she reached her room, she set her dinner tray on the floor and said to Devin, who had just caught up with her, "I'm good for the night."

"Works for me." He sounded happy to be rid of her. "I'll be back sometime in the morning to take you to breakfast."

"Don't bother. I have everything I need here," Tara replied, pointing towards her breakfast cereals.

"If that's what you want," Devin replied, sounding pleased he didn't have to worry about it. "I assume you want lunch and dinner?"

"Yes." *If you have any food left,* the voice of doubt reminded. Tara tuned it out and said, "Any chance we can go before everyone gets there?" The less people she had to deal with the better. On the bright side of things, only Miguel and Peter had gone out of their way to torment her.

"If that's what you want. Does eleven and three work?"

"If those hours are less crowded. Yes," she replied, taking her normal position at the window. Devin said a causal goodbye and left. Tara waited a few moments, then clenched her fists and hammered on the wall, letting her frustration out.

"I'm not going through that day after day," she told herself. *How do you plan on avoiding it?* the voice of doubt asked.

"Like I already said, I'll go when less people are around," Tara said, answering her own thought. The smell from the warm chicken reminded her how hungry she was. She sat down, and soon, having her first hot meal in weeks made her forget most of her frustration. As she ate, she started going through her mental checklist. *I have a noise reducer, and you might have a way to cut a hole in the wall.* Tara bolted to her feet. While in the kitchen, she had not checked to see if the knife had a dull point. She grabbed the knife from the bag and said, "Yes," looking at the sharp point. It was not the ideal cutting tool, but it was probably the best she was going to get. *Okay, have a fan and knife. Next I need to get measurements of how far it is from my room to the VIP room. Of course I don't have a measuring tape.* Tara placed her hand on her head in frustration, realizing she had nothing to put in front of the escape hole. *Should have bought a small shelf or something,* she thought in annoyance.

She looked at the air mattress and soon came to the conclusion there was no way it would cover a hole large enough for her to fit through. Tara took in a deep breath and blew out, trying to find a solution to her problem. She snapped her finger as the answer to her problem was right in front of her. *Start the tunnel in the closet.* Inside the small closet only had one shelf near the top. Tara went inside the closet and got on her knees. She jammed the blade into the wall. It took a little effort, but the blade went through. "Yes, yes, this will work!" Tara said happily. She wanted to start working right then but knew a lot more planning needed to be done first. She left the closet and looked the room over, searching for a safe place to keep the knife. *My old friend the toilet.* She went over to it, lifted the toilet lid, and dropped the knife inside, then sat back down and started eating. When she was finished, she instinctively looked for a waste basket. She huffed in frustration. *Forgot to get a trash can.* She put the tray next to the door, intending to dispose of it the next day. She walked over to the closet wall at the back of the room and started making mental notes. *Start the tunnel to the left, when you reach the room corner, make another left. What if the wall with the window is not hollow?* the voice of doubt asked her. Tara cursed, realizing her inner demon might be right.

She looked at the window. *It's a bay window.* Tara smiled. *Meaning there's a space in the wall.* That brought another detail to Tara's head. Every door and window she had seen, including hers, were on the same side of the wall, the side facing the outside world. *If this building is a square, what's in the center of the square?* The thought intrigued her, but it didn't pertain to her current goals so she soon forgot it. She got on her hands and knees next to the bay window. There were several feet of space between her back and bottom of the window seat. "Okay, there's enough room," she said out loud, pleased with the results. Having done all she could, Tara unboxed her air mattress and plugged in the electric air pump. *It will be so nice to have a soft place to sleep tonight,* she thought, listening to the humming of the motor. Once the mattress was fully inflated, she put her blanket on it and plugged her fan in. She looked at the time, which read seven-thirty-two. She set the alarm for twelve-thirty. Before bed, she brushed her teeth, never imagining a simple activity like brushing her teeth could bring such joy. After that, she set her alarm and lay down on the air mattress, which felt like heaven to her back. Surrounded by the blanket's warmth, she closed her eyes listening to the soft humming of the fan. Feeling the cool air on her face made her feel like she was home. She imagined that until she fell asleep.

At one a.m., Tara was awoken by the beeping of the alarm. She turned it off and got up. *Let's get this over with,* she thought, knowing this was probably the riskiest part of the plan. She splashed some water on her face, then moved to her door, listening for people in the hallway. When she determined it was safe, she opened the door, double checked to make sure no one was around, then headed for the mystery door. She stopped under the camera.

She looked at the door and said softly, "I'm going to reach you soon, Mr. Phone, and you're going to help me escape." She turned towards her room and got on her hands and knees, then extended her right arm as far as it would go and placed it on the ground. *One,* she thought as she moved her back legs forward, going back to a natural crawl stance. She extended her left arm. *Two.* She repeated the process until she reached her room, her final count being seventeen. It was a crude way of measuring, but it was all she had. Deciding it was worth the risk, she repeated the measurement and got the same result. She thought about taking a trip past the dining room to see if her theory about the building being square was true and to learn what was located in that section of the building, but decided against it. If she was caught, it would make her captors aware of her nighttime activities. Satisfied with her accomplishments, she returned to her room.

She went over to her snack bag and grabbed a cookie to celebrate. She looked at it for a moment, thinking about how she used to avoid cookies like the plague. *After more than a week of starving, one or two cookies won't kill me,* she thought, taking a bite. Soon a feeling of tiredness came over her. She lay back down, again taking in some comforts of home. Her situation was far from okay, but at least she had this to look forward to at night.

Chapter 11

Romy parked in the Ellwood City square shopping plaza where her business Ellwood City Hair and Nails was located. She had started the business five years ago right after graduating from college with a bachelor's in business management and a certification in cosmetology. Ellwood City Hair and Nails was opened from eleven a.m. to seven p.m., Monday to Thursday. Friday and Saturday hours were ten a.m. to six p.m. Romy chose those hours so her employees could enjoy going out with friends on Friday and Saturday nights. The salon was closed Sundays. Along with Sunday, each girl had an additional day off during the week, with the exception of Fridays and Saturdays, the busiest days of the week. Romy had two employees working for her, Mellany Kittelt and Casey Anderson. Both of them acted as either hair and nail stylists or a receptionist. At times this made things hectic, but it was never busy enough for Romy to need a full-time receptionist. Romy tapped her finger on the steering wheel, feeling when she returned to work, she would subconsciously accept Tara was gone. She also knew many of the local customers would be asking about Tara, questions she really did not want to answer.

Thinking about what Brandon and Ryan had told her, Romy pushed the car door open and started walking towards the building. *I'm going to have a load of office work to do,* Romy thought, knowing during her time off she had neglected her business, orders needed to be placed, bills needed to be paid, and a polite text from Mellany had reminded her that pay period was coming up. Romy opened the door. She saw Mellany getting everything ready for the coming day.

"Romy, welcome back!" Mellany said, excited. She walked over to Romy, quickly hugging her.

"Same as when you left it," Mellany replied. "I even had Casey give my hair some gloss," Mellany said, flipping her long black hair.

"Looks amazing," Romy complimented. Her voice got serious when she said, "Look, Mel, I want to thank you for all the extra work you and Casey have been doing and helping look for Tara."

"It was no trouble. I can't imagine how hard it must be for you. If you need more time away, Casey and I can run the store for you." Inside Romy wanted to accept the offer but knew she needed to get back to her normal routines.

"No, you and Casey have done more than enough and your checks will show how appreciative I am."

"You don't need to do that," Mellany replied.

"I know, but I want to, and besides, you want the extra money. I can see it on your face."

"Was I really that obvious?"

"Got ya," Romy replied. Mellany opened her mouth in playful surprise.

"Now get back to work and quit slacking," Romy teased.

Mellany put her hands on her ears and stuck out her tongue. Romy went to the receptionist desk to look over the clients for the day. As soon as she looked up, she focused on the missing persons poster of Tara. Her mind went back to a few years ago when Tara had worked for her. The worst employee she ever had. She remember always having to scold Tara for coming in late or using her phone at work. It drove her so crazy that she was glad when Tara had quit to work on her modeling career, but now she would have given anything to see her sitting in the receptionist chair on her phone, breaking the rules. Romy got up and walked up to the missing persons photo. *Tara, we're going to find your kidnappers and bring you home.*

◆　◆　◆

Compared to every other morning of her imprisonment, this one started off well. Waking up in a warm bed, knowing what time it was, and, more importantly, having a filling breakfast had her morale up and her mind focused on escaping. She was also relieved to be able to change clothes. She wore a pair of blue jeans and blue unmarked t-shirt. Tara spent a majority of the morning perfecting her escape plan. In her room she knocked on every inch of wall along her planned path, making sure there were no solid areas. She stopped when the sound of approaching footsteps caught her ear. *Time for lunch.* She climbed onto the window seat and sat down. Moments later, the door opened.

"Hi, Tara. I'm here to take you to lunch," Devin said in his normal neutral, uninterested voice.

"Sounds good," Tara replied, getting down and grabbing her trash.

"What were you doing up there?" Devin asked as they walked.

"Dreaming of home. What else can I do?" she replied. Devin shook his head like he had just heard something ridiculous.

"Some friendly advice, don't. Try to forget about it. You're never going to see it again." Tara felt anger flare up inside her. *Shut up. I will, wait and see.* Devin didn't seem to notice or care about Tara's lack of response and went back to playing with his phone. As they walked, an idea came to her. She smiled and asked, "What do you do around here anyway? I mean besides escorting me to the kitchen."

"At the moment, not much. Things have been pretty slow around here since the training brothel for this area got shut down." *A training brothel got shut down? That explains a lot,* Tara thought. It answered the question of why she was the only girl here. She was beginning to like Devin. He was careless, easy to get information from.

"What do you mean it got shut down? Like it went out of business?" Tara asked playfully. Devin looked around, making sure no one was in earshot.

"I didn't tell you this." He lowered his voice and said, "It got raided by police. Everyone but Nora and a few others made it out." Tara slowed down, wanting to get as much information as she could.

"Were the girls working there arrested?"

"No, after the police confiscated them, they let them go." Tara shot him a quick glare. She hated how this organization treated the people they abducted as property. That caused another question to enter her mind. *How many people were currently being held against their will by these people?* Devin must have noticed she was in deep thought because he said, "Don't get your hopes up. Omnipotent doesn't allow loose ends. Twenty girls were taken and I heard last night fourteen of them have been captured or killed. The others won't last long." Hearing that caused a jolt of fear to run though her. She had thought Nora had been exaggerating the size of the organization. *Was Devin lying as well?* His tone and casualness as he spoke made her doubt it. All sorts of questions began running though her head. When she did escape, would she be hunted for the rest of her life? Would her escape put Romy and Ryan's lives in danger? Instead of letting the thoughts overwhelm her, Tara focused on getting more information.

"So, Nora doesn't normally work here? I thought her and Joseph ran the brothel? When I..." Tara tried to find the right word. "Arrived, Nora told me Heartwood Manor was every girl's dream."

"She told you what?" Devin replied with a slight chuckle. "Heartwood Manor was the place that got shut down. Nora's only been here for about a month. Joseph's the one who's in charge of the facility." Devin paused as if thinking about whether he should say what he was thinking. "If you asked me, the sooner she's gone the better. I don't like her power plays or using our facility as a pleasure house."

"Why not?" Tara asked, wondering if he did have some human empathy after all.

"Too many unknown people coming to screw you," Devin said in a joking voice. It took all Tara had from punching him in the face. *Stay calm, Tara. Stay calm. Go back to your questioning.*

"So, if this place is not a brothel, what normally goes on here?" she asked, showing no sign of anger in her voice.

"Wouldn't you like to know?" Devin replied. Tara remained quiet for the remainder of the walk, not wanting to push Devin too far. When they arrived at the recreation room, Tara searched for Miguel and Peter, ready to leave if she spotted either of them. Four men were there, all sitting at the same table: two she recognized from the night before, two were new. Tara walked slowly, keeping an eye on them, but when she noticed no one was paying any attention to her, she walked at a casual pace over to the fridge. She saw Devin grab a bag of chips from a cabinet and sit at a table. Tara readied herself, expecting to find her bag of fruit had been stolen, but when she opened the fridge, she was pleasantly surprised to find her bag untouched. She grabbed an apple from it. Her plan was to eat a big breakfast, small lunch, and a normal-sized dinner. If everything went according to plan, that would be all the food she needed. Her eyes scanned the counter top and sink looking for anything she could use as an additional cutting tool or weapon. When she spotted nothing, she went over to Devin and said, "I'm going to walk around and explore the area a little if you don't mind."

"Okay with me," Devin replied, not looking up from the online game on his phone.

Tara walked into the recreation room, checking to see if there was anything sharp, but not surprisingly, there was nothing. The closest thing she saw was a box of darts. She thought about grabbing one but decided against it. *Too much risk for too little reward.* Tara looked up and down both empty halls. The men in the room, including Devin, were all occupied with their own activities. With no one paying attention to her, Tara's curiosity got the better of her. She wanted to see what was beyond the kitchen. She kept an eye on everyone in the room with each step moving closer and closer to the end of the dining hall. She looked back a final time to see if anyone had noticed her—no one had, so she went on. She figured when Devin noticed she was missing, he would assume she had gone back to her room. She had no doubt she would be caught. When she was, she would use the excuse she took a wrong turn, and blame Devin for not keeping an eye on her. Sweet revenge for his earlier comment. Tara walked a few yards until the hall opened up to a wide area on her left. *This looks like a hotel hallway,* Tara thought, staring at the walls that were painted light brown with grey carpet covering the floor. Twelve doors were on each side of the hall, with two doors at the end of the room. *Living quarters,* Tara guessed. Being this close to what she considered a lion's den made her very uneasy. She started to step backwards, wanting to come back at night when everyone would be asleep. She planted her back foot down to stop herself. *No, I can't risk them coming into my room to check on me at night.* Quickly and quietly, she walked past it, continuing down the hall.

As she suspected, she encountered a left turn hallway. When she walked past the turn in the hallway, a door blocked her path. She looked above it and, not seeing a camera, she cautiously opened it. The door opened to a large garage and storage area. Twenty vehicles were parked on the right and left sides of the garage, and past them, three semi trucks were parked. On the farthest side of the room were two industrial garage doors. Tara heard voices and saw four to five shadows moving towards her.

"Hey, is someone there?" a male voice said. Tara thought about rushing back. *No, they'll hear the door open and close. They'll know one of them would not run.* Tara frantically looked for a hiding spot. A few yards from her she spotted a concrete wall. She put her back up against it and followed it until she reached the back wall. Not the best hiding stop by any means. She could only hope they would keep walking and not look in her direction.

"What did you hear?" another male voice asked. Tara could now see them, four men and a woman.

"I thought I heard the door open," he replied.

"I didn't hear anything," the girl stated. She lightly punched him on the shoulder. "You're losing it, man."

"I guess you're right," he agreed, thinking it was nothing. "Come on, let's go eat before the next shipment gets here." The group of five started to walk forward. *The last person will look back and notice you right before he closes the door,* Tara's voice of doubt said.

No, they won't, Tara reassured herself in a nervous tone. She watched nervously as one by one, the people went through the door. She could feel sweat starting to fall as the final person went through. She gasped in relief when she heard the door close. *Okay, you're safe for now.* Still shaken by what occurred, she wanted to run back to her room, which to her disliking was becoming a place of comfort. However, once again her curiosity won out. She walked to the edge of the concrete wall. It ended about five feet from a drop in the floor, which led to the main garage area. Tara turned to her left and saw the concrete wall was actually a storage room. Yellow storage fencing covered the top and stretched about six feet before ending at another concrete wall. *This must be a loading dock.* Tara looked inside and saw a camera on the room's back wall.

"Shoot!" she said, jumping back to the wall. She had been in view for only a few seconds. *If they did see me, no point in running.* She poked her head around enough to see what was in the room. She saw five vertical gun racks. Each held seven machine or sub machine guns. Above them were twenty pistols hung on gun shelf hangers. In front of the gun racks were boxes of various sizes with paperwork taped to them. Along the back wall were four large ammo storage cabinets. Tara nearly ran across the fencing to find a way in. Her only thought was grabbing a gun and shooting her way to freedom. Her dream soon faded as logic set in. *The gate has to be locked.* An examination of the latch soon confirmed it. *Even if I could get in, the camera would see me, and ten to one the ammo's locked up. Plus, I'd be outnumbered twenty-something to one,* Tara reminded herself, abandoning the idea altogether. She tried to see what was on the wall adjacent to her but couldn't. *More guns,* she guessed.

Tara looked beyond the armory and noticed another row of fencing. In total she could make out four storage rooms. *How do I get past the camera?* she thought in frustration. She looked towards the garage area and smiled. Keeping out of camera view, she jumped down off the loading dock and got on her hands and knees using the loading dock wall for cover. She crawled until she thought she was at the second concrete pillar. She reached into her pocket and pulled out her makeup mirror and sat down. She tilted it upward, using the reflection to see where she was at. Turns out she was near the middle of the second fencing. She tried to see what was in the room, but the details in the mirror were not clear enough.

She positioned herself so she was in line with the second pillar. She climbed onto the loading dock, ran over to the pillar, and looked inside the second room. She saw a camera in the same place as the armory camera.

Across the side wall packages covered in white, grey, and brown tape were stacked about halfway to the celling. The back wall had a large work bench. Bags of cocaine, small blue crystals, and weed sat next to a weighing scale and packing material. *First guns, why not drugs?* She turned to look at the gun room. Gun racks with rifles and shotguns were on the wall she could not see before. Tara repeated her camera avoiding tactic for the next two rooms. The third room had two industrial freezers. *I can only imagine what's in there,* she thought, choosing to not focus on it.

The next room looked like it was meant to hold people. A bench stretched across each portion of wall. Above them eighteen chains were welded to the wall. At the end of each chain was a circular cuff. Tara felt a feeling of terror creep through her. She saw an image of herself handcuffed to the wall, with Miguel and Peter walking towards her, ready to load her in the back of a truck. *I have to get out of here before that happens,* she thought, knowing it was only a matter of time before her vision would become reality. Not wanting to stare at the room anymore, she looked straight ahead at the garage door.

"Tara, you idiot," she said out loud. Her ticket to freedom was right in front of her. She could open the garage door and escape. She was about to rush for it when she felt a hand on her shoulder, and the next thing she knew, she was spun around, now facing the tall man.

"What are you doing in here?" he asked in a menacing voice.

"I was just…"

Before Tara could continue, he cut her off, "I already know, you're snooping around, aren't you?" Before Tara could reply, he spun her back towards the room with the chains. Tara felt his iron grip pulling on the back of her shirt. "Get a good look at that room, girl. That's where you're going to end up very soon. Now let's go see Mr. Jackson." Tara felt her feet nearly lift off the floor as he drug her by the back of the shirt. Inside Tara was cursing herself. *How could I have been so stupid? How could I have not seen a simple way to escape right in front of me?* Now instead of escaping, she was going to have to face the wrath of her captors.

Inside his office, Joseph Jackson was furious. He was visibly red in the face, so much that veins were nearly bursting. Tara turned to Nora Peters's desk, noticing she was not there.

"Justin, thank you," he said, looking at the tall man. "Please wait here." He turned his attention back to Tara and said, "Tara, what were you doing out of your room and in the loading docks?"

"I was getting lunch. Devin was fooling around on his phone so I decided to go back to my room myself and got lost."

"Bullshit!" Joseph screamed, slamming the table. The sudden action startled Tara, but she soon regained her composure.

"No, it isn't. Here's an apple," Tara said, holding it up. A look of concern suddenly formed on Joseph's face. "Justin, did you search her?"

"No, didn't see a reason to," he replied.

"Do it! Do it now!" Joseph said, not in a panic, but Tara did notice a hint of concern. Justin got up without being told. Tara did the same, feeling very glad she didn't steal any darts from the recreation room. Justin padded down every inch of her. Tara cringed when he touch more sensitive areas, but to her relief he didn't linger on them. Justin placed Tara's makeup mirror on the table.

"Only thing on her," he said casually.

"Why were you carrying this around?" Joseph demanded to know.

"I always carry a mirror with me, an old habit from home," Tara replied like it was an everyday thing. Joseph looked like he didn't believe her but didn't have any proof she lying. He pulled out his cell phone and dialed a number.

"Nora, it's Joseph. Do you know where Justin found Tara?" Tara managed to hide a smirk, knowing they were going to start fighting. "Snooping around the loading dock!" Joseph shouted. Tara tried but couldn't hear what Nora was saying.

"I don't know what she was doing?" Joseph said in a raised voice.

"No, she didn't steal anything or try to escape; if she did I would have killed her on the spot." Inside a jolt of fear ran through Tara. The feeling soon turned to relief, realizing how lucky she was that Justin had caught her before she made a break for the doorway.

"It is a big deal!" Joseph said, getting up in frustration. "This event was unacceptable. Do you know how lucky we are someone caught her?" Joseph listened for a few moments, then said, "She's right here in the office." Joseph shoved the phone in Tara's face. "Nora Peters wants to have a word with you."

"Hello?" Tara said, intentionally sounding frightened.

"Tara, do you care to explain your actions to me?" Nora asked.

"I got lost, then curiosity got the better of me, so I decided to explore the facility."

"What did curiosity do?" Nora asked. Hearing both of them threaten her life did frighten her. Thinking quickly, she thought of a way to use it to her advantage. She started talking fast, acting like she was desperate for Nora to believe her.

"I swear to you, though, I didn't touch or take anything I wasn't supposed to." Tara sounded desperate when she said, "Are you coming back soon? Joseph's really mad at me. I'm afraid he's going to hurt me." Tara tried to keep a straight face when she saw Joseph's reaction. She was hoping her act would cause Nora to think she was broken and saw her as a source of authority and comfort. Her act was also making Joseph believe she feared him. She did but not as much as when she first arrived.

"I never said anything like that, you lying whore!" Tara had the phone slightly away from her ear so Nora could hear everything.

"No, please don't hit me!" Tara yelled, sounding like she was cowering. In reality, Joseph was several arm's lengths away from her.

"Tara, give Joseph the phone!" Nora shouted. With a trembling hand, she handed the phone towards Joseph.

"N…Nora wants to talk to you." Joseph ripped the phone from her hand. *Everything's going according to plan*. Joseph left the room and talked with Nora for several minutes. At first she heard shouting, but then things seem to cool down. He returned to the office and handed the phone back to Tara, still looking like he wanted to strangle her.

"Tara, I talked it over with Joseph, and I agree it was unacceptable for you to leave your escort and go wandering around the facility. We cannot have an incident like this occur again."

"I understand, and it won't happen again, I swear," Tara replied.

"That's good to hear and I understand some girls have a curious nature. However, actions have consequences. I will have to give you a small punishment so we can move on."

"I understand," Tara replied, now seriously becoming nervous.

"I'm afraid I have no choice but to keep you locked in your room until further notice. Someone will bring meals to you, and you will only shower before you meet a client." Inside Tara was jumping up and down. Nora's punishment had worked in her favor. If they thought she was locked up, no one would have any reason to check on her, and she wouldn't have to worry about getting harassed in the kitchen area.

"Why does the door need to be locked? It's not like I can go anywhere," Tara said, sounding upset. She knew if she went along with it without putting up a fuss, Nora might suspect something was up.

"You're going to stay in there with the door locked and that's the end of it!" Joseph added harshly.

"I understand. It that all you needed?" Tara said, sounding defeated.

"One last thing," Nora said. "You have a client tomorrow." Hearing that sent away any happiness or feeling of victory Tara was feeling. "I want you to use this time to mentally prepare yourself." Her voice took on a stern warning when she said, "No incidents had better occur this time."

"Nothing will happen. I learned my lesson," Tara said, this time with genuine fear in her voice.

"I know it won't," Nora replied with assurance in her voice as she looked out her car window.

Chapter 12

Nora Peters exited her luxury car, tossing a cigarette on the ground.

"Wait here," Nora ordered the driver. She pulled out her phone, snapping a picture of the building in front of her. *You're not the only one who can play mind games, dear Tara,* she thought as she entered.

"Hi, can I help you?" a young girl asked as she approached the receptionist desk.

"Nora Peters. I have a two o'clock appointment with Romy Cymric."

Mellany glanced down at the schedule. "I'll let Romy know you're here. If you'd like to have a seat in the meantime," Mellany replied, motioning to the waiting area seats. Nora grinned, spotting Tara's missing persons poster. Tara was sitting on a park wall smiling. Under the photo in large letters was, "Help Bring Our Beloved Tara Home." In smaller letters were details about Tara and what was known about her disappearance. Nora scoffed under her breath when she read the words, thinking of all the trouble Tara had already caused her.

"Hi, Ms. Peters, I'm Romy," Romy said, walking over and offering her hand.

Nora shook it. "A pleasure."

"If you're ready, you can follow me and we'll get started." Romy led Nora to the styling chair. "That accent, is it German?"

"Eastern European," Nora replied, sitting down.

"I understand you wanted to add some color to your hair?" *Now the game begins,* Nora thought.

"Yes, I'm returning home from visiting family in the area and wanted to show the people at work I can still party in my later years." Romy snickered.

"I'm sure you can," Romy replied as she placed the cutting cape on Nora. "Do members of your family come here?" Romy asked, trying to make small talk as she worked.

"No, why do you ask?"

"I wasn't trying to be nosy," Romy replied, fearing she had upset her. "For referrals, I give clients ten percent off their next visit; that's why I asked."

"I'm sure you weren't," Nora replied, waving it off. "I wanted to get my hair done before I returned home. Your business had good reviews and was close, so I came here."

"I'm glad you did. Thanks for choosing us," Romy replied, placing a hand on the chair lever. "I'm going to lay you back so I can wash your hair."

"Before we begin, do you mind if I take a quick photo? I wanted a before and after shot."

"Sure," Romy replied. Nora pulled out her cell phone and took a selfie, making sure Romy was in it.

"Thank you," Nora said, putting her cell phone away.

"Not a problem. What color were you thinking of?"

"I was thinking blue with possibly the tips of the hair dyed pink." Inside Nora laughed, watching a look of disbelief form on Romy's face. No doubt she was thinking about Tara. Tears started to appear in her eyes. Before breaking down, Romy managed to get out, "I'm sorry, Mellany will take care of you." Nora smiled a satisfied grin as Romy rushed towards her office. "Mellany, take care of Ms. Peters, will you?" Romy said right before shutting her office door. Mellany stood conflicted.

"Is everything all right?" Nora asked, pretending to be surprised. Mellany wet her lips, looking back and forth between Romy's office and Nora Peters.

She remained silent for a moment before fake smiling and saying, "Yes, my name's Mellany. I'll be taking care of you now."

"In my experience when someone runs off crying, everything is far from okay," Nora replied, enjoying watching Mellany's confliction. She could tell she was thinking of what to say next.

"Romy's sister went missing a few weeks ago, and she's been devastated ever since," Mellany replied sadly.

"That's horrible," Nora said, placing a hand over her mouth in surprise. "Don't concern yourself with me. Perhaps you should check in on her."

"Well." Mellany turned her head, clearly wanting to go comfort Romy. "I can't keep you waiting. I'm sure it's awkward enough for you already." Nora shrugged the remark off.

"Go see if your friend's alright. I don't mind waiting a few extra minutes."

"Are you sure, you don't mind?" Mellany asked, lighting up a little.

"Not at all," Nora assured.

"Thank you! Thank you, Ms. Peters," Mellany said gratefully.

Romy sat at her desk. Her head was down and both hands covered her face. She looked up when she heard someone say, "Romy, are you okay?"

Romy wiped some tears from her reddening face. "Yes, I'm fine, thanks for asking, Mellany. Did Ms. Peters leave?"

"No, she said I should go check on you, so I took her up on it," Mellany replied, hoping Romy would not become more upset. Romy gave a soft smile.

"You sure you're okay?" Mellany asked, concerned.

"Hearing Ms. Peters say she wanted her hair dyed blue made me think of Tara." Romy shook her head in embarrassment. "I can't believe I broke down like that. Sorry, Mel, I didn't mean to put you in such an awkward situation," Romy apologized.

"You don't need to apologize," Mellany reassured. "I'm not angry and Ms. Peters doesn't appear to be either. I can take care of her no problem."

"Thanks, Mellany. I should be out in a little bit." Romy gave an awkward laugh before saying, "I just want to make sure my head's clear so I don't break down again."

Nora Peters waited. *So, Romy, will you finish the task or send your employee out?*

"All right, Ms. Peters, thank you so much for waiting," Mellany said, visibly more cheerful. *A weak-minded fool*, Nora thought, beginning to wish it had been Romy she had abducted and not Tara.

"You wanted blue dye, right?" Mellany asked.

"Actually, I've had time to think and I've chickened out," Nora replied, never intending to color her hair in such a disgraceful way. "Why don't you just take a few inches off?"

"No problem," Mellany said. She washed and began cutting Nora's hair.

"I must say you're very beautiful," Nora complimented. "Do you have a boyfriend?"

"Yes," Mellany replied. "What about you? Do you have a husband, boyfriend?"

"Neither. I'm married to my work."

"What type of business do you work for, Ms. Peters?" Mellany asked between cuts.

"I'm in asset management. I match the right assets with the right people. I'm also in charge of shipping our East Coast merchandise to other countries."

"You sound very important. I wish I could hold a title like that," Mellany said, impressed.

"Perhaps one day you can. In my line of work we are always on the lookout for new talent." *Yes, you might do nicely.* For a brief moment Nora looked like a wolf staring at a lamb, a look Mellany missed.

"Are you from this area or are you attending university?" Nora asked.

"I'm local. I just graduated from a one-year cosmetology course." Mellany flipped the mirror around so Nora could see. "How's that?" she asked in a proud voice.

"Wonderful. You're very talented. I'm sure many people could make use of it."

Mellany looked a little confused before saying, "Thank you. For now I'm very happy here." Moments later, Romy exited her office and saw Mellany and Nora Peters at the cash register. Embarrassed, Romy walked over and said in an apologetic voice, "Ms. Peters, I am so sorry I ran off like that. My sister went missing a few weeks ago."

"Your talented employee here explained the situation. I completely understand why you were upset," Nora said, cutting in. "If you don't mind me asking, is that missing persons poster her?" Nora asked, pointing towards it.

"Yes, that's Tara," Romy replied, sadness returning to her voice.

Deciding to add insult to injury, Nora said in a shocked voice, "Oh, my. Her hair is the same color I wanted." Nora placed a hand on Romy's shoulder. "I should be the one who's sorry, dear. I had no idea I was bringing back traumatic memories," Nora continued with a look of sympathy. A look she had perfected over years of practice.

"There's no need to apologize, but thank you for thinking of my feelings," Romy replied.

"Sorry if this is too personal. Have you found any leads into your sister's disappearance?"

"We think she may have been kidnapped." Romy took a deep breath. "Other than that, nothing." Mellany patted Romy on the back, her way of telling her everything was going to be okay. Romy shot her a smile, showing she appreciated the gesture.

"That's horrible," Nora said sympathetically. "I can't imagine what type of monster would do such a thing?"

"We're going to keep searching until she comes home no matter how long it takes," Romy said, wiping the water from her eyes. Nora could tell she was serious. *She never will, and you would be wise to stop searching.*

"Do you happen to have a copy of that poster? I can't promise anything but I would be willing to take it to Philadelphia and hang some copies around my job." A wide smile formed on Romy's face.

"Yes, yes, I can get you one!" Romy opened a drawer and pulled out several of the posters Mellany and Casey had been handing out to clients. Nora took them and placed them in her purse.

"How much do I owe you?"

"Don't worry about it, it's on the house. I feel I owe it to you after what happened," Romy said, smiling.

"I don't like accepting charity," Nora said.

"I insist," Romy replied. "You were kind enough to want to help find my sister, and that's enough for me."

"If that's how you feel, then I accept." Nora turned around to leave, then said, "I almost forgot, I need an after shot." Nora again pulled out her phone.

"I would like you in it," she said to Romy. "You too, dear," she continued, pointing to Mellany.

"I'd be honored," Mellany replied and the three women smiled as Nora took the picture.

"Well, it is time we part ways. It was a pleasure meeting you, Romy," Nora said, shaking her hand. "And you, Ms?"

"My last name's Kittelt, but just call me Mellany."

"You did an amazing job on my hair, Ms. Mellany. You have a bright and productive future."

"Thank you again for your willingness to help find Tara," Romy added.

"Dear, I'm hanging a poster up, not a problem at all." Romy and Mellany waved as she exited.

"It's nice to know there's people out there who still care," Romy said.

"Sure is. I liked her," Mellany agreed.

Outside Nora got into the back seat of her car and lit a cigarette. "Let's go home," she commanded the driver, then pulled out her phone and made a call. "Dimitri, I'm sending you a photo. Find out as much information as you can on the girl on my left. Her name is Mellany Kittelt. Then, arrange a meeting with the Brandon Aiden. He misinformed us about Tara's personality." Nora listened while Dimitri spoke. "Also, Tara's siblings are going to be a thorn in our side. They need to be dealt with," Nora added, thinking about Romy's words.

◆ ◆ ◆

When Nora entered her office, Joseph was waiting for her.

"Was it worth the drive?" he asked.

"The look on Tara's face will make it all worth it. She believes herself in control. I will show her how wrong she is."

"Sit down. I need to show you something," Joseph asked.

"Can it wait until tomorrow?"

"No," Joseph replied with meaning in his voice.

"What is it?" she asked impatiently. Joseph played a five-and-a-half minute video showing views from all four security cameras in the loading dock. Nora didn't see anything until the end where Justin was escorting Tara out of the room. "What did you want me to see?" she asked, uninterested.

"That's the point. You didn't see anything." Joseph reversed the footage and paused it on Tara looking into the gun room. He played the video and she moved out of sight. "She got from one end of the dock to the other without being seen. It took her no time at all to find the camera's blind spot." Joseph angrily pointed at the garage door. "Those doors have no lock! She could have opened them and escaped."

"For a time," Nora replied, unimpressed. "We would have recaptured and disposed of her quickly."

"I've transported girls for you since we started working together, and all of them have been scared and broken." Joseph reversed the footage so Tara was in view. "This one is going to be a problem. If you ask me, we shoot her and cut our losses."

"Tara has a client tomorrow. We cannot disappoint him."

"Is it really worth the risk?" Joseph demanded.

"Tara is on the verge of breaking. My visit to her sister's business will assure that," Nora replied confidently. She left the room happily staring at the missing persons poster.

Chapter 13

The next afternoon, Nora Peters stood outside the dressing room.

"Tara, your next customer will be here in an hour." *Alright, I'm coming.* Tara opened the door, having just come from her shower. She was grateful to get it but also knew what it meant. "Here is what the customer requests." Like before, Tara was handed a note. The request was a blue cheerleader outfit with blue eyeliner, and the hairstyle was two pigtails. As much as it disgusted her, she thought, *Tara, you have to do it; think of your plan and concentrate on that.* She didn't say anything to Nora as she returned to the dressing room. "Oh, Tara," Nora added. Tara turned to face her. "Before changing, I wanted you to see these photographs. *What now?* Tara grabbed the two photos, expecting more instructions. Tara let out a shocked gasp. *No, this photo of Nora and Romy has to be fake. It has to be photoshopped!* Tara looked at the next photo and dropped both of them. Seeing Nora posing with Romy and Mellany and clearly seeing the inside of Romy's salon proved to her it was real.

"So, this is where you were yesterday?" Tara asked in a soft disbelieving voice, putting two and two together.

"Correct." Nora viciously grabbed Tara by the hair, slamming her into the wall. Tara whimpered in pain as Nora pulled and turned it. "You think you can manipulate me? You think you have me wrapped around your fingers?"

"No," Tara replied with agony in her voice.

"You're right, you can't do either," Nora said sternly. "Friendly warning. If you cause any problems for this client, the next picture of your sister will be…" Nora paused and shrugged. "Use your imagination." Tara gave a frightened acknowledgment. Nora released her grip. Tara closed the door. *I have to get every detail perfect,* she thought as she anxiously changed. Moments later she entered the client waiting room where Nora, Miguel, and Peter were sitting. She felt fear and tension join her anxiety, knowing what Nora's subliminal message was. Peter whistled a cat call.

"Oh, baby, you look amazing. Please mess up like last time, Tara," Peter begged. Tara nearly shouted back but caught herself at the last second.

"Tara, remember our talk," Nora said with a serious look on her face.

"I know what I have to do. Make the client happy," Tara replied.

"You're finally using that brain of yours," Nora complimented. "Go on in. The client will be here in a few minutes." Tara went in the pleasure room and sat on the bed. Breathing in and out heavily, she kept telling herself, "You have to do it. You have to do it." She tried thinking about how she was going to execute her escape plan. Every time she tried, all that entered her mind was Nora's new threat. A threat that had her considering abandoning her plan. Moments ago her plan was a beacon of hope, but now the risk of going through with it terrified her. *No, Tara, you can't abandon it. Ask once and if he's not interested, forget it,* she told herself. Tara kept repeating "you have to do it" to herself until the door opened. A man who looked to be in his mid to late twenties walked in. He was thin with blond hair and no facial hair. Tara closed her eyes and swallowed. *Okay, show time.*

"Hi, you must be Tara?"

"Yep, I'm Tara," she said, trying to smile. "And you are?"

"Alex. Alex Walker," he answered. They stared at each other for a moment before Alex said, "You ready to start?" *Here it goes,* Tara thought.

"Do you care if we talk a little first? Just for a few minutes," Tara emphasized. "I'm kinda embarrassed to admit it, but I'm shy and like to get to know people before we begin."

"Sure, I understand," he said, sitting next to her. Tara calmed down a little. He was willing to talk. Her idea might work.

"I actually only moved here a few weeks ago. Are you local?" Tara asked innocently.

"Sure am. New York born and raised." *Bingo,* Tara thought. "Where are you from originally?"

"New Castle, Pennsylvania. It's a small town near Pittsburgh," Tara answered.

"Why did you move to New York?" Tara wanted to fall apart, she wanted to tell him she had been kidnapped against her will, and beg him to help her. *If he's in a place like this, Tara, he's a scumbag. You're on a roll, keep it going!* her inner voice reminded her.

Tara managed to keep her head and answered, "Better parties, better customers. Speaking of which, do you know any places a girl can have fun around here? I mean other than New York City."

"Well, I'm sure you thought of Buffalo and Niagara Falls. I know you can find something to do there."

"I was talking about the local area, not big cities," Tara replied, then said seductively, "Come on, tell me your secrets."

"Not much to do in North Ridge." Alex thought for a moment, then continued, "If larger cities aren't your thing, Lockport would be your best bet. You can also give the local bars and concert parties a try." He placed an arm around her. "Or I could show you a good time now?" Tara gave a real smile. Her plan had worked like a charm. She decided to stop the questions to avoid upsetting him.

"Okay, I'm in the mood now. Let's start," Tara agreed, feeling disgusted. Thinking she was doing it to save Romy and probably Ryan's life helped her. Five minutes into the session, Tara felt herself becoming nauseous. *Don't throw up, push through it,* she thought, trying to will herself. Suddenly, she felt her breakfast moving up her throat. *No, get away from him!* her mind pleaded. She pulled away from Alex, but it was too late. Vomit came flooding out of her mouth, covering his chest. He screamed and grunted in annoyance. Tara quickly moved away and continued to throw up on the floor.

"Hey, are you okay?" Alex asked. "Hold on, I'll get someone." Tara was still coughing, so she didn't fully hear or understand what he said. Tara heard the sound of the door closing. *No!* Realizing what had happened, she felt another panic attack coming. She had done it again—this was the second time she had upset a client. *I need to get out of here, I need to hide!* Tara frantically thought. She searched the room, looking for someplace to hide. She knew what was coming and this time it would be far worse than before. Out of fear she crawled under the bed and curled up into a ball. The darkness and being surrounded by the bed skirts brought her a false sense of safety. Moments later, she heard the door burst open.

"Tara," she heard Nora say. Tara felt her body break out in a sweat.

"She's under the bed," Miguel said, hearing the rapid sound of her breathing. With one arm, he lifted the bed up, turning it on its side.

"Please! Please! Please, no!" Tara begged. Her body trembled uncontrollably, and her face had become ghost white with fear. Nora and Peter soon joined Miguel standing over her.

"Pathetic," Miguel said, disgusted. Between deep frightened breaths, Tara managed to say, "Please! Please! Do whatever you want to me, but please don't hurt my sister or brother."

"Well, let's get on with it. I'll go first," Peter said. Tara felt the breath leave her. She thought about hitting her head on the floor to knock herself out. It would be better than being violated while conscious.

"No, both of you get out," Nora replied. *What did she just say?* Tara opened her eyes.

"Wait, why? Doesn't she need to be punished?" Peter asked, surprised.

"I said leave the room," Nora commanded. "Miguel, please put the bed back in place. Tara, come out, you're not a small child." Tara moved to the part of the room that was farthest away from them. *She's up to something, I know it,* Tara thought fearfully. When Miguel and Peter left, Nora sat on the bed and ordered Tara to join her. Tara sat next to her, fearing what would happen if she didn't.

"Tara, what happened?" Nora asked in a calm voice.

Not knowing what to say, Tara replied, "I guess I'm sick or something." Nora touched her forehead.

"You have nerves, nothing more." Nora lit a cigarette and said, "I was expecting you to cause trouble. I even had arrangements in place to punish you." *What's she going to do?* Tara worryingly thought. *She's going to hurt Romy and Ryan, I know it.* "I will admit you surprised me. The client was pleased and wanted to continue the session another time." Tara gasped in relief. Nora scoffed and shook her head. "Joseph has overestimated you. I trust next time you will finish the session with the client?"

Tara shook her head yes. "Yes, of course I will."

"You're getting the hang of this," Nora complimented. "As you know, I must punish bad behavior." Tara gave her a frightened look. "But I also reward good behavior. Tonight you may choose food from any restaurant you want."

What? Tara thought, then replied, "Thanks," still suspecting Nora was up to something.

"What type of food would you like? Tell me and I will walk you to your room."

Playing along, Tara replied, "Lobster tail with a salad on the side is my favorite." She expected Nora to burst out laughing and tell her she wasn't getting anything.

Nora did laugh, then clapped her hands and said, "I knew it, you're a girl with class. Would you like a side of king crab to go with it?" Tara gave her a stunned look. *What's going on?* Tara thought, feeling very uneasy, knowing a trap was coming. "What would you like to drink? I'm sure you want something more than water." Tara wanted to ask her what the game was. There was no way she was being nice to her out of pity. Nora gave her a look that said she was waiting for a response.

"Red wine," Tara answered.

"Come," Nora said, gently putting a hand on her shoulder. "Let's go to the office and order your food." Tara tensed as they exited the room, assuming Miguel and Peter were going to jump her at any moment. However, to her surprise, they entered Nora's office without anything happening. Joseph saw her and shut off his monitor.

"What has she done now?" he demanded.

"She's done a good job," Nora replied.

"A good job. Yesterday we caught her snooping around the loading docks," Joseph said, raising his voice. "I want her out of the office right now!"

"She will leave as soon as I give her a reward," Nora said, picking up her phone.

"What reward!" Joseph demanded. Tara begun to understand Nora's game. Her apparent kindness was nothing more than a way to annoy her rival.

Nora didn't answer him. She dialed a number and said, "Hello, I'm Nora Peters. I would like to place an order for takeout, please. I would like lobster tail with a salad on the side, and an order of three king crab legs..... A bottle of red wine for the drink." Nora looked at Tara and asked, "What would you like for dessert, dear?"

"That meal's for her!" Joseph shouted, now visibly fuming.

"I'm fine," Tara replied, not wanting to push her luck.

"Don't be ridiculous, everyone needs dessert now and then." Nora snapped her finger. "A piece of chocolate cake." Nora flicked her finished cigarette on the floor while listening to the casher. "That will be fine, thank you," Nora confirmed and hung up. "Tara, your meal will be here in about an hour."

"Why don't I go pick her up a gold plate and crystal goblet to go with it?" Joseph said sarcastically.

"Why don't you?" Nora replied, lighting another cigarette and blowing the smoke in his direction. Tara remind quiet, trying to stay invisible.

"I want that order canceled and your whore taken back to her room. After what she did, she shouldn't be fed for a week!"

"She made a customer happy and will be rewarded," Nora replied. "Tara, return to your room."

"No, you stay here until someone escorts you," Joseph added.

"Fine, I will walk her," Nora countered. When they arrived, Tara quickly went inside her room. "Oh, Tara, I almost forgot, here's a souvenir for you," Nora said, handing Tara the missing persons poster and a small amount of poster putty. "Perhaps you can hang it up?" As Nora closed the door, Tara stared at the poster and felt herself tearing up. She started feeling the mental and physical strain of her panic attack. Not expecting to get her promised meal, she lay down and looked at her missing persons photo, seeing an old photo of herself along with the words "Help Bring Our Beloved Tara Home." This brought her to tears.

"I'll be home soon, I promise," she said quietly. She didn't know how much time had passed before she heard her door unlock. Ivan entered holding a large bag.

"Here," he said, dropping it on the floor. "Mr. Jackson ordered me to search your room, so get off the bed." Tara did as she was told. She watched as Ivan looked under the mattress and other areas of the room. She didn't show it but inside she was worried he was going to lift the top off the toilet, discovering her knife. Ivan searched for several minutes, finding nothing.

"Everything okay?" she asked casually.

"You're fine," he replied and exited the room. Tara licked her lips and opened the bag, not believing she had actually gotten her promised reward. The smell of hot lobster and crab legs caused her to drool. She hated this place, but she was going to truly enjoy this meal.

"I'm going to get wasted and forget all my problems" she said out loud in a carefree voice, grabbing the bottle of wine. *No, don't get drunk,* her inner voice warned her. *You have work to do tonight that you can't do if you're drunk.* Knowing it was right, Tara only drank a small amount while finishing the meal. For the first time since she could remember she felt amazing. She was in a horrible situation but was lucky enough to have the two leaders fighting among themselves. Tara spent the rest of her afternoon creating a mental map of her tunnels path.

◆　◆　◆

Brandon Aiden sat at a table in the Boar's Head Tavern. It was a smaller bar with a wood cabin atmosphere, located a few miles from McConnells Mill State Park, right next to the Rose Point camping grounds. Animal trophies adorned the walls. In the middle of the dining section stood a mounted grizzly bear in a standing position. Brandon was staring at a mounted cougar head when someone sat in the seat across from him. Before they could speak, a waitress came over to take their order. Many of the people working at the tavern had no connection to Omnipotent. Only the owner and head manager were part of the group.

"Hello, Dimitri," Brandon said, recognizing him from their last meeting.

"Hello, Mr. Aiden," he replied. Both men paused when the waitress returned. She handed Brandon a beer and Dimitri a pot of tea.

When she left, Brandon said in a clearly annoyed tone, "Do you mind telling me what this meeting is about? From what I understand it's highly unprofessional on your part." Dimitri poured himself some tea and took a sip. High-ranking Omnipotent members like Joseph Jackson or Nora Peters never appeared in person; a representative was sent in their place in case the meeting was a police trap. At any meeting, the representative had the authority to make final decisions on behalf of the person he or she was representing. "Mr. Aiden, I'm going to be frank with you. Currently your reputation inside Omnipotent is not good."

"What do you mean by that?" Brandon asked, taken back.

"Mr. Aiden, as you know, when purchasing merchandise, we look at four factors: age, beauty, temperament, and social standings. The higher the merchandise scores on these factors, the more we pay." Dimitri sipped his tea before saying, "We feel you were dishonest about the merchandise you sold us."

"I was honest with every detail!" Brandon replied in a loud whisper. He then gave a mocking laugh and said, "Tara's causing you problems? What? Is her constant crying and begging getting to you?"

Dimitri had a serious look when he said, "When we were acquiring her, she assaulted me and three others, resulting in her nearly escaping. Since then she broke a client's nose, and has made numerous escape attempts, nearly succeeding several times." Brandon gave him a look that showed he thought he was lying. There was no way bubbling, dramatic Tara could do that. Dimitri remained unfazed by the stare. "Tara's sibling are also becoming a cause for concern."

"What do you want?" Brandon demanded.

"You return thirty thousand of the fifty thousand dollars." Brandon looked insulted.

"You can forget that, Mr. Dimitri," Brandon said rudely. He tossed a ten dollar bill on the table and started to get up.

Dimitri opened his jacket, showing a holstered pistol. "If you'd prefer a bullet." Brandon sat back down, getting the message. Both men stared at each other while Brandon thought.

Brandon was the first to break the silence by saying, "May I suggest another option?" Dimitri motioned it was okay.

"I can get you information on Tara's siblings that Nora Peters will find very useful."

"You've already given us information on them," Dimitri countered.

"I'm talking about current information," Brandon shot back. "I'm also interested in the possibility of franchising. I want to operate one of your businesses. I was thinking one located on a California beach. Lots of tourists in areas like that. Lots of beautiful young women, and men of working age." Brandon's voice gained a cocky tone when he said, "I could become one of your top suppliers. If you recall in the past year I've given you two smoking hot girls."

Dimitri slightly shook his head. "John Baxter, our Director of Human Trafficking Operations in California, told me you wasted his representative's time with the cosplay girl, and Tara has been nothing but problems." Brandon started to become visibly defensive.

"Look, I like to plan ahead. She was supposed to be at a cosplay shoot all day. It's not my fault she caught me with Alexa and broke up with me. If I recall, Alexa worked out well for you." Dimitri dropped a five dollar bill on the table.

"I will present your request to Ms. Peters and Mr. Baxter. If they are interested, someone will contact you."

"Thank you," Brandon said politely. "Can I expect Romy or Ryan to have an accident soon?"

Dimitri shook his head. "No, we will get rid of them through nonviolent methods." That was not the answer Brandon wanted to hear. The last thing he needed was those two poking around the rest of his life.

"Why not? Your organization is large enough to remove practically anyone."

"Mr. Aiden, yes, we could remove them as you say. However, you do that too often and people start to ask questions, and soon your entire organization is exposed and taken down. Currently, the Heartwood Manor incident is taking up our time and resources. Do you have any other questions?"

"Is the situation settled?" Brandon asked.

"That depends on Ms. Peter's decision concerning your request." Dimitri looked at Brandon, darling him to come back with a counter-argument. Brandon looked away, showing he was satisfied, and Dimitri stood up.

"Goodnight, Mr. Aiden."

◆ ◆ ◆

Later that night, the ringing of her alarm clock woke Tara. She became fully awake nearly instantly. She shut it off, turned off her fan, and waited to see if she could hear anyone moving outside the room. After several minutes of hearing nothing, she was satisfied it was safe to begin working. She pulled her knife from its hiding spot, brought her fan over to the closet, and crouched down inside it. Knowing it would cause suspicion if she was sleeping half the day, her idea was to sleep from nine to twelve. Work from twelve to three and then sleep until eight or nine. Tara opened her makeup kit and used her liner pencil to make a dim outline of a two foot by three foot square. She stretched out one of her shirts on the floor next to her work area, then turned hampered her ability to hear if anyone was coming. Tara rammed the knife into the wall, then put her hands on her temples in frustration. She recalled yesterday's room search. Anyone coming in here was going to notice the square-shaped cutting lines on the wall. Tara leaned against the wall, trying to think of a solution. *I could cut out the pictures on the cereal boxes, then ask for tape to hang them.* Tara shook her head. *No, that's stupid.* She looked at her bed and saw the missing persons poster. Tara got up and grabbed it. She placed the poster on the wall. It only covered half of her square.

"Better than nothing," she said, trying to stay positive. She looked down at her makeup kit and an idea came to her. It was crazy, but crazy enough it might work. Tara rooted through the kit—it was a smaller set with only ten shades of eye shadows, a brush, eye and lip liner pencil, and seven lipstick shades. One of the lipstick colors was white. She pulled the knife out and moved the white lipstick along the cut in the wall. It was not a perfect match but good enough that no one would notice unless they were looking hard. *This will work,* she thought, pleased. If she ran out of lipstick, it would be easy to get more. She would take it from the makeup room. Tara placed the knife back into the cut in the wall and started working. The knife moved back and forth, making a loud sawing sound with every motion. Tara cut until her arms were burning with fatigue. When she stopped, she noticed she had only gotten a little over one fourth of the way across the top of the square. She breathed in and out, letting her arms rest. It was ten minutes to two when her muscles had enough. She had cut across the top of the square and halfway down the middle. This job was going to take a lot longer then she had thought. She covered the portion she had cut with her poster. Nora's idea of a cruel joke had actually proven useful. She gently folded the shirt on the floor and dumped all the paint chippings and piece of drywall into the toilet. She hid her knife and climbed back into bed. "In about a week, I'll be home," she repeated to herself, thinking of that wonderful place as she drifted off to sleep.

Chapter 14

The next day, Tara nervously sat on the examination table in Dr. Bodkin's office. She guessed he was going to make sure she was well enough to preform tomorrow. Wanting to get away from Dr. Bodkin as quickly as possible, she said, "I feel fine. I threw up due to stress."

"I have no interest in examining you. Now keep quiet and do as I say." *What does he mean?* Tara wondered as her body tensed up. She watched Dr. Bodkin remove supplies from his medical cabinet and place them on a medical cart.

He approached her and said, "Stretch your arm out. Radius bone on top."

"What?" Tara asked, genuinely not understanding what he meant. Dr. Bodkin grabbed her arm and moved it so her palm was facing upward.

"Keep it there." Dr. Bodkin scowled. "Stupid girl." Tara blocked out the insult and did as she was told. Dr. Bodkin placed a blood pressure cuff above her elbow, then dipped a medical swab in iodine. He held Tara's arm in place and started spreading the iodine over her median cubital vein.

"What are you doing?" Dr. Bodkin did not answer. He ripped the plastic off an IV needle attached to a sterile blood bag. Tara felt her body beginning to shake.

"Please tell me what you're doing?" Tara asked, frightened.

"We're getting rid of an irritant," he replied. Tara winced when the IV needle punctured her skin. She watched as the clear tube turned red. Thoughts and explanations started running through her mind. *Is Joseph trying to kill me behind Nora's back? Is he planning on bleeding me to death?* She felt her fear climb when Dr. Bodkin approached her with a pair of medical scissors.

"Stop, please," Tara whimpered softly.

"I'll stop when it is time to stop," Dr. Bodkin replied. Instinctively, Tara started reaching for the IV. Dr. Bodkin grabbed a strap attached to the examination table and moved it up and down. Tara pulled her arm away from the IV, getting the message. Dr. Bodkin brought the scissors down. *Should I start screaming for help?* Tara thought fearfully, worried this psychopath was going to start cutting her. *If Nora doesn't know about this, she might stop it, but then again if she does, I might get hit for screaming.* Tara felt the scissor blades against her hair. She closed her eyes and felt a few locks of her hair fall off. Dr. Bodkin placed the hair in a bag. *Okay? What was the point of that?* Tara wondered in confusion. She turned her head, watching as the IV bag began filling. She had no idea how much blood she could lose before she died and she had no intentions of finding out. *Okay, Tara, play along for now.* Tara looked at the blood bag. *If that bags fills and he hooks up another, find a way to escape.*

For the next ten minutes, Tara closed her eyes, trying to remain calm. The more she thought about it, the more she realized this blood drawing was not meant to kill her. Nora had no reason to want her dead, and if Joseph was behind it, he would have undoubtedly stopped by to rub it in. When the bag was nearly full, Dr. Bodkin removed the IV needle from her elbow. Tara let out a breath of relief. She felt slightly dizzy and weak. Against her better judgment, she told Dr. Bodkin how she was feeling. His reply was cold.

"I've only taken a unit of blood or one pint for the ignorant." He walked over to the door and said, "We're done." Tara got up, stumbling at first, but soon managed to walk straight. Her usual escort Devin walked her to her room. She turned around to see Dr. Bodkin leave his office with the blood bag. *What is he planning to do? What was that all about?* Tara wondered. *Is he planning on selling my blood?*

"Happen to know what that was about?" Tara asked casually.

"Nope, and never run off without me again," Devin said in an aggravated voice. "Your little stunt got me in trouble with management." *Well, I'm so sorry,* Tara sarcastically thought.

Tara spent the rest of the day eagerly waiting for nightfall. Around six o'clock she was brought a shrimp alfredo TV dinner, an orange, and a refilled water bottle. As she ate, she tried to figure out why Dr. Bodkin had taken her blood. Like earlier, her first thought was that he was planning on selling it. The more she thought about it, the more it didn't make sense. To her knowledge, blood was not worth that much, and if they were planning on selling it, why hadn't they drawn any when they first abducted her?

"Wait," she said to herself. She went into deep thought, trying to get buried memories to resurface. *When Romy talked me into donating blood at the hospital, there was a handout.* She focused harder, trying to picture the handout. *The handout had said someone can only donate blood every eight weeks. Okay, cross selling the blood off the list. Okay, why did he take it?* Annoyed she couldn't think of anything, she focused on Nora and Joseph. Nora was easy; as long as Tara did her job without causing problems and made her feel in control, she would leave her alone. The challenge was walking that fine line of acting up enough to make Nora believe she was not ready to leave this training center without acting up so much that she was beaten or get a family member killed. Joseph was the challenge. He was more cautious and probably smarter then Nora. Tara knew he suspected she was up to something, which told her more room inspections were on the way.

"Joseph believes I'm up to something. If I stop trying to escape, he'll know I'm up to something," Tara said softy. *Then give him something to find,* her inner voice told her. She looked at her door. Picking the lock was out of the question. If he found out she could do that, she knew either a camera or guard would be outside her door. Tara looked at her plastic tray, and an idea came to her. She tore a bit off and saw the plastic had a sharp point. She carefully tore another bit off, trying to make it the same size and shape as her last one. She put the two pieces on top of each other. They were a bit uneven but close enough to look convincing. Tara repeated the process with a third piece. She grabbed some of her poster putty and glued them together. She held her decoy knife up to her face and smiled. It would do its job, look like a desperate attempt from a desperate girl. She hid it under her collection of cereal boxes. She knew something would happen to her when it was found it, but a few kicks to the ribs were better than her true escape route being discovered. She went over to look at her square, desperately wanting to work on it. She guessed it would take her three days to finish cutting through her wall, then another five to cut through the back wall of the mystery door. *Soon I'll be home.* The thought brought a wave of joy through her body. *Home.*

Thinking of home brought another idea to her. She grabbed her liner pencil. She added a roof and rooms to her square, making it look like a house. She also drew another house in front of her bed. She stepped back and admired her work. If anyone questioned her about it, she would tell them it was to remind her of home whenever she went to bed.

◆　◆　◆

In Waterford Pennsylvania, Ryan Cymric drove down Comer Road. Earlier that morning he had received a call from the Waterford police. A call he had been dreading. He paid no attention to the meadows and patches of forests surrounding the back country road he drove on. His thoughts were only on the message he had gotten earlier. A housing renovator, Johnathan Herd, had phoned the Waterford police claiming to have found what he described as a torture chamber in the basement. What caught Ryan's attention was the police report clamed strands of blue and pink hair were found at the scene. He knew the hair might not have belonged to Tara—he was hoping as much but it was still a lead worth looking into. He could have waited for the Waterford police to send him the photos and official finding; however, he wanted and needed to see the location with his own eyes. As soon an old three bedroom house came into Ryan's view, he brought his car to a stop and turned into the driveway. A Waterford police car was parked in front of the house.

"Lieutenant Cymric?" a young police officer asked, exiting the house as Ryan got out of his car. He looked to be in his early twenties, probably a recent graduate from the police academy. Ryan had seen him at the Waterford police station, but they hadn't met.

"That's me," he replied.

The young officer introduced himself, "Name's Isaiah Mills. If you would follow me, I'll take you to the chief."

The inside of the house looked as bad as the outside. The structure was not in danger of crumbling, but it had seen better days. An older officer who looked to be Ryan's age came down a flight of stairs.

"Lieutenant Cymric, nice to see you again," Henry Edwards, the Waterford Police Chief said. "I see you've been introduced to half my police force." He made a joking motion to himself and Mills. The Waterford police department was a small town department with only four officers. Ryan had met with Henry Edwards when he first started looking into Tara's disappearance.

"Your report mentioned you found strands of blue and pink hair. Have you sent them away for forensic tests yet?"

"Yes, sir. We found nineteen hairs in total. I had them and blood samples sent to the forensic lab in Erie city an hour ago."

"Is it okay if I head into the basement to have a look around?" Ryan asked.

"Fine with me," Edwards replied. "I'll walk you down." A squeamish look formed on Chief Edwards's face. "I must warn you we aired the room out, but it still smells something horrible." Hearing that made Ryan cringe. Bad smells did not bother him, it was the possibility that some monster had tortured his sister to death. When Ryan was halfway down the basement stairs, the smell of burnt flesh and blood filled his nostrils. He coughed a few times before gaining control of his senses. Even with newly replaced lights, the basement's damp and gloomy feeling remained. What was left of an old burnt wooden chair lay next to an old wooden table. Several tools and knifes with dried blood sat on top of it. Blackened blood stains surrounded the chair pieces. A portion of the floor near a broken window looked to have been burnt. Ryan bent down to examine the parts of the broken chair. He picked up one of the arms and noticed the remains of burnt leather. *Holding straps.* Ryan found himself beginning to fear the worst as he picked up a drill. The bit showed a clear blood stain on the tip of the one-fourth-inch drill bit. Inside Ryan felt rage beginning to build. He looked over at the burn area near the window. It was large with deep pools of blood in certain spots. Ryan visually pictured Tara lying down in the burnt spot. Her body was around the same size. He dropped the bit and pounded the wall several times. If this was Tara's blood, these sick people were going to pay dearly.

He took a few moments to get his emotions together, then addressed Chief Edwards, who, along with Mills, was respectfully giving him space. "Where did you find the hairs?"

"Mills picked them up, he can explain better," Edwards said, looking towards Mills.

"Near the broken chair." Mills pointed towards it. "Most were half burnt but a few were intact. Wonder why whoever did this didn't burn the entire house down?" Mills pondered.

"My guess is they were trying to destroy evidence without causing too much of a scene," Edwards answered.

"Or someone walked in on them," Ryan added. "When you got here, did the fire seem recent?"

"No, we saw no burning embers and the ash was cool to the touch," Edwards stated.

"I assume you looked into the housing renovator's background?" Ryan asked.

"No need. I also know him personally, he's an honest man," Chief Edwards stated confidently.

"Who owned this place before Johnathan Herd bought it?"

Chief Edwards thought for a moment and answered, "An older couple owned the house until about three years ago. It's been abandoned since then. As you can imagine due to the condition of the house, it took a while to sell."

"And to your knowledge no one's lived here since?" Ryan asked.

"Local kids party here all the time, but none of them would have done something like this," Edwards assured. "With a house out in the woods like this, it's hard to tell who's been coming and going." He stopped, then admitted, "To be honest we don't even know if this is foul play. It could be some type of witchcraft blood ritual or even a sick prank." Ryan knotted his head, understanding where Chief Edwards was coming from.

Ryan spend the next half hour searching the house and surrounding woods. During that time, Chief Edwards headed back to the station. Ryan's search was ended when Mills approached him looking less than happy.

"I just heard back from the lab. The blood and hair were confirmed to belong to Tara Cymric." It was hard, but Ryan managed to keep his composure. He patted the young officer on the shoulder.

"At least we know," he said softly. "I'm going to be heading back home."

"Anything else we can help you with, sir?" Mills offered.

"I'm going to bring a K-9 unit up from Pittsburgh to see if they can track where Tara went from here."

"Fine with us. We'll be happy to help with the search."

"Can I get a copy of the crime scene photos?"

"I'll have to confirm with the Chief, but I'm sure it will be fine."

"Good enough," Ryan said. The two men shook hand and said farewell. Ryan got in his car and called Romy's number. He had not told her where he was going, wanting to know all the details before giving them to her. She answered after two rings.

◆ ◆ ◆

"Hey, Ryan. Did something happen?" she asked in a hopeful voice.

"Hi, Romy, are you with a client?" Romy could tell by the sound of his voice something was wrong.

"I-I'm in the office," Romy said with a slight stutter. "Ryan, what's wrong?"

"I'm in Waterford. Been here since early morning."

Knowing why he must be there, Romy asked sharply, "Why didn't you call me earlier?"

"Romy, I didn't want to tell you anything until I had all the facts. I wasn't even sure this had anything to do with Tara until a few minutes ago."

Unhappy, but understanding his reasoning, Romy asked, "What did you find?" She readied herself, dreading what she was about to hear.

"The local police found blood stains and some hair in an abandoned house's basement." Romy felt her legs getting weak, so she sat down, trying to remain calm.

"They belonged to Tara, didn't they!"

"Yes, the forensic reports just conformed that." Ryan felt his anger return.

"How bad were the blood stains? What did the basement look like?" Romy asked bitterly.

"Romy, that's not important." He didn't want to repeat what he saw.

"Ryan, what did it look like!" Romy yelled. "Sorry," she said right away. "Please, I need to know what they did to our sister." Romy could hear him trying to form words.

He finally said, "There's a good chance Tara was tortured to death." Romy gasped partly from shock, only managed to let some of it out.

"You sure?"

"No, I'm not sure she's dead," Ryan answered, wanting to believe it himself. "We only know the blood and hair were hers. Tomorrow, I'm planning on coming back with a K-9 unit."

"Count me in," Romy said seriously.

"I'll get the details worked out and get back to you."

"I'll let Brandon know," Romy said. After she hung up with Ryan, she called Brandon to tell him the bad news.

◆　◆　◆

Brandon Aiden grabbed his ringing phone, hoping it was Dimitri. He snarled when he saw who was calling. This time he was at work and Romy was truly interrupting something.

"Romy, I'm busy at work. Can I call you back?" he asked, trying to sound polite.

"Brandon, Ryan thinks he knows where Tara is." Brandon felt himself becoming nervous; suddenly his work didn't seem so important.

"That's great to hear," he said, trying to sound convincing. He moved his chair towards the window to see if any police cars were in the parking lot.

"Not really," Romy continued, sadness creeping into her voice.

"Why, what happened?" He tried to make himself sound upset. "Is she…?"

"We don't know. The Waterford police found blood and hair belonging to her in the basement of an abandoned house."

"Are you sure it was Tara's?" Brandon asked, sounding concerned.

"Positive," Romy said, assurance in her voice. *Dimitri, you sly devil,* Brandon thought, understanding what had happened. A slick smile formed on his face. Romy had driven him crazy with her daily calls about Tara. He was going to return the favor and have some fun at Romy's expense.

"Romy, how much blood was there, was there evidence she escaped?"

"I don't know. I didn't ask." Brandon could tell by Romy's voice she was getting more distressed. "All I know is Ryan said it looked like a torture chamber and there's not a very good chance Tara is alive." Brandon felt his curiosity go up. *Had Dimitri really had Tara tortured to death, or was it some type of cheap trick?*

"I don't know if I believe that," Brandon said. "Things like that don't happen in the real world."

"Ask Ryan to explain it if you don't believe me," Romy said, clearly crying.

"Sorry, Romy, I didn't mean to make you upset. If someone really did torture Tara to death. I'll… I'll kill them myself."

"Ryan and I feel the same way," Romy said softly. "Tomorrow Ryan's going to search the surrounding woods with a K-9 unit; if you want to join in, you're welcome." He thought about saying no, but he knew how bad it would look they might even begin to suspect him. Yes, he could deal with this one last encounter with Tara's siblings, who had become nothing but a nuisance to him.

"Of course I'll come. When are we meeting?"

"We're meeting sometime early tomorrow. I'll text you the time and directions when I get them."

"I'll be waiting," Brandon replied.

Chapter 15

<hr>

The following day, Ryan and Romy Cymric, along with Chief Edwards and Brandon Aiden, stood outside the abandoned house. Ryan, Romy, and Brandon were clustered around Ryan's SUV while Edwards waited inside his patrol car. Ryan had his tactical carbine strapped across his shoulder. K-9 Officer Donald Sorenson and his tracker dog Cappy, a one-hundred-and-ten-pound bloodhound, were in the basement, hoping Cappy could pick up Tara's trial. The group had decided to let the dog handler go in alone to reduce the chances of the dog becoming confused, plus no one who had previously been in there wanted to go back in anyway.

"I hope the dog finds something," Romy said, shifting her weight from side to side. A nervous habit of hers.

"What happens if they took Tara away in a car?" Brandon asked.

"We're out of luck," Ryan said in a dejected voice as he leaned against the SUV. *Ryan, don't say that, please.*

"Do you think the scent will be too old?" Romy asked nervously.

"Believe it or not, Cappy can track scents up to three hundred hours old." Romy gave him a playful snack on the shoulder.

"How long is that in days?"

Without having to think about it, Ryan replied, "Twelve and a half."

Romy gave him an impressed look. "That long?" Romy noticed the nervous look on Brandon.

"You alright?" she asked.

"Yes, fine, just hoping we find Tara." The conversation was ended by the loud sound of a bloodhound baying. Cappy came rushing out of the house, his ten-foot leash stretched to the limit, his nose fixed to the ground. *He found something!*

"Does he have a scent?" Romy asked. Her voice was filled with hope.

"He sure does, strong one too," Sorenson replied, in a running sprint. He left the driveway and headed down Comer Road.

"Do you want to take the car or walk?" Romy asked Ryan.

"Walk. We don't know if the trail will stay on the road," Ryan replied. Romy started jogging after Cappy. "Chief Edwards, we're following on foot," Ryan yelled.

"Okay, I will follow in the patrol car," Edwards replied, leaning out of the car.

"Brandon, you coming with us or riding with Edwards?" Ryan asked, walking backwards toward the road.

"I'll come with you," he replied, rushing after them. Cappy followed Comer Road to Old State Road. The dirt road turned into a single lane paved road. Cappy followed the scent for several miles, occasionally giving a bay to let the humans know he was still on the trail. The temperature was a pleasant seventy-six degrees with a light cloud cover.

"Reminds me of the walks we used to take as kids," Ryan said, tossing Romy a water bottle. He was trying to keep the mood light and people's minds off what they might find. Romy caught it and took a long drink.

"Those were fun times." She noticed a patch of tiger lilies growing off the side of the road. Reminding her of Tara, she picked one and placed it in her hair. "Biggest decision was taking the road or the forest home." She handed the bottle to Brandon. "I remember you would get so annoyed when Tara came along because no matter what, you would always have to carry her home." The siblings continued to reminisce about their time as kids. Brandon stayed back a few steps, listening to the radio songs coming from

Edwards's patrol car. At around the three and a half mile mark, Cappy made a turn onto Smedley Road, the modern asphalt once again becoming dirt. The farm fields and meadows turned to thick forest on both sides.

"It's two thousand and twenty-two, can't these people pave their roads?" Brandon complained.

"Hey, Romy, remember this?" Ryan asked, kicking at the dirt, sending a cloud of dust flying towards her.

"Yes," she replied, smiling and kicking some back. "You always found it funny when Tara or I would complain about dust getting in our hair." The mood changed when Cappy came to a stop. He circled, sniffing the ground. *Had he lost the trail?* Romy wondered. Like he answered her, Cappy let out a loud bay and rushed into the wood. Edwards parked the cruiser.

"Those woods are part of State Game Lands Number 192. In several yards you're come across a cluster of creeks and ponds." Cappy and Sorenson broke through the thick tree line into a grassy embankment. As Cappy approached the bank, several green frogs leaped into the water. Cappy went into the water, heading towards a cluster of cattails. Officer Sorenson could see something out of place amount them. Bits of pink and black were hidden under the cattails. He stepped into the shallow water and made his way towards the object. Four turkey vultures flew from the cattails. Cappy sat down and let out a single bay, showing he had found what he was looking for. A strong smell filled Sorenson's nostrils, a smell he was all too familiar with. He could hear the others making their way through the tree line. He bent down, placed a hand over his mouth, and readied himself for the unpleasant sight he knew he was about to see. He parted the cattails. In front of him, a naked female body lay face up. The bottom half of the body was submerged in water. Bloating had begun to occur. Bloody foam protruded from the mouth and nose areas. Light black carbonized tissue covered the body. Pink spots and rips dotted it, marking where the vultures had fed. Sorenson walked back slowly and turned around to face Ryan, who was at the edge of the creek. The look on Sorenson's face told him everything he needed to know.

"We found what we we're looking for," Sorenson said unenthusiastically. He looked down at Cappy and said, "Good boy," rewarding him with a treat. Sorenson and Cappy moved to the side.

"Romy, stay on the bank," Ryan said, moving forward. Edwards already approached the scene. *Like I'm going to do that.* Romy ignored his request and followed close behind. Edwards was the first to see the body. He stumbled backward, losing his balance on a submerged log, falling into the creek rear first. Cappy tilted his head in confusion, wondering why the man was retreating.

"Ryan, I'm afraid it's not pretty," Sorenson said. Ryan saw the body and started huffing in frustration. He let out a scream of rage as Romy peered over his shoulder.

"No, Tara!" she screamed in horror. The body may have been unrecognizable, but she knew who it was. Romy fell on her knees, breaking down. Ryan got on his knees and hugged her, comforting himself as much as it comforted her.

"I'll bring a bag," Sorenson said softly, momentarily placing a comforting hand on Ryan's shoulder. Ryan gently pulled Romy up, and everyone returned to the stream bank. Sorenson left Cappy under the shade of a large tree for a well-deserved rest.

Romy sat on the bank, staring out into space from shock. *Tara's dead. She's really dead.* Ryan placed a blanket around her and sat down. She smiled a small smile of thanks but said nothing. Neither of them did; neither of them was ready to. Romy heard Edwards on the police radio, most likely calling an ambulance or a homicide unit. She saw Sorenson heading towards the water with a body bag.

"I'm going to help him," Ryan said. Romy shook her head with acknowledgement. "Hold up," Ryan said, getting up.

"Ryan, you sure you're up for this?" Sorenson asked.

"Yes, I need be a part of this." Ryan and Sorenson searched the area for additional evidence. During that time, Chief Edwards informed them he had called for an ambulance to take the body to the coroner. He offered to help, but seeing how disgusted he was at the sight in front of him, Ryan told him to wait for the ambulance and to brief them on what occurred. While they worked, Romy went over to Cappy's tree and started petting him.

"Thanks for finding Tara," she said softly. Cappy moved his head so her fingers went over his ears. She looked over at Brandon, who was standing next to the patrol car. *I should go talk to him.* Romy patted Cappy on the head and got up. She walked over to him and shared a quick hug. "How you holding up?"

"I don't understand how could someone could do this?" Brandon said.

"Neither do I," Romy replied. She didn't say anything, but she was wondering why he didn't seem nearly as upset as she thought he would be.

After finding nothing, Ryan and Sorenson photographed the area and conducted the unpleasant task of moving the body out of the reeds and placing it in a body bag. Before the body bag was closed, Ryan tried to find some type of identifying mark, but the body was burnt to the point of unrecognition. The one odd detail he did notice were all the teeth had been removed.

"Did you find any teeth on the first search?" Sorenson asked, noticing it as well.

"No," Ryan replied. "I'm guessing the teeth were removed so it would be harder to identify the body after she was killed." He hoped for Tara's sake it occurred after she was killed. The two men grabbed opposite sides of the bag and carried it ashore. Romy heard the sounds of approaching sirens in the distance. She walked over to Ryan.

"Ryan, please open it a little. I need to see Tara again. To say goodbye." Ryan gave her a reluctant look.

"Romy, you don't want to—"

Romy cut him off before he could finish. In a serious voice, she said, "Please, I need to say goodbye!" Ryan did as she requested and opened the bag, exposing the head. Brandon approached, acting like he was paying respects. Romy didn't look away but stared at it closely.

"I can't tell if it's her." She felt a tear roll down her cheek. "Tara, I'm so sorry we didn't find you in time." Her and Ryan gave silent goodbyes, then motioned it was okay to close the bag. The newly arrived ambulance crew took possession of the body.

"Is it okay if we take the body to our coroner in Erie city?" one of the medics asked.

"That's fine," Ryan replied. Romy rested against his shoulder.

"The forensic lab will run DNA and blood tests. We'll know who this was by the end of the day," Chief Edwards assured.

"Thank you," Ryan said, wiping a stream of tears from his eyes. "Think we can get a ride back to our car?"

"Of course, anything you need," Chief Edwards replied.

As he and Romy walked, he said, "There's still a chance it's not Tara." Romy kept staring straight ahead.

"Thanks, but I know you don't believe that. You wouldn't be crying if you did." She glanced over at Brandon, still wondering why he wasn't crying.

Chapter 16

Tara sat on the pleasure room bed. The fact that she knew who was coming made the situation a little easier. She knew Alex was a pervert, but the devil she knew was better than the devil she didn't. She had spent most of the day mentally preparing herself. She had gotten lucky last time, but if she messed up again, she knew there would be consequences. *If everything goes according to plan, I'll only have to do this once more,* Tara thought, trying to make the best of the situation. She remained in thought for several minutes until Alex opened the door.

"Hi," Tara said, bubbly.

"Hello again," Alex answered. "Feeling better?"

"Much. Sorry about last time," Tara replied, making a sad face to reinforce the point.

"No problem. Do you need to talk this time?"

Tara smiled and seductively shook her head no. "I know you already. Did you have any trouble getting here? I know some people have a hard time finding the road."

"No, not at all, from the highway get on Daniels Road. The driveway was the hardest part; it's like you're traveling down a dirt road through the forest for miles," Alex replied. Tara was ecstatic that little scrap of information would help narrow the search. "I'm eager to get started," Alex continued. Knowing she had no choice, Tara went on with the session. She closed her eyes and thought of Brandon. Half an hour later, the session was finished. Tara left the pleasure room and went straight to the showers, feeling violated and disgusted. She let the warm water comfort her. *You had to pay for information, only you used your body instead of money. It's the price of getting home,* Tara thought, trying to make herself feel better. She put on her clothes, wiped the fog from the mirror, and looked at herself.

"You're going to get through this," she said softly. "Tonight you'll be through the first section of wall, in about three days you'll be through the second, you'll get to the phone, and in less than a week you'll be home." Tara exited the shower area to find Nora Peters waiting for her. She had a pleased look that told her she had done alright.

"Tara, I'm impressed," she said sincerely. "It took a while, but you managed to finish a session with a client." Nora's face turned neutral. "However, the client made a comment that you seemed upset at the end. Try to be happy during the entire thing. If you need to cry, do it in your room."

"Okay, I understand," Tara replied. *You'll be the one crying soon,* she thought.

"I know you do." Nora patted her on the shoulder. "Now run back to your room. Someone will bring you dinner."

"Thanks. Do I need to wait for someone?" Tara asked, suspecting this was a test, because no one was around to escort her.

"No," Nora replied. "If anyone stops you, tell them I…" She stretched the "I" out. "Said it was okay." *So this is power play,* Tara thought.

"Good to know," she replied. She turned and walked off smiling, knowing fireworks were about to go off between Nora and Joseph. *Now if I know Joseph, I can expect someone to search my room sometime today. He's probably worried I stole something from the client or during my trip to my room.*

◆ ◆ ◆

Joseph Jackson sat at his desk, wishing things would go back to normal. He liked to run a simple facility: items came in, upper management told him where to send them, the items were shipped out, and the cycle repeated itself.

That's how he liked it. He cursed the day Nora Peters and what was left of her crew was thrust upon him. To add to his misery, she had to abduct Tara Cymric and turn his facility into her personal pleasure house. He had contacted management several times about removing Nora, but to his displeasure the answer was no, facilities would be opened until the traitor in Omnipotent was found and disposed of. Joseph hoped it would be Nora. That power hungry women would do anything to get ahead, even compromise her own facility. He began fantasizing about killing her. His thoughts were broken by her phone ringing. Since Nora was out of the office dealing with a client, he went over and answered it.

"Hello, Joseph Jackson speaking," he said.

"Mr. Jackson, please put Ms. Peters on," Dimitri said.

"I'm in charge of this facility, you will speak to me," Joseph said in an authoritative voice. "I will pass any important information on to Nora."

"Fine," Dimitri replied in a voice that showed he did not care.

"I trust everything went according to plan?" Joseph asked, hoping for good news, but when dealing with one of Nora's men, who knew how badly he messed things up.

"Everything went fine," Dimitri replied calmly. "The local police found the decoy site and the body of one of the former Heartwood Manor girls. Our asset in Erie city used the blood and DNA we took from Tara to create a fake match."

"What guarantees do we have that someone will not realize the results were faked?" Joseph asked, concerned.

"The body was under our control until it was placed in a casket. A body in that condition will not have a viewing. It will be buried and that will be the end of it."

"That's fine," Joseph replied. "Is that all you wanted?"

"One more thing," Dimitri said, and he heard Joseph huff. "I would like to recommend we allow Brandon Adin to work for us in California. That way all leads involving Tara will be gone from the area."

"That's not my department," Joseph replied. "Anything that removes evidence is good enough for me." He was about to hang up when Nora walked in. "Nora, it's Dimitri," he said, handing her the phone. Nora took it, and Dimitri explained everything he said to Joseph.

"That will be fine; if he doesn't work out, we can always have him removed," Nora said, sitting down. She spoke business with Dimitri for a few moments, then hung up.

"Did everything go alright with your customer?" Joseph asked, expecting to hear Tara had caused problems again.

"Yes, Tara performed her duties." She looked at Joseph and said in a proud voice, "You see, she is under control."

"I assume you searched her before she returned to her room?"

"No, there was no need," Nora replied, grabbing for her pack of cigarettes. "After she performed, I sent her back to her room."

"Alone?" Joseph asked, stunned.

"Yes," Nora replied nonchalantly. Joseph cursed.

"Is she in her room now?"

"I assume so," Nora said.

"You assume!" Joseph yelled. Nora scoffed. Joseph's attention went to his computer he opened the camera feed. He checked the camera feed that covered Tara's room. A camera he had installed since he ordered Tara locked in her room. He reversed the footage until he saw Tara enter the room and shut the door.

"Satisfied?" Nora asked, smartly glancing at it.

"No!" Joseph snapped. "She could have grabbed something; there are dozens of blind spots."

"What could she have possibly grabbed?" Nora asked.

"Who knows?" Joseph yelled.

"Which means nothing," Nora replied sarcastically.

"We'll see what Ivan finds tonight," Joseph said, going back to work, and ended the conversation.

◆ ◆ ◆

At home, Ryan Cymric sat in front of his TV, doing his best to distract himself from reality. His son was sleeping and Krista sat next to him, providing what support she could. She was a pretty blond-haired girl in her mid-twenties. The buzzing of his cell phone brought the news they both knew was coming.

"Hello," Ryan answered.

"Hello, Ryan Cymric? This is Dr. Philip Spitz. I'm the forensic specialist with the Erie city police department. Is this a good time to talk?"

Ryan got up and went to this office. "Yes, do you have the results?"

Dr. Spitz maintained a professional voice when he said, "There's no easy way to say this, so I'm going to tell you the facts as is. As you know, the body was too badly burned for visual identification, and the lack of teeth prevented identification by dental X-rays. I conducted blood and DNA tests, and both matched Tara Cymric." Ryan had tried to prepare himself for this, but the news was still like a dagger to the heart.

"Thank you," he said, trying to remain composed. "Is that all you found?"

"Do you want me to give you the full autopsy details?"

"Go ahead," Ryan replied. After hearing the report, he hung up. Hearing his cries of pain, Krista went in to comfort her husband. In their five years of marriage, she had never seen him cry like this. Ryan waited until his head was clear enough to think and speak clearly.

"I need to tell the news to Romy," he said, picking up the phone.

"Do you want me to leave?" Krista offered, knowing the siblings would want privacy.

"If you don't mind. Thanks, Krista." She released his hand and left the room.

◆   ◆   ◆

Romy saw Ryan's number and knew why he was calling.

"It was Tara, wasn't it?" she said in an upset voice.

"Yes. The DNA and blood tests confirmed it," Ryan replied in a teary voice himself.

"Do they know what happened?" Romy asked.

"No, all they could confirm was the body was Tara's." Romy could tell by the tone of his voice that he was lying.

"Ryan, there's something you're not telling me. What is it?" she said in a voice that showed she was not going to let it go.

"Okay, Romy, I received the full autopsy report. Trust me, you don't want to know the details," he replied.

You're right, I don't, Romy thought.

"I don't want to know, but I need to know. Please tell me what happened," Romy replied. Ryan gave in and gave a quick description of the report.

"Several of the ribs and the left leg were broken."

Romy let out a yell of frustration.

"Do you want me to stop?" he asked, wanting to himself.

"Geez, what else did they do to her?" Romy shouted.

"Let's forget it, Romy."

"Ryan, tell me!"

"Her teeth were most likely pulled out before she died." Hearing that made Romy wish she had listened to Ryan. Neither sibling spoke for a while.

Romy broke the silence by asking, "Ryan, how did she die? Was she alive when they burnt her?"

She heard Ryan tear up before answering, "Yes, she died from extreme burns to her respiratory system."

"Who would do this? Who would want to torture and kill Tara?" Romy asked, barely able to speak.

"I don't know," Ryan admitted. "All I can promise is we're going to catch the sick bastards who did this and make them pay."

"Yes, we will," Romy agreed, equally determined.

"Romy, why don't you come over to my house. We should be together at a time like this."

"Agreed. By the way, did you notice Brandon acting strangely earlier?"

"You mean like he didn't seem as upset as he should have been?"

"Yes," Romy confirmed, "I might be overthinking it, but it seemed odd."

"We can talk about it in person," Ryan suggested.

"Okay, I'll be over soon," Romy said before hanging up. *It's over,* she thought. Finding out Tara was dead was devastating to her, but the burden of not knowing had been lifted. Now Tara could be laid to rest.

◆　◆　◆

Ivan walked in Tara's room and handed her a chicken enchilada with mixed vegetables dinner. Tara took it and sat down. Ivan lifted her bed up—as Tara had predicted, he was here for an inspection.

"What are you doing?" Tara asked, pretending she didn't know what was going on.

"Room inspection," Ivan replied, setting the bed down. He pointed to the drawing on the wall.

"What's this?"

"My apartment," Tara replied.

Ivan walked over to her. He crossed his arms and asked, "Where did you get a marker?" He expected she had stolen it.

"I used my liner pencil." Tara got up and showed it to Ivan. He took it, examined it for a moment, then dropped it on the ground, giving no more thought to it. Tara sat back down by her cereal boxes, using her body to hide where the plastic knife was. When Ivan opened the closet, Tara started eating, showing no interest or distress. Inside she was a basket case. If he pushed on the section of wall she was working on, he would know she was cutting into it. *Don't touch the wall, please don't touch the wall.* For a few tense moments, Ivan ruffled her pants and shirt, seeing if he could shake anything loose. Tara's body relaxed when he closed the door.

"Nearly done?" she asked, not moving from her spot.

"Nearly," Ivan replied, coming over to her. "Move," he said, motioning for her to get up.

"Why? Only my cereal's here," Tara asked, intentionally showing a hint of nervousness.

"I'm not going to take them; now move," he said, giving Tara a slight kick. The kick didn't hurt, but Tara yelped and moved out of the way.

As soon as Ivan started his search, Tara asked, "So, Ivan, anything new going on around here?" Ivan gave her a look that said *I know there's something here you don't want me to find.* Ivan moved the small boxes around. Tara tried talking to him, doing anything to distract him. She exaggerated her look of fear and disappointment when he found her half-made plastic knife.

"Really?" he asked, picking it up.

"Um," Tara said several times, like she was thinking of an excuse. The attempt at a knife was more pathetic than threatening so Ivan found it somewhat amusing. "Let's go see Mr. Jackson," he said and ordered Tara to follow him.

Moments later, Tara sat between Nora and Joseph's desks. Ivan was standing behind her. Joseph Jackson tapped the half-finished attempt at a plastic knife on the table. He was about to speak, but Nora cut him off.

"Tara, what were you planning on doing with this?" she asked in a disappointed voice.

"What do you think she was going to do with it?" Joseph shot back. "I told you from the beginning this girl is nothing but trouble. I mean, look at this." He continued waving the knife in front of Nora, resisting the urge to test the blade's sharpness out on her.

"It's a piece of plastic," Nora said, unimpressed.

"It's an attempt at creating a knife," Joseph yelled.

"I made it for defense," Tara added calmly. Inside she was loving it. *Keep creating tension between them, Tara.*

"Did I tell you to talk?" Joseph asked.

"I was answering Nora's question." A smirk formed on Nora's face. Joseph clenched his fists.

"Defense against whom?" Nora asked.

"I was worried someone would try to force themselves on me," Tara replied, giving a hint of fright. "I wasn't trying to escape." Tara gave a look of defeat. "As you know I tried several times and learned it's impossible." Joseph was not buying any of it.

"Let me tell you what I think," Joseph said, getting in her face. "You were planning on ambushing the person bringing you food, then escape through the garage area during the confusion."

Tara made a scoff, intentionally sounding like Nora. "If I'm so smart, don't you think I would have learned that to get to the garage I would need to go through the recreation center and living quarters?"

"You take me for a fool?" Joseph asked.

"I'm sure she does, Joseph," Nora added. *For once I agree with you,* Tara thought. "Tara is my problem. Sit down and worry about yours." The way Joseph looked, Tara expected the situation might turn to blows.

Joseph turned to Nora and said fiercely, "Get her out of my sight."

"Tara, where did you get the material to create this?" Nora asked calmly.

"I used some of the plastic from my dinner trays and held them together with the wall putty you gave me."

"You are a clever girl," Nora said, impressed. "Tara, dear, I understand your reasoning, but you cannot be making weapons."

"I understand," Tara replied.

"To make sure you get the point, no supper for two days," Nora said, tossing the knife in the trash.

"That's fair, I guess," Tara replied in a not-too-thrilled tone. She glanced at Joseph, who had his face buried in the computer, tuning out the situation.

"You may go now," Nora said, waving her off.

"Thank you," Tara replied.

Tara was about to exit the room when Nora said, "Tara, come here a moment, I want to show you something." Tara walked over to Nora's desk. Her guard was up, and she could tell by the look on Nora's face she was about show her something she didn't want to see. Nora handed her a piece of paper.

"This was emailed to us by our contact in Erie city."

"Why don't you tell her the names of all our police contacts?" Joseph yelled in disbelief. Tara thought the paper she was holding was a joke. It was her death certificate.

"Funny," she said, handing it back to her.

"Keep it, it's yours," Nora said before lighting a cigarette. "You're dead to your family and the rest of the world. In fact, your funeral will be in a few days." The confident way Nora spoke told Tara this was no joke. Her mind started racing. *I have only been missing a few weeks—no way anyone would declare me dead. Even if Omnipotent did manage to fake my death, Ryan would see through a trick like that in a second. They would need my DNA.* Suddenly, she remembered the blood and hair Dr. Bodkin had taken from her. Somehow, some way, they had manage to fake her death. Truly heartbroken, Tara turned to leave again.

When she was at the door, Nora spoke.

"Tara, your next customer will be in four days."

Now Tara clenched her fists. Nora always had a way of adding a cherry on top of an already bad situation.

Moments later, Tara lay on her mattress and started to cry. Now no one was looking for her. Romy and Ryan both thought she was dead. Brandon would cry for her every night and she would cry for him. After letting her emotions out, she calmed down and sat up. *It's all up to you now, no help is coming.* She looked towards her closet and set a new goal for herself. In three days, she was going to be inside that mystery room.

Chapter 17

At quarter past two, Tara was wide awake, as her knife cut and grinded through the wall. Tara closed her eyes in pain as her sweat-covered arms were again screaming in pain, but she couldn't stop… she was mere inches from finishing. The knife continued its grinding sound until it suddenly stop resisting. Tara sighed a happy sigh and wiped the sweat from her forehead. *I'm through,* she happily thought as she carefully pulled the section of wall out and laid it to the side. She got to her hands and knees and shined her flashlight inside the wall space, hoping she was right about there being enough space inside the wall for her to move through. She cursed when she noticed a major problem. The crawl space was too narrow for her to crawl on hands and knees. She was going to need to move her body sideways and shuffle her way through the wall.

"Getting inside is going to be fun," she said in dismay. She lay down on her side, placed the flashlight in her mouth, and started shuffling forward. She winced in pain every time her exposed skin scraped against the unsanded wooden floor.

When her entire body was through the hole, Tara looked up and reached for the wooden stud. She carefully pulled herself up, knowing what would happen if she made a hole in the wall. When her feet touched the ground, she pulled out a few splinters, then placed the flashlight in her left hand. She could see the curve in the wall. *Please let the hole under the window be large enough for me to get through,* she thought, worried. At a slow pace, she started moving forward. She could feel the tight space getting to her. *Relax, Tara, you never had a problem with tight spaces before.* Tara breathed in and out, trying to calm herself. The voice of doubt, of course, had to rear its ugly head. *What happens if someone comes in to check on you while you're in here?* Tara felt herself move backwards a few steps. "Go forward," she commanded herself. She moved forward until she reached the bay window. The top section looked to be solid wood, but under it was a square crawl space. Tara tried to get to her hands and knees when she felt a sharp pain in her shoulder. "Ow," she said, clenching it. She shined the light on her hand and saw blood on her fingers. She moved the light on her shoulder and saw a small cut. She thought back to when she had her normal life, when she would have freaked out over a cut like that. Now it barely hurt.

She moved the light beam on to a rusty nail. *Good thing I'm up to date on my tetanus shot.* Tara struck the nail a few times with the end of the flashlight, knocking it down. She tried several times but couldn't get to her hands and knees to crawl through. She moved back a few steps and lay sideways. "It's going to be so much fun doing this every night," Tara said out of frustration. Like before, she placed the flashlight in her mouth and moved through the tunnel head first. Everything was going fine until she felt something stringy and sticky cover her face. Her body tensed. She could feel the eight legs of a large spider run from her face into her hair. Tara tried to swat it off, but she couldn't move her arms in the close quarters. Still feeling the spider moving, she broke into a panic. She moved out of the crawl space screaming, frantically swiping at her hair, trying to get the spider off her. She finally felt it fly off her body. Once she calmed down, she realized how much noise she had been making. "Shoot! Shoot! Shoot!" she yelled, rushing back to her room. *Someone must have heard that. I'm finished,* she thought, trying to move as fast as she could.

She got back to her closet, put the wall paneling back, and ran to her bed, waiting for someone to come storming in. After a few hours of intense waiting, no one came. "Jeez, I was lucky," she said gratefully. *The camera might have picked up the sound,* the voice of doubt added. Easy fix. *If the camera heard the screams, I'll tell them the spider was in my room,* Tara counter-thought. She debated between sleeping or going back into her tunnel. Finally, she decided to go back to the tunnel; she at least needed to get to the mystery room. She was about to enter the closet when she started cursing and stomping her feet in frustration. The distance between her room and the mystery room she had taken so much time to memorize was her crawling on all fours. Now there was a camera outside her door, which meant she couldn't go outside and redo her measurements. She tried to think, but nothing would come to her. She was tired and still a little freaked out by the spider incident. *I know you want to figure this out tonight, but right now the best thing you can do is sleep.* Tara knew her inner thoughts were right. She lay down in bed, threw the blanket over her body, and drifted off to sleep.

◆ ◆ ◆

It was two o'clock at New Castle Cemetery. Romy sat between Ryan and Brandon. In total, forty-two people attended the memorial service. While family members and Tara's close friends cried, the sight of Tara's gravestone surprisingly brought a sense of closure and relief to the siblings. Now they knew their sister was no longer suffering. She was at peace and had been laid to rest. After the service was over, people laid flowers on the grave. Soon the fresh dirt was covered with red and white roses. Ryan laid a red rose on the ground, and his wife Krista did the same.

"You okay?" she asked, surprised that neither he nor Romy shed a tear.

"Yes," he replied, looking up from the grave. He gave Krista a kiss on the check. He saw Romy taking to Mellany and Casey and noticed Brandon mingling with some of Tara's female friends. Ryan placed his arm around Krista as they stared at a white rose wreath with seven pictures of Tara in the center. Four pictures were Tara as an adult, and three were from when they were kids. A feeling of deep regret came over Krista. She regretted the fact she never got to really know Tara. She had always thought of Tara as Ryan's spoiled partying sister. She had never told Ryan, though she was sure he knew, that she didn't like Tara, and in some ways hated her. The cause of her resentful feeling came from the few weeks she was bedridden from her C-section. When Ryan was working, Romy was always there, helping take care of the baby and cooking meals. They were lucky to see Tara once a week, and when she did come, she'd bring takeout from a fast-food restaurant, talk for a few minutes, then leave. Despite this, Krista knew how much Ryan loved her. He had always told her there was more to Tara than her party girl appearance. She had always meant to get to know Tara, but kept putting it off due to her bitter feelings. Now it was too late. Romy finished talking to Mellany and Casey and rejoined her brother.

"I always loved that picture," Romy said, pointing to a picture of Tara sitting in front of a tiger exhibit at the Pittsburgh zoo. Before Ryan could speak, Brandon joined the group.

"How are you two doing?" he asked in a dejected voice.

"Honestly, I'm glad we found her. Even if she's not with us anymore, the pain of not knowing was so much worse," Romy replied.

"I hate to bring this up at a time like this, but what do you guys want done with Tara's belongings?" Brandon asked.

"Obviously we need to sort them out. What time would you like us over?" Ryan replied.

"Anytime this week works for me," Brandon answered. "Do you two need a couple days to heal?"

"Why don't we do it tomorrow? No need to wait on an unpleasant task?" Ryan suggested. He looked at Romy. "That okay with you?"

"Ya, works for me," Romy agreed.

"Tomorrow around one o'clock?" Brandon asked. Ryan and Romy both agreed the time would be fine. "Do you want me to rent a truck?"

"For the amount of clothes Tara owned, better rent two," Ryan said. Everyone laughed. A low rumble of thunder was shortly followed by drops of rain. "Don't worry about the truck, my SUV should be able to hold everything."

"Alright, see you tomorrow," Brandon replied, walking away.

"Sorry about Tara," Krista said to Brandon.

"Think it's time to go," Brandon suggested. Everyone walked towards their cars.

Romy briefly looked back and said, "Bye, Tara, we'll come visit soon."

◆　◆　◆

Tara turned on her flashlight and worked her way through the wall. That afternoon she solved her measurement problem. While in her crawl position, she left markers where her feet and hands were, then side shuffled between the two markers. She found that two shuffles were equal to one of her crawls. When she reached the crawl space under the bay window, she shined the flashlight down it, looking for cobwebs or her good friend the spider, whom she was sure was still alive. After seeing nothing, she worked her way through to her delight, spider free. She righted herself and made a left shortly after that. Tara felt her heart rate increase. *I'm past my room.* She placed a hand over the flashlight beam, fearing any hole in the wall would give away her location. She continued to move through the wall counting her steps, and when she got to thirty-four, she stopped. If her estimates were

correct, behind the wall was the mystery room. Tara felt her worries and anxiety starting to build. *I don't even know if I'm at the room.*

"Don't get overwhelmed, think," she whispered, trying to calm herself.

The lights in the hallway were always on, and if no one was in the mystery room, it should be dark. At least she hoped it would be. Tara used the knife to make a small hole in the wall; no light came out. "Yes! Yes!" Tara said a little too loudly. She relaxed against the back wall, staring at the drywall in front of her. Behind this sheet of drywall was the end of her nightmare, her ticket to freedom. She soon left her moment of victory and got back to work. Tara looked at her knife and looked at the drywall. *People can't see the cut in the wall,* she thought. Tara put her head against the wall, thinking of what to do. She had never seen anyone enter the room, but there was no guarantee it would stay that way. *Should I rush the process? Break through the wall, call for help, and hope no one sees it?* She quickly created a counter-argument. *No, I can't risk it. If someone finds it before help arrives, they'll move me to another location for sure.* The voice of doubt had to add the point, *You don't even know if a phone's inside there.*

"Shut up! Just shut up," Tara quietly yelled at herself. She knew the voice of doubt was right. This whole plan of hers was based on the idea, the hope, that the room had a phone. "No, there will be. There has to be!" Tara said to reassure herself. *Wait, if there's a phone, there has to be a desk and other furniture in the room.* Tara smiled; this was something she could go on. *If I make the hole behind a larger piece of furniture, it will be hidden.* Tara pushed the knife though the wall. She didn't feel it hit anything, so she pulled it out and tired again a few feet from her first cut. Again she felt nothing. *Wish I had one of those snake cameras Ryan showed me.*

Wanting to know what was inside the room, Tara placed the knife in the second hole and turned it until the hole was circular in shape. *No one will think anything of a small hole in the wall; it will look like normal wear and tear,* Tara thought. She pulled the knife out, closed one eye, and looked through. Her eye being adjusted to the dark was able to make out furniture shapes: one was tall and rectangular, a refrigerator, and the other looked like a table or desk. A wide grin formed on Tara's face. She was sure she was right, and the room was reserved for important visitors. She drove the knife through the wall a third time. The blade was nearly halfway through when it stopped with a thump. She moved the knife back and forth, hearing a thumbing sound each time it went forward. "Yes!" she said, wanting to jump up in celebration. *Don't get too excited yet, you don't know how big this is.* She drove the blade into the wall every few feet, getting an idea of how big the object in front of her was. When she reached the end of the object, she made an X. When she finished, she guessed the size of the dresser was just under three feet. *It's going to work!* Tara thought, feeling ecstatic. Tara laid her flashlight on the ground, using its light as a guide. Tara starting cutting. *To be safe, I'll cut halfway through the top tonight.* She now found herself regretting she didn't get a battery powered clock. Tara started cutting, finding that in her excitement she was cutting at a much faster rate. Suddenly she stopped cutting, thinking she heard what sounded like a tarp moving in the wind. *I've heard that before,* she thought. She listened for a few seconds, then nothing.

She shook her head. *No, you're being paranoid.* She was about to start cutting again when she thought she heard another sound. She pressed her ear against the wall. She heard something but couldn't make out what it was. It sounded like soft footsteps but not like the sound a shoe or even a foot would make. *Okay, that's it,* she thought, feeling uneasy. She wanted to keep working but couldn't risk getting caught. She examined her night's work: she had cut a little less than halfway through the top. *At least you nearly reached your goal,* she thought, trying to make the best of the situation. She backed up, striking her head against the wall. She grunted in pain, holding the back of her head. When she got back to her room, she saw it was only a little past one o'clock.

"Great, I've wasted a whole day," Tara said, frustrated. Tara lay awake, thinking of the sounds she heard. *Maybe someone went in to clean the room? No. If it were a person, he would have said something.* Tara continued to think until she drifted off to sleep.

Chapter 18

With the funeral behind them, Romy, Ryan, and Brandon got an early start removing Tara's things from her apartment. Brandon offered to keep all the furniture with him. Ryan and Romy agreed, as neither of them had any interest in it, plus it saved them from having to haul it to the secondhand store. Tara's personal stuff was sorted into three piles. Junk and less valuable items were going to be donated. Romy came up with the idea of selling Tara's more valuable items at auction and donating the money to a group that helped victims of human trafficking. Her most valuable items were her computer, camera, and necklaces and rings, some being worth several hundred dollars each. Ryan and Romy split sentimental items like photos and family heirlooms. Inside Tara and Brandon's room, Romy opened Tara's closet. She shook her head and smiled at the sight of her many knock-off designer brand coats, shoes, and purses. She then opened her jewelry box and took out a matching necklace and bracelet she had bought Tara.

"Romy, do you want any of Tara's shampoo and whatever else is in here?" Ryan asked as he cleaned out the bathroom.

"What else is there besides shampoo?" Romy replied, wanting to see if Ryan would take the time to read off every shampoo, conditioner, and perfume Tara had.

"I don't know, come see for yourself," Ryan replied, not taking the bait. Romy giggled, went in, and took half. "Take the rest home to Krista," she suggested. Ryan placed the items in a separate pile, while Romy sorted a pile of Tara's physical pictures Brandon had set on the table. Many of them were photos from their childhood or of memorable events. *I can't believe you're gone,* Romy thought.

"Ryan, how do you want to divide these photos up?" Romy asked.

Ryan picked up a photo of Tara's first modeling shoot and said, "I'll take them home and scan them; you can keep the originals." Romy gave a grateful smile.

"I'll get Tara's digital photos and send them to you," Brandon offered.

"That'll fill up my computer," Romy joked. "Brandon, do you want to keep the photos of Tara and you?"

"Yes, I would," Brandon replied. Romy handed three photos to him. He looked them over, then set them back down. Then he said, "Ryan, Romy," getting their attention. "I have something important I need to tell you."

"Do you want us to sit down?" Ryan asked.

"If you don't mind." Romy and Ryan sat down, wondering what it was about.

Brandon waited until both were seated, then said, "This is not easy for me to say, but with Tara gone, there's nothing more for me in this state. I got offered a job as branch manager with California Sacramento bank, which I accepted." Brandon waited, wanting to give either Ryan or Romy a chance to speak. They looked at each other, seemingly surprised by the news.

As Brandon expected, Romy was the first to lash out.

"Sorry for sounding cruel, but I need to ask. Did you accept the position before or after you found out Tara died?" Romy asked with a cold stare.

Brandon hesitated for a moment. "Before," he replied. "I learned about it last week. I didn't say anything because of the circumstances."

Romy became visibly angry. "Did you even consider how Tara would feel if she came home only to find out her boyfriend had moved to another state?" Brandon put a hand up to his face. Ryan placed a hand on Romy's shoulder, a gentle way of saying *calm down*.

"Look, Romy," Brandon shot back in a raised voice, but he quickly changed to a softer tone. "I can't pass up a promotion like this. I loved Tara, but tragically, she's gone. I'm explaining my decision out of respect for your curiosity, not because I had to."

Romy, snapping her finger, sarcastically replied, "Wish I could write Tara off just like that." *You had an affair, didn't you?* Romy thought but didn't bother to share her thought.

"Okay, you two, let's stop before things get out of hand," Ryan cut in.

"Brandon, you're not family," Ryan said, his way of showing he agreed with Romy. "So I understand how it's easier for you to move on. If you accepted a new position, I respect your decision."

"Thank you for understanding," Brandon complimented. He looked at Romy and asked, "Do you have anything else to add?"

Deciding it was not the time to be fighting, Romy smiled and said, "Sorry I shouted. I'm still upset about losing Tara. Sorry for taking it out on you. Congratulations on your new job."

"Thank you, and don't worry about it. Tara's death has affected us all," he said in his charming voice. *Sure it did,* Romy thought.

"When do you leave?" Ryan asked.

"I'm leaving later this week," Brandon replied. "Look, guys, I really don't want to leave on bad terms. While I was with Tara, you two became like family to me."

"We feel the same way," Ryan and Romy agreed. Both gave each other a look that only they could read. A look that said they were only agreeing with him to be polite.

"So, with that out of the way, do you need to find any more of Tara's belongings?"

"I think we got everything. Only thing that's left is to load it up," Ryan said.

"I'll help you carry the boxes down," Brandon offered. It took each person two trips to load everything into Ryan's SUV.

Ryan got into the driver's seat and said to Romy, "I'll have the photos to you tomorrow."

"That would be great," Romy replied, wanting them.

"Brandon, do you want me to send you the copies?" Ryan asked.

"Sure," Brandon answered. "Hey, if we don't see each other again, it was a pleasure knowing you guys. If you're ever in California, drop by. I'll take you out to the finest restaurants in the city."

"I'll keep that in mind," Ryan said.

"It was Tara's dream to become a Hollywood star. She would have loved moving there," Romy added, daydreaming Tara was still alive, standing next to Brandon.

"Thanks for letting me keep the furniture and several photos of Tara; it will help me remember her," Brandon said.

"Don't forget her," Romy said seriously.

"I won't," Brandon replied. He shook Ryan and Romy's hands and waved when they left.

As soon as they turned on the road, Romy said, "Ryan, I know this is going to sound bad, but did you find it odd Brandon seemed to move on so quickly?"

"To be honest, Brandon never struck me as the most loyal guy." Romy laughed out loud because she was thinking the same thing.

"I thought I was the only one who thought that," she said, surprised. "Do you think he was having an affair?"

"I don't know, but it wouldn't surprise me if he did. Speaking of which, did you notice him talking to the girls at the funeral?" Romy shook her head yes. After that, both their thoughts focused on Tara for the rest of the ride.

◆ ◆ ◆

Once again, Tara made her way to the mystery room and crouched down. She knocked on the wall and listened. She didn't know what she heard last night, but she needed to be sure no one was inside. Hearing nothing, she knocked again, much louder this time. To her relief, nothing stirred or called out from the other side. Satisfied it was safe, she got to work. She had started her work half an hour earlier that night, with the goal of finishing her cutting tonight. Tara cut through the remaining portion of the top part of the wall quickly, then got to work on the second portion, taking small breaks to relieve her aching arms. Tara didn't worry about the time; her full focus was on the task in front of her. She kept cutting and cutting. Her arms burned, her hands were covered in sweat. Tara suddenly stopped cutting, letting the knife drop. She relaxed back against the wall and let out a happy sigh. She picked up her flashlight, shining it on the beautiful square shape she had created. She had done it.

Tara was about to rip the section of wall out and grab the phone when her inner voice said, *Tara, wait. You don't know what time it is—go back and check. You can always come back tomorrow night.* Tara ground her teeth, wanting more than anything to go on. However, she knew her warning thought was right. Rushing into things was when mistakes were made. Reluctantly, Tara went back to her room. After emerging from her tunnel, she checked the clock and saw that it was nearly a quarter to three.

"This is more than enough time," she said happily. Minutes later, Tara was back at the rectangular portion of wall. She carefully removed the panel. Joy, anticipation, and nervousness ran through her. She tilted her head, looking through the hole. Several inches of space were between the dresser and the wall. Tara placed both hands on the bottom left side of the dresser and pushed. *Come on, you can do it!* she willed herself. She pushed with all her might until she felt the dresser move, then repeated the process on the right side. The carpeted floor brought the sounds down to nearly nothing. Tara got on her knees and noticed she was taller than the hole. "No, it can't be too small! It can't be too small!" she whimpered. Through the cloud of panic, she managed to think. *Tara, it's too small because you're upright, crawl on your stomach.* Her feeling of disappointment was replaced by feeling foolish. *I'm so stupid sometimes.* She got to her stomach, and it was tight, but she wiggled her upper body through.

Tara grabbed on to the top of the dresser and started pulling herself up. She moved her head sideways to prevent her face from scraping against the dresser. She pushed and wiggled her way forward, every moment taking a strain on her tired muscles. Suddenly, she felt she couldn't move forward. She tried to move backward but couldn't do that either. *Don't panic, don't panic,* she told herself. *Have you checked your hair for spiders?* her voice of doubt taunted. She began to feel spiders moving across her body. *Nothing's there, Tara, ignore it!* Her voice of doubt changed tactics. Images of Miguel entering her room filled her mind. After realizing she wasn't there, he entered the mystery room and found her stuck between the wall and dresser. *They never came in at night,* Tara countered. *Of course Murphy's Law would cause them to come in on the night of her ticket home,* she thought and started to believe it might be true. *No, that is not going to happen! After weeks of hell, this is my time, my moment!* That thought cast out any feeling of doubt, replacing it with a determined fire. She grunted and pushed her upper body, forcing herself to squeeze through the tight space between the cabinet and the wall. Tara felt her head and upper body break into the open air. She got to her knees and turned her head to see the room layout. The room was completely dark. She was expecting to see the small lights from an internet box or computer monitor, but there was nothing. She could only make out shapes of furniture and a bed, but it was too dark to tell if anything was on them. Tara cursed under her breath, realizing she had left the flashlight behind. "Not a big deal, Tara," she told herself. She got off her knees and felt her feet plant beneath her. She felt a wave of happiness and victory come over her. She had done it. In moments, she would be on the phone with Ryan or Romy. The thought of hearing her siblings' voices made a tear of joy fall down her check. "I did it! I actually did it!" she said happily.

"Did what?" a voice in the darkness asked.

Chapter 19

Tara gasped in horror. She heard the click of a light switch, then a circle of light lit the area around her. The feelings of hope and joy left her body and were replaced by a feeling of complete hopelessness. Tears of despair started to fall uncontrollably. Her legs began to wobble, as her head sank to the dresser.

In a soft, helpless voice she cried, "No.… No." Everything she had worked toward was over. She waited for the shouting to start, for someone to grab and hit her.

"Uh, hi," the voice said in a gentle but slightly confused tone.

Did he say hi? Tara asked herself, wondering if she heard right. She could tell the voice came from a man, but it didn't sound like any of the men she had unfortunately come to know. Tara slowly looked up. The light coming from the lamp blinded her, small rainbows forming in the water in her eyes. She placed an arm above them, trying to see who he was. She could only make out a dark figure. *This is a trick from Nora, it has to be,* Tara thought, figuring she must have known about her tunnel since the beginning. *Soon I'm going to be raped and beaten to within an inch of my life! Everyone thinks I'm dead, so no one's going to come rescue me. I'm going to spend the rest of my life in another country trapped inside a pleasure house!*

"Sorry, guess I am shining the light in your face," the voice continued. The lamp turned off. Tara stopped sulking and focused. She saw a human figure jump off the bed towards the wall near the door. *This is my chance to escape,* Tara thought, nearly making a break for her tunnel. *What's the point of running? They'll find you anywhere you go.* Although the thought of hiding in the walls, forcing them to tear the building apart searching for her, was pleasant. *No, I can't run, my escape plan failed. The only thing left to do is fight. I'm done for anyway. I'd rather die fighting than be a sex slave the rest of my life.*

The main room light turned on. Tara was ready to release a battle cry and charge whoever was in front of her. Tara's scream stopped before it left her throat. She tried to breathe but couldn't. Her eyes grew wide with fear and disbelief. The being standing a few feet from her had grey skin with an almost transparent texture to it. He had straight ear-length silver hair. His face and body were human, though his eyes were unnaturally circular with light red irises. His ears were large and bat-like. His feet were like an ape's only with bird-like claws. Tara stared at him, unable to move from the shock. Rapid imagines of the statue and photos she had seen in Dr. Bodkin's office entered her mind. The creature jumped forward, landing on all fours. Tara tried to scream, but her throat muscles were paralyzed with fear. This room was not her salvation; it was her demise. She had wandered into the layer of Dr. Bodkin's nightmarish creation. Tara quickly pulled her body back, desperate to get to the tunnel. Suddenly she felt herself unable to move. In a panic, she started screaming, desperately trying to move. Tara's body hit the floor when the dresser was effortlessly moved to the side. Tara whimpered and closed her eyes, readying herself for the mauling from this inhuman creature.

"Don't worry, you're not stuck anymore. Are you ok? How did you get in here?" *Wait, is this thing talking to me?* Tara wondered, opening her eyes. The being had moved to an Indian squat, his elbows on his knees. His arms fell between his wrists, and unnaturally long outstretched fingers touched each other. His head tilted from side to side, curiously watching her. Tara's body struggled on the first few attempts, but she finally managed to stand.

"Yes, I'm fine," Tara whispered. *And still alive.* The being or creature still had a curious look rather then a menacing one.

"My name's Katahdin. What's yours?" Again Tara took a moment to answer, still not believing what she was seeing.

"T…Tar…" She tried to form words but couldn't. She closed her eyes and finally managed to get out, "Tara Cymric."

"Tara Cymric, that's a long name," Katahdin said. "Do you want to come out, Tara Cymric? I can't imagine it's too comfortable back there?"

"Okay… sure," Tara replied in a slight state of shock. Katahdin moved to a standing position, now a little taller than average height. Tara guessed he was around six-foot-one or six-foot-two. Katahdin effortlessly moved the dresser, creating a wide opening.

"That explains how you got in," Katahdin said, pointing to the hole in the wall. Tara didn't react to his discovery, her mind still trying to process what was going on. She walked to the corner of the room, remaining a cautious distance from Katahdin. He moved the dresser back to its original position. That frightened her; he had taken away her only means of escape. *I think if he wanted you dead, you'd be dead*, Tara thought, looking at him closer. For the first time, she realized he was wearing clothes, grey sweatpants and a matching grey t-shirt.

Katahdin turned to her and said, "You seem tired and look sad." Tara shook her head yes, still finding it hard to speak. "Would you like a glass of milk? That always helps me sleep."

Tara closed her eyes and said, "S-Sure, that would be great," worried what would happen if she refused him.

"Okay, Tara Cymric, sit down at the table." Tara followed his request and sat down. She watched Katahdin open the fridge and grab two bottles of strawberry milk. "See, it even has a smiling rabbit." Katahdin placed the bottle in front of Tara, before opening his own. Tara placed the bottle in her hand and stared at it. She felt her eyes beginning to water, which soon turned to a stream of tears. This was the first true act of kindness anyone had shown her in over a month, and it had come from this creature.

"Hey, don't cry, Tara Cymric," Katahdin said, his confused tone returning. "Do you not want the milk?" Tara moaned and held it close to her body. "Oh, I know why you're upset, I was rude." He grabbed a box of chocolate chip cookies from the cabinet and placed them on the table. "Here, milk and cookies." Tara let out a tearful laugh, oddly feeling slightly less frightened.

"Thank you," she said softly, caring more about the act than the cookies. Katahdin leaped into a chair across from her. He didn't sit but crouched in the position he was in earlier.

"No trouble, Tara Cymric," Katahdin said, opening his own milk. "I've never seen you before, but then again, I haven't seen a lot of people living here." Tara flinched when one of Katahdin's fingers went inches from her hair. "I like your hair. I've never seen someone with blue hair." Tara gave a genuine smile.

"Thanks. I dyed it blue, blonde is my natural hair color."

"I get it, I can change my hair color too. Watch." Tara watched in amazement as Katahdin's silver hair started to turn the same shade of blue as hers.

"How...How did you do that?" Tara asked. Her voice was full of amazement, not believing what she just saw.

"I think about it and it happens." Noticing her surprised look, Katahdin said, "If that surprised you, watch this." Katahdin got out of the chair and started taking off his clothes.

"Katahdin, what are you doing?" Tara asked, worried, having become all too familiar with this sight from the pleasure room.

Katahdin smiled. "Watch."

Tara dropped her cookie and let out an astonished yelp when Katahdin disappeared before her eyes.

"Katahdin," Tara said, standing up. *What's happening. What's happening!* Tara wondered, knowing this entire situation was impossible. *That's because it is,* Tara thought, suddenly figuring out what was going on. "I'm dreaming," Tara she said out loud. *I must have fallen asleep when I went to look at the clock.* Tara closed her eyes. "You're asleep in bed, wake up," Tara shrieked when she felt a pinch on her left shoulder.

"No, you're awake," Katahdin confirmed. Tara looked over her shoulder to see Katahdin had reappeared.

"How." Tara took a deep breath; this was real, all right. "How…How did you disappear?" Before Katahdin could explain, she asked, "Can you please put your clothes back on?" To her delight, Katahdin dressed quickly. Tara sat back down. She took a long drink of milk, wishing it were booze. Katahdin jumped in his chair and grabbed two cookies.

"I can change the color of my skin. Dr. Bodkin says." The mention of his name sent a chill down Tara's spine. "It's like those ancient animals, the squid or a chameleon." Tara was still giving him a look of disbelief. Now Katahdin looked surprised. "I don't see why it's so shocking to you; you changed the color of your hair."

"I dyed my hair this color. I can't change it by thinking about it."

"What's dyed your hair mean?" Katahdin asked. Wanting to keep him happy, Tara explained the process of getting her hair done, and soon even found herself enjoying it. Talking about something like that brought her back to her natural element. Once she finished, her mind went back to who she was talking to. *What are you? Where did you come from?* Tara thought about how to word her next question.

"If you don't mind me asking…" She paused, hoping her question would not upset him. "What are you?"

"Father says I'm a special human."

"I agree with him," Tara replied, feeling herself disgusted by the sight of him. "Who's your father?" Tara continued, wondering if other beings like him were around.

"Dr. Bodkin." Tara a felt a look of fright form on her face. *Dr. Bodkin's your father? Did he experiment on his own son?*

"What wrong, Tara Cymric?" Katahdin asked.

Mainly out of anxiety, Tara lashed out. "Look, my first name is Tara, just Tara! You don't need to say my last name!"

"You have two names?" Katahdin asked, puzzled.

"Ya. A first, middle, and last, like everyone else."

"Katahdin is my only name. Dr. Bodkin gave me it, since it's close to *konchen*, the German word for bone." Not wanting to explain every detail about her three different names, Tara changed the subject.

"How's Dr. Bodkin your father?" she asked, seriously wanting to know the answer.

Tara noticed a slight look of sadness form on his face when he said, "He's not my actual father. I never met my real parents. Dr. Bodkin said they died when I was very young." *I know how you feel,* Tara thought, recalling how she lost both her parents. "Now Dr. Bodkin takes care of me. I'm very sick. That's why I need to stay isolated from everyone else." Tara shot him a serious look.

"Sick with what?" Tara asked, worried he was contagious.

"I have a rare bone disease that I'll die from without treatment. If I'm outside the room too long, Dr. Bodkin says I'm in danger of infection because my immune system is so weak. I go to see him every other week for treatments. In fact, I go tomorrow." Katahdin smiled at Tara. "I'll let him know you're feeling sad."

"No, that's okay!" Tara said quickly. She thought for a moment, then smiled. "The milk and cookies made me happy."

"I'm glad they did," Katahdin replied. Tara mentally went over what Katahdin had told her. The story made no sense. *The room is not hermetically sealed. The space under the door confirms that. Okay, they're lying to him, but why?*

"Katahdin, if you don't mind me asking, what type of treatment are you on?"

"I take pills twice a day. When I go visit Dr. Bodkin, he gives me a shot to help control the disease." Tara was no medical expert, but that didn't sound right either. She recalled something else he had said, something about chameleons being ancient species.

"Why did you call the chameleons ancient animals?"

Katahdin looked at her like she had asked an obvious question, then answered, "All known animal life went extinct around one hundred years ago."

"What?" Tara replied, not having a clue what he was talking about. Katahdin again looked at her like she was crazy.

"Did you just wake up from a cryo chamber?" Katahdin asked seriously. *No, have you been living under a rock?* "You must know what I'm talking about. The nuclear war that wiped out nearly all life on Earth. The people in this place are the only humans left—that's why I was surprised to see you. Then again, I've only seen around four people."

Tara gave him a look of pure confusion. "What are you taking about?" she asked, dumbfounded. "There are billions of people and animals running around as we speak." She was about to tell him to look outside a window before realizing there were none.

"You're thinking of prewar times," Katahdin replied, undeterred.

"Where are you getting these ideas?" she said out loud. *Dumb question,* she thought, knowing where.

"Dr. Bodkin tells me about what happened, and I read a lot of history books," Katahdin said, pointing to a bookshelf. Tara felt herself wanting to scream: he's lying to you. *No, Tara, there's a better option.*

"Do you care if I look at some?" Tara asked, wanting to know what he was reading, hoping to poke his logic full of holes.

"Sure. No offense, but you ask a lot of strange questions." *No, you believe a lot of strange stuff.* Tara went over to the bookshelf. The books were a mix of fiction about nuclear wars, and nature and wildlife books. The only supposed history books were clearly typed on a computer and stapled together. Tara grabbed one of the fiction books and, hoping to show Katahdin it was a work of fiction, she turned to the author page only to see it had been removed. She cursed. *These people think of everything.*

"If you want to read more, I have some files on my laptop." *Did he just say...?*

Tara quickly turned around to face him. In an excited voice she asked, "You have a computer?"

"Ya, it's over there," Katahdin replied, pointing to a newer gaming laptop. "I like to watch movies and play games on it."

Tara nearly ran over to it before asking, "Can I used it?"

"Sure," Katahdin replied. Tara jumped in excitement, which made Katahdin look at her like he thought she was an idiot. She didn't care. *This could be it. I'll email Romy and Ryan everything I know.*

Katahdin turned on the computer while Tara watched, anticipation building as it loaded. Her look of excitement soon turned to a frown when she saw the computer was not connected to the internet.

"Can this connect to the internet?" Tara asked, fearing she already knew the answer.

"What's the internet?" Katahdin replied.

"Never mind," Tara said, disappointed. "You can turn the computer off; it doesn't have what I needed." Tara snorted in frustration. "I don't suppose you have a phone."

"Sorry, I don't. I have more cookies if that will make you happy," Katahdin offered. His comment managed to bring a smile to her face. She glanced at the room clock, which read five-thirteen.

"Shoot!" she said. With everything going on, she had forgotten about the time.

"I'd better get back to my room. I'll take a rain check on the cookies." Tara walked over to the dresser and pulled it out enough to fit behind. *If he tells anyone about this, I'm dead.* Her concerned feeling returned. She turned to Katahdin, who was still sitting at the computer table. "Do you mind not telling anyone I came to visit you? I want to do it again and I'm afraid they won't let us if they find out."

"Secret's safe with me," Katahdin replied, getting up. "I spend almost all my time locked in this room. It gets really lonely sometimes. It's nice to have someone to talk to." Tara smiled, knowing exactly how he felt.

"I'm locked in my room too. Yes, it is nice to have someone kind to talk to." Tara thought about explaining her situation to him, but she needed to be careful. He had told her Dr. Bodkin was like a father to him. If she started telling him who Dr. Bodkin and everyone really were, he might get angry. She seemed to be on friendly terms with Katahdin and didn't want to ruin that. "I should probably be going now. Please don't say anything about the tunnel either."

"It's our secret," Katahdin confirmed, waving goodbye. Tara waved back.

"I'll stop by soon." She ducked down and crawled into the hole. She picked up the section of drywall, putting it back into place. She sat against the wall. Now that she was alone, she started to wonder if any of that had happened. "What I saw was impossible. I must have fallen asleep here," she told herself.

"No, you were awake, Tara," Katahdin said though the wall.

Tara shrieked slightly before saying, "I know. Thank you. Goodnight." She knew Katahdin was real, but her mind was having trouble accepting it. When she returned to her room, she started to worry Katahdin would use the tunnel himself. *No, he's too big to fit through the hole.* That settled the matter for her. When she lay down, a new reality hit her. Her entire escape plan was based around a phone being in the room. *What do I do know?* she thought. Again, hopelessness started to creep in. *You can't think like this, Tara. You can't give up.* With the possibility of getting a phone out of the question, she started focusing on Katahdin. At least he seemed kind and in a way to care about her well-being. He didn't seem dumb either; he seemed to be brainwashed and taught a world of lies. *He knows Dr. Bodkin, which means he probably knows Joseph and Ivan,* Tara thought. *What do they want from him? There is no way they are keeping him out of the kindness of their hearts. Wonder if Nora knows about him?* Tara continued to wonder. *If she doesn't, that might be a good way to further pin Joseph and Nora against each other... she could even slip up and tell Katahdin something Bodkin didn't want him to know.* Tara spent the rest of her time awake thinking about Katahdin and how she could use him to escape.

Chapter 20

A few hours later, Tara was woken up by Ivan entering the room. She groggily opened her eyes.

"Dr. Bodkin wants to see you in his office," he said, remaining in the doorway. *Right, I have a client today,* she remembered. She pulled the blanket off and looked at her clock. It was only a little past nine.

"Do you mind waiting outside so I can change?" Tara asked.

"You'll be back soon enough," Ivan replied. Since changing clothes didn't really matter, Tara went along without a fuss. She had been cycling through the outfits since she got here.

"Do you normally sleep this late?" Ivan asked. *Do they know what happened last night?* Tara thought, feeling nervousness return.

"Time really doesn't matter to me anymore," Tara replied.

When they got to Dr. Bodkin's office, he was standing near the examination table, and Joseph Jackson was sitting in a chair. Tara knew this was not a routine checkup; they were up to something. She looked over her shoulder to see Ivan standing in the doorway. His massive body blocked her only exit.

"What's going on?" Tara asked, trying to hide the nervousness in her voice. Despite her best effort, some of it slipped out.

"Sit down," Dr. Bodkin said in his disdain-filled voice. Tara did as she was told. Joseph was eyeing her like he had caught the cat eating the canary. She began to fear the worst. *Do they know where I was last night?* Tara quickly shot the thought down. *No, if they did, Ivan would have torn my room apart. What if someone's going through it right now?* the voice of doubt added. The fact that Nora wasn't here made her fear her doubts were right. *Stay calm, Tara, don't act like anything unusual happened.*

When she sat down, Dr. Bodkin said, "I understand you saw Katahdin this morning." Tara felt her body tense. He told them about last night. Inside, she started cursing her stupidity. *I should have known not to trust him.*

"Um. Uh." Tara tried to create words, but nothing would form. She tried not to think about what would happen to her when they found her tunnel. "I don't know who that is," Tara replied, playing dumb. It was foolish, but it was the only card she had. Dr. Bodkin walked around her, smiling like he knew she was lying.

"I'm sure you remember seeing him. It was less than an hour ago." *Wait, why did he say I saw Katahdin less than an hour ago, and neither of them have said anything about the tunnel?* Tara felt herself starting to relax. Maybe Katahdin had not betrayed her trust. Dr. Bodkin stood in front of her and said, "Katahdin says he saw you in the hallway when he was coming for his examination. He also told me you talked for a while."

"You're talking about that freak?" Tara replied, acting shaken up. "Yes, I saw him and I never want to again. Who was he? Why does he look like that?"

"That is none of your concern. I want to know what you talked about, and what you told him," Dr. Bodkin said in a serious tone.

"I wouldn't say we talked; it was more like he asked me questions and I replied to them."

"What kinds of questions did he ask?" Dr. Bodkin demanded. Tara could sense a hint of fear in Dr. Bodkin's voice. *Afraid I undid the brainwashing?* Tara wanted to say, but instead said, "I was scared out of my mind. I honestly don't remember." She then acted like she was thinking hard. "It was basic stuff. Like 'what's your name, I never saw you before.'" To her relief, that seemed to satisfy him.

"Doctor. If I may step in?" Joseph asked.

"Of course," he replied as he started conducting the routine examination Tara went through before seeing a client.

Joseph got up, went up to Tara, and asked sternly, "You were told not to leave your room without an escort. What were you doing walking around the halls this morning? More importantly, how did you get past the camera?" *Great,* Tara thought, knowing she needed to think of an excuse for something she didn't do.

"I got bored and went for a walk," Tara replied in a smart tone. She was taking a chance talking to him in that tone, but she was coming up with a new plan. An idea that might get her out of performing today.

"Don't you lie to me!" Joseph yelled.

"Enough!" Dr. Bodkin cut in. "I need to make something very clear to Tara!" Dr. Bodkin moved his hands to her face as if checking for broken bones. "Katahdin is very important to my work." He slowly moved his hands from her face to her throat. "In the future, if you see him, you will not speak to him. Forget you ever saw him. Understand?" he asked, momentarily applying pressure to her throat. It was not hard enough to choke her, but she got the message.

"I understand," Tara replied. *No, I don't. I'm sick of cowering at every threat, my only plan of escape failed, so why not make life miserable for these people?* In a way, they had overplayed their hand. They had already beaten, starved, and raped her. There was not much else they could do to her. She recalled seeing Dr. Bodkin holding that large needle. Now she thought she understood what it was used for. "You're harvesting bone marrow and using him as a lab rat, aren't you?" Tara said softly. Dr. Bodkin gave her a look that said *how did you know that*? "And what's his connection to that bone statue?"

That set Dr. Bodkin off. He started violently shaking Tara and yelled, "You will never speak of him **again!**" By his response, Tara knew she was right. There was nothing wrong with Katahdin. He was Dr. Bodkin's brainwashed cash cow. He released her and yelled, "Physically, you're okay, now get out!"

"I'm sorry, doctor," Joseph added in a furious tone. "I'll get her out of here." He ordered Ivan to escort Tara to her room. Dr. Bodkin glared at Tara as she exited the office. Joseph followed them out. *I must have hit a nerve,* Tara thought as she heard the door slam. Now it was time to start. Instead of going towards her room, Tara started walking towards the office area.

"Where do you think you're going?" Joseph demanded.

"I need to ask Nora something," Tara replied, making a Nora-like hand wave, telling him to move.

"No, you don't. She does not need to be disturbed," Joseph replied. "You're going straight to your room and if you come out again, I'll have you chained to a wall!"

"In case you forgot. I answer to Nora Peters, not you," Tara said smartly.

"What did you say?" Joseph asked. Ivan looked stunned, not understanding where her sudden boldness came from.

"I said I don't answer to you." She changed to a more confident tone when she said, "If I want to leave my room, I don't need your permission, and if I want to go see Nora, I will."

Joseph clenched his fists in anger, then screamed, "How dare you speak to me that way! I should beat you within an inch of your life!" *So far, so good,* Tara thought as she grinned at him. Now was the time to strike. She noticed a decorative vase on a table a few feet from her. She grabbed it, holding it up like she was ready to throw it. Ivan was about to step in when Joseph waved him off. He took off his suit jacket.

"You want to go! Bring it, Tara!" Joseph yelled. He rolled up his sleeves, looking like he wanted to kill her. Tara slowly walked along the wall. Joseph followed, daring her to do something. "If you're going to do something, do it! I'm sick of your games." Before Joseph could react, Tara ran closer to the office area, and as she expected, he chased after her. She turned around, tossed the vase against the wall, and let out a frightened scream.

"I'm sorry! Please don't hit me!" She made a fist and smacked it against her hand, creating a punching sound. Tara then smacked her face against the wall. In true pain, she cried, "Please stop, please stop hitting me!" She saw Joseph standing stunned a few yards from her. She smashed her face into the wall twice more. She felt blood coming from her nose. She raised her voice and cried in a desperate shriek, "No, please!" Tara screamed until she heard the sound of footsteps coming from the main office. Tara let some of the blood from her nose fall into her hand. With Joseph still stunned, she rushed him. She brushed her bloody hand across his knuckles and fell down in front of him. She huddled into a ball, and again she started crying and begging.

"Get up! What are you doing?" Joseph asked, completely confused.

"What's going on?" Nora Peters demanded as she exited her office. *Keep up the act, Tara, be convincing.*

"Nora?" Tara said weakly. Tara looked up and started to crawl towards her. Blood poured from her nose, her face starting to bruise.

"Tara? My god, what happened to you?" Nora asked, predictably shocked by what she was seeing. Tara fell in front of her and sobbed.

"J-Joseph said I needed to stay in my room all day. I told him you wanted me to perform this afternoon, then he got mad and threw that vase at me, then he kept hitting me and hitting me!"

"You lying whore, I never touched you!" Joseph yelled. Nora glared at him.

"Yes, you did!" Tara whimpered. She grabbed Nora's leg like a frightened child. "Oh, Nora. I thought he was going to kill me."

"You started this! You attacked me! Right, Ivan?" Joseph raged. Ivan agreed with Joseph's story.

"Be quiet!" Nora yelled.

"There, there, Tara," she said, gently patting her on the head. "Doctor, get her something to stop the bleeding," Nora said to Dr. Bodkin, who had left his office to see what the commotion was about. Dr. Bodkin returned to his office, grabbed a towel, and threw it in front of Tara. Nora grabbed the towel, bent down, and said, "Tara, use this, dear, you're getting blood all over the carpet." Tara put the towel over her face and leaned on Nora's shoulder. "Keep that on your face," Nora ordered, not wanting blood to get on her white business attire.

"If you ask me, that whore deserved every bit of this," Dr. Bodkin said, showing his hatred towards Tara.

"No one asked you," Nora countered. "Thank you, doctor, you may leave."

"No, you stay here!" Joseph ordered, wanting to show he was in command. The towel hid Tara's grin. *Everything is working like a charm.*

"What is the purpose of me remaining here?" When Joseph couldn't give him an answer, Dr. Bodkin added, "I have things to do."

When he returned to his office, Nora scolded Joseph. "Joseph, you assaulted one of my girls, when she has a client coming in three hours!"

"I didn't touch her!" Joseph countered, moving towards her. Keeping up the act, Tara yelped in fright.

"Don't let him hurt me anymore!" she begged, moving behind Nora. With Nora's back to her, she wanted more than anything to stick her tongue out at Joseph.

Nora turned around and looked her in the eye. "He will never touch you again, I promise," Nora said reassuringly. Her face turned more serious when she said, "Now, Tara, you must tell me the truth. What were you doing out of your room? You know you're not supposed to be walking around unsupervised."

When Joseph started to speak, Nora lifted her finger. "I was asking Tara." Tara removed the towel from her face, holding it under her nose so she could speak clearly.

"This morning I was going stir crazy, so I left my room to go for a short walk. Just up and down my hall," Tara reassured. "When I was walking, I saw the strange man."

"Shut up!" Joseph cut in.

Undeterred, Tara continued, "Who's in the room next to mine. Joseph and Dr. Bodkin were questioning me about him, and they told me not to say anything to you. When I said you should know about the strange man, that's when he started hitting me." *That will start some fireworks,* Tara thought. Nora slapped Tara across the face.

"Joseph already told me about what's in that room. He hit you because you left your room and saw something you shouldn't have. Does that sound more like the truth?"

Knowing she had overplayed her hand, Tara looked down and said, "Yes, sorry I lied. I'm just angry about getting hit."

Nora pulled Tara's head up and asked in a disappointed voice, "Tara, have you learned nothing?"

Before Nora could continue, Tara said, "When I misbehave, I get punished, when I behave, I get rewarded." *Please be what you wanted to hear,* Tara thought, seriously concerned Nora was going to do something to her for lying.

"You were listening," Nora replied, pleased.

"Are you going to buy her bull crap?" Joseph asked, stunned. "She's learned nothing, she's only telling you want she knows you want to hear. How you're handling this is unacceptable." Unintimidated, Nora got in his face.

"Hitting one of my girls is unacceptable! Especially right before a performance!"

"Nora, in case you have forgotten, you are in my facility. You have four people loyal to you, the rest are loyal to me. If I wanted to, I could have you and everyone from Heartwood Manor shot right now!" Nora scoffed.

"You don't have the guts." Joseph turned to Ivan. "Ivan, come back here with a loaded pistol." *Have I gone too far?* Tara wondered. She wanted Nora dead, but not when she was surely going to be in the cross fire. In response, Nora backed away and pulled out her phone.

"Dimitri. Joseph Jackson has just threatened my life and the life of a valued company asset." *I'm a human being, you know,* Tara thought, now wanting to kill Nora herself. "Report this to corporate, tell them I wish to press full charges, and call me once every daylight hour for the next two days. If I don't pick up, Joseph Jackson and everyone at his facility is to be killed for murdering a company employee." She hung up and gave Joseph a look that said "your move."

Joseph turned to Ivan, defeated. "Ivan, forget my last order."

Nora lit a cigarette.

"As you know, the charges I'm about to press will cost you your position. If you would like me to drop them, I want full control of Tara, movements and activities."

"Fine," Joseph reluctantly agreed, knowing he had no choice. "But I want you to sign a letter stating I was against this idea and cannot be held accountable for any negative consequences that result from it."

"Whatever," Nora replied unfazed. Joseph and Ivan left the room.

She turned to Tara and said, "Starting right now, you may come and go as you please."

"Thank you," Tara said happily, knowing full well Nora's act of kindness was only a ploy to anger Joseph.

"How's your nose? Do you need to see the doctor?"

"Most of the bleeding stopped," Tara replied, not wanting to be anywhere near Dr. Bodkin. Nora looked at her face.

"A minor bruise, some makeup will cover it up. I trust you're well enough to perform?"

Tara's first thought was to say no, but the idea of moving freely was too good to ruin. Knowing she had no choice, Tara said, "Yes."

"Excellent. I'll see you in a few hours."

Before she walked away, Tara said, "Nora, can I ask a small favor?"

"What is it, Tara?" Nora asked in a neutral voice.

"I don't want Joseph's men coming in my room anymore. As revenge, I'm worried one might hurt me."

"It's an understandable concern. Consider it done."

"Thank you," Tara replied.

"One more thing, Tara." *Here comes the cherry on top,* Tara thought. "Know that the privileges I've given you will go away if you misbehave. Today, I expect nothing more than a happy client." Menace came into her voice. "Or else."

Chapter 21

Later that afternoon, Tara exited the shower room. She was angry and feeling violated. Her client this time had been a massively overweight man in his late forties who treated her like dirt. She was heading for her room when she heard the voice she didn't want to hear.

"Tara, come here a moment," Nora ordered. *Does she always wait outside the showers?* Tara wondered. Figuring Nora was here to give a performance review, Tara approached her. Nora didn't appear angry, but Tara had learned her temperament could change quickly.

"Once again, your customer was happy. You have shown great improvement since your first days with us," Nora complimented, her look changing to pleased. "I believe you will be ready for graduation soon." Dread filled Tara's body.

"What do you mean 'graduation'?"

"Moving on from this place. The opportunity to travel the world," Nora replied, selling it like it was some type of vacation. "I think a nice European country would suit you nicely. We have many wonderful offices there." It took all of Tara's mental strength to keep calm. Right now she needed information, not conflict.

"When will I graduate?" Tara asked.

"We will see how you do with your next client. After that, a week, maybe less. It will be nice to have Joseph out of your hair, won't it?"

Tara didn't answer her question; instead, she asked, "What if I don't graduate?"

A scowl formed on Nora's face.

"In the unfortunate event I feel you're not working out as a sex asset, we have clients who prefer torture to sex." A jolt of fear entered Tara. "Either that or I will allow Joseph to have his way and dispose of you or your act as entertainment for the boys. Either option will be fine with me."

"I'll perform well for the next client," Tara replied, unable to hide the distress in her voice.

"I know you will," Nora replied.

"What day am I scheduled to perform?" Tara asked, needing to know how much time she had.

"Two days from today. Now I have some business to take care of. Enjoy the rest of your day." Nora pulled out her cell phone and walked towards the office area. Tara had been planning to get something to eat, but her appetite was gone. When she got to her room, her only thoughts were on Nora telling her she would be shipped off to another country soon. In a panic, she started pacing back and forth.

"I've got to get to a phone. I've got to get out of here. I've got to get out of here." She pounded the wall, grunting in frustration, knowing all her work and careful planning had been for nothing. Tears of stress and frustration started to fall. "I thought you were done crying, Tara." She wiped a tear from her cheek. "No, there's plenty more tears and beating to come," Tara said, changing the tone of her voice, acting like someone else was talking. She changed back to her normal voice and cried. "Ryan, Romy, please just get here! You've had long enough to figure it out!" Tara started to laugh and fell onto her mattress. Her voice changed to sarcasm. "I forgot they're not looking for me. They're mourning me because they think I'm dead." Tara started to laugh again. "I wanted a modeling career, and now..." Tara sat up and stretched out her arms. "And now I have the best job ever!" She lay back down and hugged her pillow. "I am so screwed," she said, depressed.

Out of the corner of her eye, she noticed her closet door was halfway open. Noticing it brought her back to reality because she knew the door was closed when she left. *Someone searched my room when I was gone! Did they find the tunnel?* Tara thought, worried. She rushed over to the closet. The door suddenly burst open. Tara felt the wind on her face.

"Booo!"

Tara shrieked and fell to the ground.

"Sorry, too good to pass up," Katahdin said, appearing before her.

"Oh, Katahdin," Tara said, calming down. A look of shock and worry formed on her face. "Katahdin, what are you doing in here! How did you get in here?"

"Same way you got into my room: the tunnel in the wall." Tara heard footsteps coming down the hallway, then her doorknob started to turn. *There isn't enough time to tell Katahdin to leave or tell him to hide inside the closet. I'm dead.* She desperately tried to think of a solution but knew there was no way she could get out of this.

A male guard came in. Tara did not know his name; she had only seen him a few times in the recreation hall.

"What's going on?" he asked. Tara wondered why he was not saying anything about Katahdin. She glanced over to see he had disappeared. Thinking quickly, she gave an embarrassed laugh.

"A bird or something banged into the window. It nearly scared me to death," Tara replied, patting her heart. The man gave her a look that said "thanks for wasting my time," then left. "Good thinking," Tara said, turning to where she thought Katahdin was.

"I remembered you said you didn't want people to know we talked." Katahdin reappeared and went into the closet to put on his clothes, which were lying on the closet floor. When he came out, he smiled and shook his head. "Tara, the only living birds are in the biodome. So you might want to think of better excuses next time." *Okay, I'm sick of this,* Tara thought.

"Katahdin, come here," Tara said, walking over to her window. It was time to end Katahdin's delusion once and for all. "Look out the window and tell me what you see."

Katahdin looked out the window. "I see grass, trees, and the sky," he replied.

"Exactly, I thought everything was wiped out," Tara replied, thinking she had found a loophole in his logic.

"Not near us. Dr. Bodkin told me they're working hard on terraforming operations. Everything inside the walls is replanted." Tara grunted in frustration. From her window the wall was too far to see. She scanned the area, hoping to see a bird or a small animal. Of course none were around.

"Just keep looking. I'm sure a bird will fly by."

"What's the point? None are out there." Tara accidently gave him a look that showed she thought he was nuts. "Sorry for being direct, but there might be a good reason you're locked in here."

"What reason is that?" Tara asked, a little upset.

Katahdin spoke in a caring tone. "Earlier you were walking back and forth, screaming, and talking to yourself in different voices. I'm physically sick, and you seem to be mentally sick."

"Look, Katahdin!" Tara started to say, wanting to unload on him. He was the one who was mentally sick, believing all the nonsense he did. Before things got out of hand, she stopped herself. Katahdin was the closest thing to a friend she had, and possibly her only hope of getting out of here. Calmly she replied, "You're right. I guess I am a little messed up. Anyone would be in my situation."

"I know it's boring being locked in our rooms all day with hardly anyone to talk to." Hope filled Katahdin's voice. "One day our illness will be treated, and the world will heal. When that day comes, the two of us can go explore it. Like the people I read about." Katahdin's optimism had a calming effect on Tara. She had nearly given up hope of escape. *Somehow, some way, I'm getting out of here.*

"Katahdin, thank you," she said gratefully.

"Thank you for what?" Katahdin asked, confused.

"Reminding me there's still hope." She placed a gentle hand on his shoulder, like Ryan would always do to her. "Look, Katahdin, I'm glad to see you, but you can't come in my room anymore. You're sick remember? I don't want your sickness to get worse. They keep you in that room for a reason, remember?"

"Good point," Katahdin agreed. "Are you going to visit tonight? I have a surprise I wanted to show you."

"Sure, see you tonight," Tara replied, expecting a new type of snack, which she would not mind. Katahdin went back to the closet. "Katahdin, how did you get through the hole, anyway?"

"Apparently I have a collapsible skeleton. Makes it easy to fit through small holes." Katahdin placed his head inside her hole. Tara cringed at the sound of his bones snapping as soon as his shoulders moved upward and he effortlessly went through.

"Katahdin, are you okay?" she yelled, concerned he was seriously hurt. Katahdin wrenched his head back until his back was nearly folded in half.

"Yes, collapsible skeleton, remember?" Tara smiled at him and shook her head that she understood. After covering the tunnel entrance, Tara sat down, still shaken by the close call. *I have to convince him I'm in danger and these people are using both of us. If I can do that, I know he'll help me.*

◆   ◆   ◆

Later that night, Tara sat at the entrance to Katahdin's room. She took a deep breath and swallowed, hoping she would be able to convince him to help her. She had spent that afternoon planning and rehearsing different things to say. She removed the section of wall and pounded on the dresser twice, figuring it would be easier for Katahdin to move it than to force her way through. Moments later, the dresser moved.

"Hey," Tara said, crawling out.

"Hey," Katahdin replied. "Ready to see the surprise I told you about?"

"Not yet." Tara's tone turned slightly nervous when she said, "Katahdin, I need to talk to you about something."

"Sure, sit down. Want anything to drink? I have water, milk, and soda."

"A bottle of red wine to drown my problems in," Tara responded jokingly.

"Sorry, don't have any of that."

"Milk then," Tara said, sitting down. Katahdin grabbed two plastic milk bottles and sat down.

"What do you want to talk about?" Katahdin asked. Tara tried to say the lines she had been rehearsing, but her mind was blank. *Forget about your script. Talk to him like you're asking a favor from a friend,* her inner voice suggested.

Tara took a deep breath and said, "Katahdin, yesterday I was not completely honest with you, because I was not sure if I could trust you." Tara showed a slight smile. "Now I believe I can." *Here it goes,* Tara thought. "A little over a month ago I was kidnapped, taken from my home and family. Now I'm forced to stay here where…" Tara tried not get emotional when she said, "I'm being forced to have sex against my will." *Please let him know what sex is, please. I don't want to have to give a lecture on that.*

Katahdin looked at her, confused. "What's sex?"

Tara stomped her foot and shook her arms back and forth in frustration.

"Hey, I'm only kidding," Katahdin said, wondering why she was so upset. "From what I understand, sex is something people do for pleasure and reproduction."

"Yes, exactly. The people here are forcing me to do it against my will," Tara stressed.

"Who is?"

"Joseph, Ivan, Nora, Miguel, and Peter." Tara left Dr. Bodkin's name out, knowing it would be easier to convince him that way. Katahdin tilted his head slightly as if thinking about what she said.

"If you don't like it, why don't you just say no?" It took all Tara had to force her next words out.

"If I don't do what they say, they beat me, rape me, and threaten to kill my family." Tara got up, giving herself some time to calm down. "Do you know the trauma and humiliation I feel every time I'm forced to perform?"

"Tara, I've met Joseph and Ivan a few times—they seem like nice people. If they brought you here, it was probably for your own good. The outside world is very dangerous." Katahdin's foolish beliefs nearly had Tara at her wits' end.

"Katahdin, the world is not a barren wasteland. There are billions of people and animals alive right now." She pointed to the door. "Those people who work here, they're keeping you here so they can profit from you." The look on Katahdin's face showed he didn't believe her.

"Tara, why should I believe you over people I have known for years?" Tara didn't reply, not having an answer to his question. "I asked Dr. Bodkin about you." Katahdin's face showed a look of compassion. "He said you had only recently been found, and mentally you are very sick."

"I'm not mentally sick!" Tara responded, her voice more menacing than she intended.

"You were talking to yourself in your bedroom, and you cried when I gave you milk because you didn't get a cookie," Katahdin countered. *You've got to cool down, Tara. Go regroup.*

"Do you mind if I use the bathroom?" Tara asked, knowing the conversation needed a break.

"No, not at all," Katahdin replied. Tara closed the bathroom door, put her arms on her head, and let out a silent scream. *What do I have to do to make him listen? Do I have to drag him outside? Good luck trying that,* she countered, again shaking her arms in frustration. *I'd have better luck* explaining my situation to a child. *Wait, that's it! Explain it to him like you would a child.* Tara came out of the bathroom.

"Katahdin," she spoke in a soft gentle tone. "These people do a lot of things to me that makes me hurt bad."

"Why are you speaking to me like I'm a child?" Katahdin asked. Tara just gave a blank, frustrated stare. *Bad idea.*

"Sorry, I was kidding," she replied with a smile. Wanting to take a break from the current subject, she asked, "I was wondering, how did you not hear me when I was cutting that hole?"

"The answer to your question involves the surprise, so I'm not saying anything yet," Katahdin replied, showing no signs of being angry. *I wish you'd tell me what this surprise is,* Tara thought. She sat back down and asked a question she had been wondering since she met him.

"I was curious about your bone power?" *Bone power?* Tara thought, knowing she had chosen a silly word.

"What do you want to know?" Katahdin asked.

"Like how do you break your bones without getting hurt? Or can you stretch your limbs like that guy in my brother's old comic books?"

"According to Dr. Bodkin, I can only manipulate my own tissue, bone structure, and calcium. I can't grow new limbs or make them longer. When I reshape my bones, it brings a little pain."

"What do you mean you can manipulate calcium?" Tara asked, wondering if she really wanted to know the answer. Katahdin lifted his right arm, and a sharp piece of bone resembling a sword began extending out of his elbow. The bone stopped moving at thirteen inches. Katahdin moved his arm towards Tara. She touched the end of it, feeling its razor sharp edge.

"How long can you make it?" Tara asked, stunned.

"As long as I want," Katahdin replied. Now it was Tara's turn to give a look that said *I don't believe you.* "I'm kidding. This is about as long as I can extend it; otherwise, the bone becomes too brittle and it cracks."

"Can you make bones came out of all parts of your body?" Tara inquired, generally curious.

"Only my elbows, knees, ribs, and back," Katahdin answered. "It hurts to do it so I'd rather not show you." Tara noticed the wound on Katahdin's elbow.

"Sorry," Tara apologized. Feeling bad she made him do it, then she noticed the wound was not bleeding. "How are you not bleeding?"

"I learned if I grow a small layer of bone over the wounds, it helps seal them." Tara still found herself having trouble believing Katahdin was real, yet there he was sitting in front of her. Wanting to get back to the subject of her escape plan, Tara tried a different idea.

"Katahdin, do you think you could get me a phone?" She made a face like she was remembering something pleasant. "I used to have one and it would really help me adjust to my new situation if I had one again."

"Sure, I can get you one," Katahdin replied like it was no big deal. Tara felt like hugging him. "In about a week when I see Dr. Bodkin, I'll ask him to get you one." Tara's brief feeling of victory soon faded.

"Can I sit on the bed?" Tara asked. Katahdin showed no signs of objecting, so she did. She lay back and looked up at the ceiling. "I just want to go home. I just want see my family and friends again. I want to see Romy and Ryan, be held by Brandon." *Nora was lying about him, she had to be,* Tara thought, knowing she always played mind games.

"You found this place. If they're still out, there maybe your family will find you here," Katahdin suggested.

"I wish. My family thinks I'm dead. No one is looking for me," Tara answered sadly.

"You're clearly alive." *Thanks for always pointing out the obvious,* Tara thought. "Why do they think you're dead?"

"The people here faked my death and want to send me to another country."

"Wait, if your family and friends think you're dead. How can you get home?" Tara put a hand over her eyes, pretending none of this was happening.

"I can't go home because I can't leave here."

"No, I mean if everyone thinks you're dead, don't people get rid of dead people's things?"

Tara shot straight up. A look of dread slowly formed on her face, knowing Katahdin was right.

"Katahdin, why do you have to bring things like that up?" Katahdin gave her a look that said "I only asked a simple question."

All my stuff better be there when I get back, Tara thought, becoming angrier.

Seeing she was again becoming upset, Katahdin said, "Tara, that surprise of mine might cheer you up."

"Katahdin, sorry, but unless you have a phone, I don't think you have anything that can cheer me up," Tara said, again burying her face in the pillow.

"You won't know until you see it," Katahdin replied. He got up and went over to the space between the bed and wall. Tara looked up to see what he was doing. She noticed a set of double doors. That caught her attention.

She got of the bed and asked curiously, "What's behind there?"

"The surprise I told you about." Katahdin pointed to the door. "Go ahead, you go first."

"Why do I go first?" Tara asked suspiciously. She doubted Katahdin had bad intentions, but not knowing what was behind them made her nervous.

"Because I've seen it hundreds of times. I don't want to block your first view of the place." *If Katahdin wanted you dead, you'd be dead already. Can't argue with that,* Tara thought, mentally agreeing with herself. With her worrisome thoughts conquered, Tara gripped the knobs with more curiosity than fear. "You're coming, right?" Tara asked, looking back at Katahdin.

"I'll be right behind you." Tara began opening the doors, wondering what was behind them. *Another one of Dr. Bodkin's monsters?* her doubts whispered. *No, the way Katahdin acted it was probably a storage closet filled with janitor supplies.* The thought made her snicker. A stream of crisp spring air touched her skin. She could smell the outdoors.

Tara pulled the doors open. Fields of grass and wildflowers were in front of her. Several rabbits stopped eating to look at her. The meadow extended about twenty feet and became a forest. *I'm outside. I'm free!* Tara thought, getting her hopes up way too much. She rushed into the meadow only to see a dome covering the area. "Great, it's a biodome," Tara said, disappointed.

Despite her disappointment, it felt good to feel grass under her feet. In the distance she thought she heard the pleasant sound of a small waterfall, then another sound caught her ear. It sounded like a tarp blowing in the wind. The same sound she had heard before.

"Hang on," Katahdin said. Before she could answer, Tara felt Katahdin's talon feet latch around her shoulders and armpits. Tara let out a gasp of surprise as she was lifted off the ground. Tara looked down to see the ground becoming farther and farther away.

"Katahdin, put me down," she said in a slightly frightened voice. She guessed she was twenty to thirty feet off the ground now.

"Look down. If I drop you at this height, you'll fall and break something." Tara found herself laughing at his response. The kind of fear she was feeling was an excited fear, not the scared-for-her-life fear she felt when she was around Miguel or Nora. Katahdin flew to one of the four large pine trees located in the middle of the biodome. He hovered over a large branch near the top. "Put your feet on the branch and grab on to the tree. I'm going to let go of you."

Tara let out a frightened yet excited moan, the kind she always made when the rollercoaster reached the top and was about to go down. She planted her feet firmly on the branch, which was easily two feet around, and hugged the tree tightly. She felt Katahdin release her, and soon he landed on a branch next to hers. His feet gripped the branch like an ape would. *Don't look down, Tara, don't look down.* She looked above her. The moon was full and the stars were shining in all their glory. If she didn't know the true horrors of this place, she would have thought it was beautiful. Against her warning thoughts, she did look down, and butterflies filled her stomach. She was easily fifty feet off the ground. One glance was enough for her. She moved her head around to get a full view of the dome. The dome was square shaped, fifty feet high with one hundred and fifty yards of land inside it. The forest area took up a large portion of the dome with sections of meadows on the dome's outer portions. Tara noticed another interesting detail. What she thought was glass was actually small wire fencing.

"Do you like the surprise?" Katahdin asked.

Tara looked at him, truly smiling. "Yes. Do you bring all the girls up here?" she asked as a joke.

"No, you're the first person I've brought up here; or carried, for that matter."

"Then how did you know you could lift me?" Tara asked.

"I didn't. I figured if you were too heavy, I'd drop you before we got too high," Katahdin replied like it was no big deal.

"Well, that's comforting to know," Tara said sarcastically.

"I spend most of my time out here. On warmer nights, I sleep out here. That's why I never heard you tunneling." Katahdin pulled out a bag from his pocket. "Tara, hold your hand out." She did as he asked. A pile of bird seed fell into her hand.

"Katahdin, I don't eat bird seed," Tara said, expecting Katahdin to start eating the pile in his hand.

"Neither do I," Katahdin answered, then he started to whistle different bird songs. "I can't promise any will be awake, but maybe some will be hungry." Katahdin whistled several more times, then a painted bunting landed next to him. It flew onto his hand, took a seed, and flew off.

"What kind of bird was that? It was beautiful," Tara asked.

"A painted bunting," Katahdin whispered. "Shh, they don't like people talking." He pointed to a branch next to Tara. Before she could turn, a yellow parakeet landed on her hand. Instead of flying off, it stayed picking at the seeds.

"Hi, little fellow," Tara whispered. Before she knew it she had forgotten about her situation and was having fun. The painted bunting returned. To Tara's delight, this time it landed on her hand. She smiled, admiring the patterns of purple, red, and yellow. She looked at Katahdin, who had a goldfinch, and a Baltimore oriole on his hand. After several minutes, the seeds were gone, and so were the birds.

"How many birds are in here?" Tara asked, her bubbly, happy voice returning for the first time since she was captured.

"Thirty, eleven different species," Katahdin answered.

"I can't believe you trained them to eat out of your hand. How long did it take?"

"Depends on the bird; mostly a month or two. Newer arrivals watch the other birds and I guess learn I'm not dangerous." A new kind of grin formed on Tara face. She had finally found a flaw in Katahdin's logic.

"If nothing exists outside the biodome, where do these new birds come from?"

Without hesitating or thinking, Katahdin replied, "Dr. Heinrich Bodkin is in charge of the facilities cloning program, and they're bringing back some of the extinct species. So far he's been able to bring back eleven species of birds, seven species of mammals, and two species of fish." *Oh my god,* Tara thought, rolling her eyes. She thought about arguing the point but decided against it. For the first time in far too long, she was enjoying herself and didn't want that feeling to leave her anytime soon.

"Do you want to get down and see the rest of the biodome?" Katahdin asked.

"Sure," Tara replied. Before she knew it, Katahdin lifted her off the branch and was lowering her to the ground. Feeling much calmer, Tara looked at the talons locked around her shoulders. The tips were visibly sharp, while the rest of the talon was dull. A fact she was grateful for. When they reached ground level, Katahdin released her.

"Some of the animals might be still awake. Do you want to find some or go to the pond?"

"Let's go to the pond," Tara suggested. "We can find some animals along the way." While they were walking, Tara noticed a patch of flowers with light blue petals and white sepals. "What are these?" she asked, picking one and placing it in her hair.

"Those are Colorado blue columbines. The humming birds love to feed on them." Katahdin pointed to a patch of bushes. "We have a visitor." Tara noticed the head of a kangaroo peering above the bushes.

"You have a kangaroo?" Tara commented, not expecting to see something like that. The kangaroo disappeared behind the bushes and they continued their walk. Tara begin thinking about the different animals she saw. Her knowledge of animals was limited, but she knew parakeets and kangaroos couldn't stay out here during the winter months. "Katahdin, what happens to the animals during the cold winter months?"

"Most of them stay out here. I move the animals from warmer climates into a holding area at the other end of the dome."

"What's the area like?" Tara inquired, hoping there would be a door to the outside.

"It's a heated room with three or four cages. The food for the animals is also kept there."

"How does the food get to the room?"

"About every other month someone brings it to my room and I take it there." Katahdin extended his hand, pointing ahead. We're at the pond." The woods ended and again became a small meadow that surrounded a large pond. At the opposite side of the pond was a large stone wall where two small waterfalls fell from the top into the pond. Tara knelt down. The water was crystal clear with a depth of five feet. She could see different colors of koi and goldfish swimming around. On the surface two swans and a group of seven wood ducks swam.

"Want to go for a swim?" Katahdin offered. Tara was tempted but decided against it.

"Actually, can we go back? I should get back to my room," Tara said, slightly worried. She had been having fun and again made the mistake of losing track of time.

"Sure, do you want to fly or walk?"

"We can walk. I'm in no real rush," Tara answered, moving ahead with a skip in her step. She stopped when she noticed a herd of small deer walking out of the woods towards the pond. "What kind of deer are those?" Tara asked, seeing a pair of fangs on the upper jaw.

"Muntjacs," Katahdin replied. They watched the muntjacs for several minutes before moving on. As they neared Katahdin's room, he stopped near a patch of long grass. "Hold on, I see something." Katahdin reached into the long grass. "Tara, hold both your arms out." Tara did as he requested, expecting a bunny to be placed in her arms. "Ready?" Katahdin asked. Tara shook her head yes. Katahdin lifted the animal up, and Tara's eye widened with shock as Katahdin casually dropped a skunk in her arms. *Help,* Tara thought, frozen in place, not daring to move, not believing she was holding a skunk. A skunk that if agitated could spray her. "Isn't he cute?" Katahdin asked, rubbing the skunk's head. Tara's feeling of surprise started to become concern. If the skunk sprayed her, everyone would know where she had been.

Managing to remain calm, Tara replied, "Yes, he's lovely. Do you mind taking him? His claws are digging into my arms." Katahdin took the skunk. *Thank you,* Tara thought in relief.

"Do you have sharp claws?" Katahdin asked the skunk in a baby voice before putting him down.

"Never thought I would hold a skunk," Tara commented, watching it disappear into the grass.

"Bet you never thought someone would fly you to the top of a tree either," Katahdin added. Tara snickered.

"No, not in my wildest dreams." Before leaving the biodome, Tara removed the flower from her hair. She glanced back at the biodome, wanting to keep her pleasant feeling awhile longer.

"Everything all right?" Katahdin asked, noticing her gloomy look.

"Just wishing I could stay longer," Tara replied as she started to walk.

"You can come back tomorrow," Katahdin reminded.

"I'll take you up on that," Tara assured. After saying goodbye for the night, Tara returned to her room. She lay down and started thinking of all the pleasant memories in her life. As odd as it was, what she experienced in Katahdin's forest had to be one of the best moments of her life. Flying through the air, feeding birds near the top of a fifty-foot tree, getting frightened by a skunk. Her experience in Katahdin's forest gave her more than a good time; it reminded her what it was like to live without fear and enjoy life. When her plan to get a phone didn't work, she had nearly given up. Now a fire was relit inside her. She was going to escape this place before Nora could send her off to another country or die trying.

Chapter 22

It was late morning. Tara sat by herself at a table in the kitchen. She had spent all morning going over her new escape plan. Right away she crossed off trying to escape through the garage doors in the loading area. Joseph was suspicious of her, and after her first journey to the loading docks, it was now undoubtedly guarded. Even though Katahdin was becoming a friend, she couldn't count on his help. He was too brainwashed to turn on the people he thought were the good guys. The only idea she had involving him was stealing cutting tools and making a hole in the biodome wall. She doubted it would work, mainly because any hole large enough for her to get through, the animals could escape through, and she knew Katahdin would never allow that. As unpleasant as it was going to be, she planned on spending all of her time in the kitchen and recreation room. Watching people, learning who would be easiest to manipulate. Of the people she currently knew, only Devin could be manipulated. Peter and Miguel were too cruel, and Ivan was too careful. She had encountered others but didn't know enough about their personalities to try anything.

She was watching a female trafficker who had pulled out a laptop. Wanting to see what she was doing, Tara causally walked around the room, coming closer and closer until she could discreetly see the laptop screen. She was looking at a national news website. The heading was "Maui Hawaii residents hold first Alexandria disaster remembrance memorial." *Nothing of interest,* Tara thought, moving on before what she was doing became obvious.

At noon, Tara returned to her room for lunch, mainly because Peter and Miguel had shown up. Around two o'clock, she returned to the recreation room, where she remained until dinner. After eating a grilled chicken TV dinner, she went back to the recreation room around eight o'clock. She noticed Devin sitting alone at a table, playing a game on his phone, surrounded by multiple cans of beer. Several other people were in the room, four in the recreation room and two sitting at a table away from Devin. *This is my chance,* Tara thought.

She walked near him and pleasantly said, "Hi, Devin, what are you up to?"

"Hey, Tara," he answered, clearly drunk. "Want to come over here and watch movies? I have a lot to drink." He continued pointing to the beer cans.

"Depends on what you're watching," Tara replied, putting her dinner tray in the trash. She grabbed a small bag of chips and went over to him. "Any good movies come out recently?"

"I know a few," he replied. Tara noticed his phone screen was unlocked. *This could be the break I need.* Pretending to set her bag of chips down, she moved her arm, knocking the phone on the floor.

"Devin, I'm so sorry!" she quickly said. She picked the phone up, shutting the screen off before giving it to him.

"Be more careful with people's things," he replied, annoyed. He opened the screen and rubbed his temple. "What was the password again?" he asked himself in slurred speech. Tara watched in anticipation as he typed it in: one, one, five, five, eight, seven. A look of hope formed on her face. *Yes! Yes! Yes!* she thought, smiling widely. This was it. The break she had been waiting for. *The next part would be easy,* she thought, ecstatic. *Devin is wasted. All I have to do is make sure he has a little more to drink.*

"Devin, before we watch movies, I have to admit I don't like the taste of beer. Care to point me to the other drinks?"

"There in the liquor cabinet, where else would it be?" Devin pointed to a large cabinet against the wall separating the kitchen and recreation room. Tara walked over and opened the cabinet. She looked over the drinks. *This will do nicely,* she thought, grabbing a bottle of strong vodka. She returned to Devin, waving the bottle playfully.

"Devin, can we go to a place a little more private to enjoy our night?"

"Sure, we can go to my room. Maybe you can give me one of your performances?"

Sicko. Tara found herself wanting to say her thought. Instead, she gave a seductive smile and said, "Who knows what will happen?" Devin got up and began staggering towards the living area. Tara walked next to him, showing false signs she was into him. When they stopped at his room, Tara asked, "Do you live here?"

"Yes, saves me money on rent," Devin replied, looking for his keys.

"Does everyone live here?" Tara asked, wondering if even the traffickers could leave.

"It depends. Some people do, others have houses or apartments—it's up to you." Devin unlocked the door and opened it. "Welcome to my castle." The room was around the size of a standard hotel room with a bathroom. Trash and clothes littered the floor. A half-eaten plate of food rested on an arm stand. *Disgusting,* Tara thought. "Sit down. I'll get some glasses, then we can watch a movie, then move on to other things."

"Sounds good," Tara replied, keeping up the act. The couch looked dirty and was littered with crumbs. Without hesitation, she sat down. *A month ago I would have refused to sit on anything like this,* Tara thought, finding herself liking her new attitude. Devin returned with two glasses. He laid them on the table and sat next to her.

"What do you want to watch?" Not caring what was on, Tara grabbed the remote and turned on the TV. "I want to drink," Tara replied. She grabbed the vodka and poured both of them a drink, making sure Devin had plenty more than she did.

"This show sucks," Devin said, changing to videos on demand.

"You know what I like to watch." Tara moved closer and whispered in his ear. "Men drinking. Really gets me in the mood." Devin downed his glass, then picked up the bottle and started chugging. Tara started to cheer him on. *This is too easy.* Before Devin realized it, he had finished half the bottle.

"That's all I can take," he said, the alcohol clearly getting to him. He handed the bottle to her, and minutes later he lay down and passed out.

"Devin? Devin?" Tara asked, playfully shaking him. Devin grunted once, then didn't move. When she was sure he was out, she grabbed the cell phone and went into the bathroom. She sat down and punched in the passcode, the numbers burned into her mind. After she hit the last number on the keypad, the phone unlocked. Tara nearly screamed a joyful *yes.* She started to dial Ryan, then she realized she didn't know his number. She couldn't remember Brandon's or Romy's either. Her second thought was to dial 911, but she remembered Joseph and Nora had both bragged about having contacts in the police department. If she talked to one of them, he or she would tell everything to Nora or Joseph. Stress and frustration started to set in. She was holding a phone and didn't know anyone's number. She felt like vomiting.

No, don't panic. Whatever you do, don't panic, she told herself. *Think, Tara. Calm down and think.* She tried to, but the stress clouded her thoughts. Tears of frustration started setting in. *Devin could wake up any second. Come on, think of something.* After several tense moments of fighting through the panic, she managed to calm down enough to think clearly. *At home, what do you do when you don't know someone's number?* she asked herself. *I asked someone or looked it up on their social media account.* That was it. She saw Devin used a different social media site then she did. She downloaded the app of the site she used and put in her email and password. *Someone could have deactivated it, if they think you're dead,* the voice of doubt taunted. *Be quiet,* she retaliated as she clicked to log in. Her page opened just as she'd left it. Only she noticed someone had added her missing persons poster. She read the message above the page.

"I'm posting this to inform everyone my girlfriend Tara went missing." She stopped.

"I'll be home soon, baby, don't worry," Tara said, nearly breaking down. She knew Ryan didn't have social media accounts, and Brandon was most likely at work. So she went to Romy's profile and clicked on it, then clicked on her contact information. "Got it," Tara whispered, overjoyed looking at her sister's number. She was about to hit call when she remembered Romy got annoyed by telemarketers and would block unknown numbers. *I can't risk her blocking me.* She thought about messaging her the information, but that could also be interpreted as a cruel prank. *I need to hear her voice.* Tara thought for a moment, then sent a text.

◆　◆　◆

Romy was at home casually loading dishes into the dishwasher. She had the last plate in her hand when her phone pinged. She pulled it out of her pocket, expecting it to be from Ryan or Krista. The sound of the plate breaking on the floor filled the room. Romy stared at the text:

"It's Tara, answer the phone!" Seconds later, it rang. A New York number appeared on screen. Romy thought about ending the call. This had to be a cruel prank by some low-life who had heard about Tara's story, and gotten her number off Tara's missing persons photo. *What if it isn't?* she thought. Knowing she would wonder about the call for the rest of her life if she did end it, she reluctantly hit the accept call button.

Come on, pick up, pick up, Tara thought.

"Hello," Romy said, readying herself for the prankster's cruel joke. Tara heavily sighed with relief.

"Romy, it's me," she said softly, hardly able to speak from the emotions she was feeling. Romy gasped in shock, nearly dropping the phone at the sound of her sister's voice.

"Tara?" Romy's teary voice said. For a moment both were speechless. Remembering her situation, Tara soon snapped out of it. "Romy, grab a pen. I have a lot to tell you and not much time."

Romy struggled to comprehend this was real. She quickly blurted out, "Tara, where are you? Are you okay? I thought you were dead! We found a body and…"

"Romy, focus!" Tara said seriously. "I need you to write down what I'm about to say and give it to Ryan."

"Hold on," Romy replied, grabbing a pad of paper and pen from the side of the fridge. She found herself having trouble believing the calm and focused girl she was talking to was actually Tara. She sounded like her, but the Tara she knew would be acting hysterical, crying and begging for help. "I have it." Before Tara could speak, Romy asked with a little suspicion, "Tara, I forgot, what's your favorite food?" At first Tara didn't understand why she was asking that, then she got it. A test to be sure it was her.

"Chicken caesar salad with red wine. If I'm in the mood for junk food, I eat Hawaiian pizza. Any more security questions, Mom?" Tara called Romy "Mom" whenever she would give her a lecture. Romy broke down. She was talking to Tara. Tara could hear her crying, which nearly made her do the same.

"Tara, where are you? Are you in danger?" Romy asked in a tear-filled voice.

"Yes. My life probably depends on his call. I have I lot to tell you and not a lot of time, so I need you to focus," Tara emphasized, barely keeping it together herself. Romy wiped her eyes.

"Tell me what you need?"

"Write all this down."

"I'm ready," Romy replied.

"The human trafficking group that kidnapped me is called Omnipotent. I'm in New York, somewhere around Buffalo and Niagara Falls. I think a town called North Ridge is near me, but I'm not sure." Tara waited a few seconds so Romy could finish writing.

"Omnipotent, New York. Got it," Romy confirmed.

"I'm in a square building. It's some type of castle or mansion with a bidome in the center of the square. The building should be located on a Daniels Road, and it should have a long dirt driveway that runs through a small forest. I imagine it's located away from any towns."

"That should be easy to find," Romy said, trying to give Tara hope.

Tara's voice got more serious when she said, "Tell Ryan to come prepared to fight. They have an armory and vehicle garage on the west side of the building. I've seen machine guns, sniper rifles, shotguns, and body armor." Hearing that sent a wave of fear though Romy. "I'm being held on the east side. If I need to, I can hide in the walls, so don't come for me first, get to the armory and cut off all escape routes." Determination filled Tara's voice. "I don't want any of these people getting away."

"Tara," Romy tried to get in.

"Romy, I'm not done!" Tara emphasized. "These people might have contacts in the police department, possibly even in Ryan's unit. Do you have all that down?"

"Yes," Romy replied.

"I'm guessing there's twenty to twenty-five people here. The leaders are Nora Peters—"

"Who!" Romy screamed as memories of the nice lady she met at the hair salon came back to her.

"Yes, the same women who went to your hair solon. Romy, write these names down!" Tara said in a stern voice. "Joseph Jackson, and a Dr. Heinrich Bodkin are the facility leaders. Nora used to run a place called Heartwood Manor. That's all the information I have. Get that to Ryan, and whatever you do, don't call this number again!" Tara paused, her voice becoming emotional. "I have to go now."

"Tara, wait," Romy pleaded, wanting to talk to her sister.

"Romy, I'm sorry I can't talk any longer, just tell Ryan to get here soon, and tell Brandon I love him and I'll be home soon." Romy gasped, not knowing how to tell her the truth.

"Tara, I don't know how to tell you this—"

Tara cut her off, "I love you, and sorry I didn't listen."

Romy broke down into tears.

"I love you too, Tara," Romy said before hearing the line disconnect.

Tara gathered herself, wishing she could have talked to Romy longer. *Don't get complacent; put that phone back,* her inner voice warned. Tara deleted the app and Romy's number from the call history. She cautiously left the bathroom. *Don't be up, don't be up.* To her relief, Devin was still passed out on the couch. She placed the phone next to him.

"Thanks," she said in a cocky voice and left the room.

Chapter 23

"Tara! Tara!" Romy yelled. She saw the call had ended. She sat down, still trying to process what had happened. She opened the call history, needing to confirm the call was real. There it was: on top of the recent call list was a New York number. She wanted to redial it to talk to Tara again. Her judgment and Tara's warning overpowered her temptation. She went to her contacts and called Ryan.

"Hey, Romy," he said casually.

"Ryan, I know what I'm about to tell you is crazy, but it's the truth." Romy's voice became happier when she said, "I just heard from Tara."

"What!" he replied, surprised. "Romy, when did this happen?"

"A few minutes ago," Romy replied.

Ryan's voice showed some disbelief when he asked, "Are you sure it was her?"

"Yes, I'm sure! I wouldn't have called you if I wasn't!" Romy shouted more out of urgency than anger. "Ryan, she's in trouble and needs our help!"

By his voice, Romy could tell he believed her when he asked, "Romy, what did she tell you?" Romy passed on all the information Tara had given her.

Once she finished, Ryan said, "Now that we know she's alive and where she is, we can begin planning a rescue." Ryan spoke with determination. His voice lightened a bit when he said, "I'm really impressed by her attack plan—guess I was right about her talent for strategy."

"I honest thought I was taking to a different person. Good to know she hasn't given up," Romy agreed. "What's our next move?"

"I'm going to start looking into Omnipotent and speak to several members of my unit I trust."

"Are you sure you can trust them?" Romy asked, remembering Tara's warning about Omnipotent having spies in police stations.

"With my life," Ryan replied with assurance in his voice. "The good news is I know for sure Omnipotent has contacts in Erie city."

"How?" Romy asked, confused.

"The lab results told us the dead body we found was Tara's. Someone had to plant some of Tara's blood or fake the results." The obvious answer made Romy feel stupid.

"What can I do to help?" she asked, needing to do something.

"Look at satellite maps of the area Tara described, then try to locate the building she was talking about."

"I can do that." Romy walked into her room to get her laptop. "I'll call you back when I have something." Romy set the phone down and typed in "North Ridge New York, Daniels Road" in her virtual map site. She saw a rural area. A pleasant mix of farm country and forests. Romy zoomed in close and followed Daniels Road, a one-lane road country road, to the end. She saw several farm and country homes, but nothing like Tara had described. She zoomed out and again followed it, but this time she noticed something different. About half a mile away from the road was a large square building. The forest that surrounded it made the dirt driveway nearly invisible from the street. Romy zoomed in and saw a wall surrounding the building and the biodome. Tara was in there, Romy knew she was. She wished she had the hand of God. Wished she had the power to reach in and pull Tara out of there.

Romy went to redial Ryan when she read a text from him that said, "I'm on my way to the station to speak with my commander. I'll call you when the meeting's over."

Romy replied with, "Ryan, I found the building! It's right where Tara described it! Sending over a screen shot."

Romy waited for several tense hours for Ryan to call her. During that time, she went between worrying about Tara's safety and being overjoyed her sister was alive. She tried to call Brandon, but every time the call went to voicemail. When she finally saw Ryan calling, she grabbed the phone and asked, "What's going on?"

"Good news! We worked out the first details of a rescue mission. My unit's going to New York for a joint operation with the Erie city SWAT team."

"Ryan, are you sure working with them is wise?" Romy asked nervously.

"Already thought of that," Ryan answered confidently. "We're convinced our unit is clean. We told Erie SWAT that a terrorist cell is operating in their area, and will give them more details when we arrive tomorrow morning."

"Great, when are we leaving?" Romy asked, grabbing an overnight bag from her closet.

"We?" Ryan questioned.

"Yes, Ryan, I'm coming to New York," Romy said, determined. "Whether it's with you or I drive to Erie city myself."

"I've leaving my house within the hour."

"I'll be there in half," Romy said as she began tossing things in the bag.

"I'll be waiting. If we're lucky, the operation will be completed tomorrow." The word "tomorrow" hit them both. Tomorrow they would see Tara again.

◆　◆　◆

Tara returned to her room. "Yes! Yes!" she said, jumping up and down from joy, then breaking into a happy dance. She had done it. Soon, so very soon, she would be out of this place, this hell she'd been in for over a month.

She looked at her drawing of home on the wall. *It will feel so good being back in my own home, sleeping in my own bed, knowing all these people are dead or behind bars.* An image of Katahdin entered her mind. *What's going to happen to him?* she thought, wondering what he would think when strange people suddenly kicked down his door. She knew the sight of him would be enough for someone to open fire. She wasn't going to let that happen. Tara pondered how she could help him. She knew explaining the situation to him would be useless and risky. She trusted him but knew she had to be careful about what she said. Katahdin trusted her captors. Even if she asked him to keep it a secret, he might unintentionally let something she didn't want known slip. She burst out laughing. She pictured Katahdin sitting in Dr. Bodkin's office asking, "What's a SWAT team? Tara says one's on the way." Joseph would panic, and Nora would be proven to be a complete fool.

"Shoot!" Tara said out loud, realizing she had told Romy the wrong facility layout. The armory was on the east side, she was on the west side. *Not much I can do now.* A little before eight, Tara tried to sleep, wanting to spend time with Katahdin later that night. As much as she tried to sleep, her excitement kept her awake. She turned her focus back to helping Katahdin. She figured when help did arrive, she'd go to his room, and that way she could explain things to him and hopefully prevent anyone from getting hurt. When this was over, maybe she would sue and get control of the place. That would allow Katahdin to keep his forest. If that did happen, she was definitely taking Katahdin out to see the world. She finally fell asleep and woke up a little after eleven, then headed for Katahdin's room.

Katahdin sat on his bed, knowing Tara normally came around this time. Soon Tara knocked for him to move the drawer.

She entered the room holding a bag. She stood up and said in a bubbly exited voice, "I brought us some candy. Got any more milk and cookies?" Katahdin seemed to notice something was different about her, and there was.

For the first time since she met him, Tara Cymric found herself truly smiling, nearly beaming and genuinely happy.

"What are you so excited about?" *I'm going home.* Tara tossed the bag of candy on the table and lay down on the bed stomach first and crossed her legs. She let out a happy sigh.

"I had a fantastic day."

"What was so good about it?" Katahdin asked, going through the bag.

"Wait, do you care if we eat by the pond?" Tara asked, jumping up. Moments later, Tara was Indian sitting by the pond. Her legs acted as a table for her strawberry wafers. Katahdin sat next to her, occasionally tossing something to the fish and ducks. Tara looked out at the calm water, enjoying the crisp spring air, thinking in less than a week she'd be home and going out to eat at a fancy restaurant surrounded by her friends and family, celebrating her return home. Tara's daydream was interrupted when she felt something nibble at her knee. She turned to see several of the ducks biting at her wafers. "Hey, those are mine!" Tara said, gently shooing them away. She looked at the nibbled wafers and tossed them to the ducks. *Greedy thieves.*

"What were you thinking about?" Katahdin inquired. Tara started to say "dreaming about seeing my family soon," but she stopped herself. Instead she rephrased it.

"Dreaming about what I'm going to eat next week."

"What are you planning to eat?" Katahdin asked, looking at her like it was a silly thing to be in deep thought over. Tara started to lay back, noticed some duck poop, repositioned, and lay down.

"I'm going to get a strawberry milkshake and two slices of Hawaiian pizza with a large side of fries, and for dessert I'm getting a giant hot fudge sundae with marshmallow crème and rainbow sprinkles." Katahdin gave her a weird look. "I know, not the healthiest meal, but after what I've been through, I deserve a junk food meal."

"What's a hot fudge sundae?" Katahdin asked. Tara sat up and opened her mouth in exaggerated surprise.

"You don't know what a hot fudge sundae is?" Katahdin shook his head no. "It's ice cream with melted chocolate, rainbow sprinkles, and nuts, and melted marshmallows." Tara clapped her hands and licked her lips. "So good."

"What are rainbow sprinkles?" Tara found herself laughing as she tried to think about how to describe them.

"I don't know how to describe them, they're rainbow sprinkles." Tara snapped her finger and said, "Small colorful straight lines of goodness." Again Katahdin looked at her, confused. Tara put her hands up in surrender. "One day I'll get you a hot fudge sundae and you can see for yourself."

"Where would you find one?" he asked, interested. Tara was about to say: when we get out of here in a few days, I'll show you. She stopped herself, remembering what was going to happen soon. How Katahdin's world was about to be turned upside down.

Her tone became more serious when she asked, "Katahdin, can I ask you something personal?"

"Sure," Katahdin replied.

"If something were to happen to this place, the biodome and the room you live in. What would you do? Where would you go?"

Katahdin shrugged his shoulders. "I guess we'd both be dead. You can't live in the outside world." *You're going to be in for a big surprise*, Tara thought. She wanted to see the look on his face when he saw what the outside world was really like. When that happened, an "I told you so" was in order for sure.

"Don't worry, nothing going to happen to this place, and we'll have many more nights like this." Katahdin's words caused a sudden feeling of sadness to come over Tara. This or the next night would probably be the last night she would see him.

"Katahdin," Tara said emotionally, nearly tearing up. "Thank you for being kind to me and, well, becoming sort of a friend. It meant a lot to me."

"You think of me as friend?" Tara smiled and shook her head yes. "Then I consider you one; actually, you're the first friend I've ever had."

"I thought Dr. Bodkin was your friend?" Tara asked, trying again to change his mind about the people holding them captive.

"He's more like a father. He's a brilliant man that is trying his best to cure me, but he's not the type of person you can have fun with." Katahdin grabbed a candy wrapper and playfully threw it at Tara, hitting her on the head. She picked it up and tossed it back. *I'm getting you out of here. No matter what happens, you're coming with me when I'm rescued.* That led her to another train of thought. *After I am rescued, what will happen to him?* She started to seriously think about that. The way he looked, it's not like he could get a normal job and live like everyone else. She worried the police would hand him over to some military lab to be experimented upon. She would never let that happen. He had been kind and had done what he thought was best to help her. For that, she would be forever grateful.

Chapter 24

Dr. Philip Spitz sat in the Pennsylvania Erie city police station's forensics laboratory. He was working late running DNA analysis found at a recent burglary sight. The sound of the laboratory door opening caused him to look up.

"Who are you?" he asked the man who had entered the room.

"First Lieutenant Ryan Cymric. We spoke a few days ago about my sister Tara Cymric." Dr. Spitz took a moment to think.

"Oh, yes, the Tara Cymric case. I'm so sorry for your loss, First Lieutenant. What happened to that poor girl was unforgivable."

"Thank you," Ryan replied, sitting down.

"What brings you back to Erie city so late?"

"I have business with, coincidentally, the Erie County SWAT team in New York. Since I was traveling through, I thought I'd stop by and ask you a few questions in person." For a brief moment, Dr. Spitz showed a look of surprise.

"Does it have anything to do with your sister's case?"

"Yes, myself and several officers from Pittsburgh SWAT are conducting a joint operation with Erie County SWAT."

"That sounds like a big operation. Drug bust, I'm assuming?" Dr. Spitz replied.

"In a way, but that's not what I came to talk to you about. I was hoping you had a few minutes to talk about the evidence you found from my sister's body."

"I can make a few minutes." Dr. Spitz answered, his tone hinting he had work to do. "What do you want to know?" Ryan stood up.

"The funny thing is we did our own DNA tests on tissue samples from the body. Those tests did not match Tara's DNA."

"How did you get tissue samples?" Dr. Spitz asked, visibly becoming flustered. "From here the body went straight to a casket."

"We dug it up," Ryan replied calmly. In reality he was lying about running any tests. He slowly started to walk around him. "Now that leaves one of two possibilities." He raised one finger. "One, you faked the evidence." He raised a second finger. "Or two, you're really bad at your job." Ryan gently patted him on the shoulder. "And I don't think you're bad at your job."

"That is odd. Hold on, I'll look over the test results again." Ryan moved back as Dr. Spitz got up and started walking towards a file cabinet.

Suddenly he burst into a sprint, heading for the exit door. Chief Edwards and Isaiah Mills stepped out from hiding, blocking the exit. Dr. Spitz cursed in a panic. He changed direction, hoping to jump out the nearest first-story window. From behind, Ryan tackled him to the ground. Spitz cursed and screamed, knowing he had lost. Ryan handcuffed him, keeping a watchful eye on the approaching Edwards and Mills.

"Listen!" Ryan said authoritatively, pressing Spitz against the floor. "Tell me right now who told you to fake the evidence and maybe the judge will go easy on you."

"I'll go to jail!" Spitz said defiantly. "It's better than what will happen to me if I talk."

"We can place you in witness protection. Omnipotent won't be able to get you there," Ryan offered. When he said "Omnipotent," he kept Mills and Edwards in view. Neither of them reacted to the name. Spitz laughed a little.

"It doesn't matter; they'll get to me no matter what." Spitz let his body relax, refusing to say any more. Ryan handed him over to Chief Edwards, figuring if either of them, him or Mills, were allied with Omnipotent, they would have made a move.

"We'll let you know if he decides to talk," Chief Edwards assured. "What do you plan to do next?"

"Heading to New York, getting a few hours of sleep, then continuing the investigation."

"Best of luck to you," Edwards said, extending his hand. Ryan shook it.

"Thanks. I'd better get going. Romy's mad enough I made her wait in the car."

"Some advice," Spitz said in an angered voice. "You have no idea what you're facing. Forget your sister and worry about your own life."

"Mills, get him out of here," Edwards ordered.

◆ ◆ ◆

Romy Cymric sat on a bench in Perry Square Park. She held two plastic coffee cups she had gotten from a local coffee shop. When she saw Ryan leaving the police station, she swallowed the last of her coffee and tossed the cup into the trash.

"Did you get him?" she asked, nearing the car.

"Romy, why aren't you inside? I thought I asked you to stay in the car."

"I just went out to get coffee," Romy countered, handing him his. "Back to my question: did you get him?"

"Yes and he basically confessed," Ryan answered, getting into the SUV. "Thanks for the coffee." "No trouble," Romy replied, getting into the passenger seat.

"Did you ever manage to get a hold of Brandon?" Ryan asked.

"No." Romy shrugged. "I guessed when he moved to California, he said to hell with us."

"I wonder...?" Ryan said. Romy could tell he was thinking hard.

"What?" she asked as he started the SUV.

"Nothing, just an idea I'd rather not go into until I can prove or disprove it." Romy raised an eyebrow, showing she wanted to know. "Okay, remember it's just a theory, which probably holds no merit."

"Alright, let's hear it."

"The thought occurred to me: what if Brandon is the one who sold Tara to the traffickers?" A look of shock formed on Romy's face.

"Ryan, why would you even think that?"

"Well, think about it. Brandon got Tara the job and knew that Dimitri guy, then he suddenly moved to California?"

Could he have really done that to Tara?

"Romy, I'm not saying this is true or not. Just a lead worth following."

I knew something was up with Brandon since Tara disappeared. Could this be it? Romy thought, now looking concerned.

◆ ◆ ◆

The next morning, Ryan and Romy entered the Buffalo Police Department's briefing room. Romy took a seat at the back of room, trying to get over her feelings of drowsiness. She and Ryan had arrived in Erie City, New York late last night, and had gotten a few hours of sleep at a local hotel. At six am they checked out and walked to the Buffalo Police Department to begin the day's operations. The briefing room was an average sized room with eight tables arranged in two rows of four with a middle aisle going between them. Four seats were at each table. Excluding Romy, twenty-seven people were in the room. Nineteen officers from Erie City SWAT and eight from Pittsburgh SWAT. The room was a little cramped, but everyone managed. Ryan and the Erie City SWAT Commander Jeff Banner stood in front of a white board. Jeff Banner got everyone's attention and started the meeting.

"Everyone, as you know the upcoming mission is a joint mission with members of Pittsburgh SWAT. First Lieutenant Ryan Cymric and myself will be leading those respective teams. Right now, First Lieutenant Cymric will explain the upcoming operation."

Ryan moved to the center of the room and explained what had happened to Tara, and how Omnipotent was responsible for her kidnapping. He intentionally left out anything about Omnipotent having contacts in the police department. After Ryan finished speaking, he took a seat.

Commander Banner directed everyone to the white board that had a drawing of the facility. Several photos of the surrounding area and a satellite photo of the facility were taped to the left side of the white board. "Earlier this morning a surveillance team confirmed there are multiple people inside the target building. Surveillance also conformed the driveway has a gate and guard post. Although unconfirmed, we believe these people to be heavily armed." Commander Banner stopped when an officer raised his hand.

"Do we know what type of weapons we may be facing?"

Ryan explained the information Tara had given him. Banner then explained the attack plan, which used elements of Tara's suggested idea. "When we arrive, both teams will storm the armory, cutting off the traffickers from their weapons. The teams will then split into two groups. Erie City will engage and arrest the traffickers while First Lieutenant Cymric's team will rescue Tara Cymric. The estimated mission time is thirty minutes. There is also a chance this will develop into a hostage situation," Banner reluctantly added. "Alright, ladies and gentlemen, grab your gear and lock and load. We're leaving at oh-eleven-hundred hours."

When the meeting ended, Ryan kept an eye on everyone. Many of the officers went to gather and load their gear. One man caught Ryan's eye; he had a cell phone in his hand and was walking towards the station exit. Keeping his distance, Ryan followed the officer. When he got outside, he started to dial. Out of sight, Ryan watched as a look of annoyance formed on his face.

"Why don't I have a signal? It works any other time," he said out loud.

"Who are you calling?" Ryan asked, stepping into view. The man turned, visibly shaken by his appearance.

"Um, no one. Calling a friend, that's all," the man replied, showing signs of stress.

"What's your name?" Ryan asked.

"Private First Class Ethen Jones, sir."

"Why do you look so nervous, Private Jones?" Ryan asked.

"I'm making a personal call. So, with respect, do you mind giving me some privacy?"

"If your phone's not working, you can try mine," Ryan offered, wanting to see if he would take it.

"No, thank you. I'd rather use mine."
"Hey, real quick," Ryan continued. Jones looked visibly irritated at him. "Just wanted to give you some information we didn't go over in the briefing."

"What information is that, sir?"

"My sister also mentioned Omnipotent has spies in several police units. In fact this morning we picked up one of them, Dr. Philip Spitz." Jones was looking down so Ryan didn't get his reaction. "Dr. Spitz was given a plea bargain. He would be released and all charges dropped if he gave us the names of the other informants. One of the names he gave was yours." *Let's see if he takes the bait,* Ryan thought.

"Informants don't know each other's names!" Jones stopped, realizing his mistake. He reached for his pistol. Ryan and four other officers were on him before his hand touched it. Like the informant before him, he screamed, struggled, and cursed, but soon he was on the ground, handcuffed.

"The fact that you caught me doesn't matter, nor will your raid. Omnipotent sees everything and they never forget!" A crazed look was on his face. "Omnipotent will kill every one of you for this!"

"They can try," Ryan taunted.

"Is brainwashing part of the recruitment?" Banner asked, listening to Jones's threats as he was taken away.

"I have no idea," Ryan admitted. "How long has he been stationed here?"

"A little over a year," Banner replied. The four officers Ryan trusted spent the next half hour watching the Erie City officers. Ryan went through Jones's call history. Right away he noticed at least once a week Jones had made calls to prepaid phones whose owners could not be traced. He looked over the other officers' call history, but with a few rare exceptions, none had made calls to prepaid numbers.

Ryan entered a SWAT van where Romy and Donald Sorenson were watching the station's surveillance videos.

"See anything suspicious?"

"Other than people wondering why they're not getting a cell signal, not really," Sorenson replied. Ryan radioed the other officers who also confirmed seeing nothing unusual.

Satisfied he had gotten all the Omnipotent plants, he turned to Sorenson and said, "That appears to be it. We can turn off the cell phone jammers." He patted Romy on the shoulder and said, "You can go back to the hotel, and we'll be back with Tara in a few hours."

"Ryan, I'm not—" Romy began to say before Ryan cut her off.

"Romy, I leave in less than fifteen minutes. I don't have time to discuss this. I'll call you when we have Tara." A frustrated look formed on Romy's face before she took his keys and left the SWAT van.

Ryan went inside the station, quickly putting on his gear and loading his weapons, while Commander Banner gave an explanation about what happened to Ethen Jones. When Ryan returned to the SWAT vans, officers were either doing final equipment checks, loading guns, or studying the planned route and facility map. Seventeen of them carried assault rifles or submachine guns. The other members of the group were two snipers, the hostage negotiator, Owen Adams, and the seven officers who carried shotguns and breaching equipment. He passed by the sniper on his team, Allyson Davis.

"Find a good vantage point, Allyson?"

"No, this terrain is flat with trees every few feet. Probably going to have to set up on the van."

"Good luck," he replied. They fist bumped, and Ryan moved a few feet and began his final weapons check. Donald Sorenson set his gear down next to him.

"You ready to go?" Ryan asked.

"Yes, we do have a small problem, though."

"What kind?" Ryan asked. Sorenson moved his eyes to the left. Ryan looked. Romy was approaching the SWAT van. Her hair was in twin braids, and she was wearing a blank tank top and hiking jeans. Her belt had a holstered pistol, knife, and medical pouch. "My sister's like you, never listens," Ryan whispered, joking. He got up and went over to her.

"Romy, what's with the gear? Why aren't you at the hotel?" Ryan asked despite already knowing her intentions.

"It's my combat gear," Romy replied, then gave Ryan a serious look. "Ryan, I'm coming with you."

Ryan pulled her out of earshot of everyone else. "Romy, sorry, I can't allow that."

"Why not?" Romy demanded. "She's my sister too! I want—no, I need—to be there when she's rescued!"

"Romy, this is probably going to get ugly. I don't want you getting hurt."

"I'll sit in the van until it's over, and if someone unwanted does get in, you know I know how to shoot."

"Romy, I can't risk it," Ryan stressed. "The operation is probably going to take less than an hour. We'll be back with Tara before you know it."

Knowing time was short, Romy replied, "Ryan, like you said earlier, we don't have time to argue, so I'm giving you two options: either you're going to let me come with you, or arrest me and handcuff me to a cell!" Her serious look that said *I'm not changing my mind* remained strong. Ryan laughed a little.

"Okay, you win," he caved. "However, you're going to follow these two rules. You wear body armor and you stay in the van, and don't came out until I say it's clear."

"Fine with both those things," Romy replied. She rushed by him towards a SWAT van.

"Romy," Ryan said with amusement in his voice. "You're rushing towards the Erie City SWAT van." Romy playfully smiled and walked toward the Pittsburgh van.

◆　◆　◆

Minutes later, both SWAT vans left the station, beginning their forty-five-minute drive to Daniels Road. No one in the Pittsburgh SWAT van said anything about Romy coming along, since they knew who she was and why Ryan allowed her to come. Romy found herself thankful she had not yet sold Tara's car or more valuable items. She could get her apartment and furniture provided Brandon had not sold them. Ryan's theory reminded in her head. She thought about bringing it up, but knew everyone had more than enough on their minds.

"How mad do you think she'll be when she finds out we gave her clothes away?" Romy asked Ryan, trying to keep her mind off the upcoming operation.

"She won't care. She buys a new set every month anyway."

Romy burst into laughter. "True. True," she replied.

"Krista's planning a welcome home party for Tara," Ryan added.

The look on Romy's face looked more sad and serious when she asked, "Ryan, how do you think Tara will be like? I mean, will she be the same?" Ryan wanted to say she would be the same as when they last saw her, but he knew that was not true.

"I know she'll have a lot of mental and probably physical healing to do." He then added in a voice of reassurance, "Tara's stronger than people give her credit for. It might take a while but she'll pull through and get back to her normal self."

"So, when you bring Tara out of the building, is it okay if I leave the SWAT van to give her a hug?"

Ryan started to give the technical term and explain how a doctor needed to examine her first. He stopped himself and said, "I'm sure Tara will love that."

Chapter 25

Tara headed for the makeup room, annoyed she had a last-minute performance; of course this place had to give her an unpleasant goodbye. Earlier that morning she was informed she would be performing for a special client. Probably some celebrity or athlete. She found it odd that her instructions stated she needed to wear her own purple sports bra and pants. Earlier in the day someone picked them up for washing. When she entered the makeup room, she found them neatly folded, waiting for her on the makeup stand. She put them on and headed for the pleasure room. When Tara reached the pleasure room door, she put on a fake smile. *Stay calm, Tara, you can do it, it's the last time. Don't cause any problems.* When she opened the door, her pleased look quickly turned to a look of shock. Sitting on the couch next to Nora was Brandon. *No, it couldn't be! Nora was telling the truth the whole time!* Tara thought, not believing what she was seeing. Brandon smiled and stood up when he saw her.

"Hi, Tara, nice to see you're doing well," Brandon said. Tara could tell by the way he looked he expected her to be overjoyed, thinking he was here to rescue her. Tara's body remained still as her mind tried to process the emotions she was feeling. The sadness of betrayal and the reality that someone she believed loved her and was doing everything in his power to search for her had sent her to his place, knowing what would happen to her. She put her head down, not wanting to give them the pleasure of watching her cry. *How could he do this me? Why would he do this to me?* Memories of fun times they had began flooding her mind. She remembered Brandon always told her she was the star of his life and wanted nothing more. *Was he *using me from the beginning?* The sorrow Tara was feeling turned to an overwhelming anger. She looked back up at him with a glare of pure hatred.

She let out a bloodcurdling scream and charged him. Startled, Brandon stumbled backwards. Dimitri, who was standing next to the couch, jumped in her path, intercepting her. Tara fought to get past him, screaming and cursing at Brandon. Miguel entered the room and lifted Tara off the ground. Like she was expecting it, Nora causally ordered Miguel to take Tara out of the room. Tara looked up, locking eyes with Brandon, who still looked like a deer in the headlights.

"You'll get what's coming to you, Brandon. I promise you'll pay for this!" she said in a nearly crazed voice as Miguel carried her out of the room.

"You'd better calm her down. I didn't pay good money for that!" Brandon said, still stunned.

"One moment," Nora replied calmly. Dimitri spoke with Brandon as she exited the room. "Miguel, put her down," Nora ordered. The moment Miguel put Tara down, she tried to run past him. Miguel pushed her to the ground. "Tara, stop!" Nora yelled. Tara remained still and looked at Nora. *Calm down, Tara you're nearly home free, don't get cocky, these people are still dangerous.* Nora motioned for her to get up. Tara reluctantly obeyed. "Tara, I knew this client was going to be difficult for you. Since you have been cooperating, I will give you half an hour to go to your room and cool off before the session." Tara shook her head no with a pleading look.

"No, I can't do him! Please, anyone but him!"

"Tara, don't take advantage of my kindness." Nora pointed in the direction of her room. "Half an hour. Go."

◆ ◆ ◆

Middle-aged Ron Edwards sat inside his security hut. He knew what went on in the facility he guarded, but as long as they kept the money flowing, he was keen on keeping his mouth shut. The job was easy: let authorized people in, keep curious local kids out, get the mail, and wait for someone to pick it up. Knowing he had no scheduled arrivals for the day, he read his favorite swimsuit magazine to pass the time.

The sound of a cocking gun caught his attention. He lowered the magazine to see a fully armored SWAT officer pointing a shotgun at him. Before he could hit the alert button, two officers grabbed him from behind. Staying out of view, Ryan disabled the camera facing the driveway. He signaled it was okay to open the security gate, then got back in the van.

"Everything went smoothly, that was the only guard," Ryan confirmed. He glanced at Romy, noticing her nerves. The reality that in minutes she might be in the middle of a gun fight was starting to sink in.

"We'll be fine, Romy." She looked down, embarrassed he had noticed her concern.

"Do you think we'll catch them off guard?" Romy asked.

"Maybe," Ryan honestly answered. "This bought us a few seconds, which could make all the difference."

In her room, Tara banged the wall. "No, I can't, there's no way I'm doing it with Brandon." She was walking back and forth trying to think of something but was so upset nothing would form. When she passed by the window, out of the corner of her eye she noticed two blue objects. She rushed towards it and saw two SWAT vans coming to a stop. Feelings of hope and joy filled her body. She smiled widely as an ecstatic look formed on her face. They had come—her rescue was here. From her viewpoint they were small, but Tara could clearly see people exiting the SWAT vans. *Wonder which one is Ryan?* she thought, filled with excitement. She started to picture how the situation would play out.

First there would be a small fire fight. Her captors would try to fight back and would fail. She would wait for several tense moments as the officers secured the area, then her door would be kicked in, and for the first time in over a month, she would see Ryan. She would jump into his arms and break down. He probably would as well, and then Ryan would carry her out to the SWAT van. She would pass a handcuffed Nora Peters and anyone else who survived the battle. She would be sure to shoot them a victory smile and tell them to enjoy their life in prison, then Ryan would drive her home where she would see Romy. She pictured both of them breaking down as they ran to each other and embraced. She would then begin her road to recovery. One of her siblings would stay with her for a few days as she readjusted to normal life. She would most likely need some sort of trauma counseling to help her through everything. In a couple of weeks she would be ready to go out with friends, and in a few months her life would go back to living a somewhat normal life. Tara burst into short loud laughter and jumped up and down in excitement when she remembered Brandon was here, trapped like the rat he was. *I'll be sure to give him a goodbye slap,* she thought.

◆ ◆ ◆

Joseph Jackson looked over the new shipment of supplies scheduled for next week. If Nora was telling the truth, Tara would be gone by the end of this week, and that was fine with him. Things were slowly getting back to normal. The computer alerted him the outdoor motion sensors had detected something. He opened a monitor showing a camera feed on the west side of the facility.

"Nora!" Joseph screamed in near hysteria. "Nora!" Nora Peters, flanked by Dimitri, came in.

"I'm with a customer; what is it?" she demanded.

"Get over here!" he screamed! "Look at what the outdoor camera system is picking up, look at it!" Nora looked at the screen, her annoyed expression turned to worry. "That's right, the police are here. Two SWAT vans!" Joseph yelled, pointing at the screen. Nora reached for her phone. "No, don't bother calling anyone. Corporate will deny knowing anything about this facility." Nora dropped it, knowing he was right and how it would look to corporate. This would be the second facility she was involved with that got raided by police.

"Why didn't our contact warn us this was happening? How did they find us?" Nora asked out loud. Joseph glared at her.

"I know exactly how. That girl you have under control, the girl who has done nothing but scheme since she arrived."

"Tara." Nora snarled, knowing Joseph was right, knowing she had been made a fool of. Joseph put his hands out like he was about to say something important.

"Or like last time someone from your facility tipped the police off."

"Don't you dare accuse me of doing this!" Nora calmed herself and asked, "Do we have enough men to handle them?"

"No, we don't have enough men," Joseph replied, slamming the table. He then picked his own phone up and said, "Ivan, we have a situation: two SWAT teams just arrived. Start arming everyone."

"Do you want us to attack right away?" Ivan asked, concern in his own voice.

"I don't know!" Joseph screamed in a panic. "Get everyone armed and wait for orders!"

"What is happening?" Dr. Bodkin asked, hearing the commotion from his office.

"Take a look for yourself," Joseph said, pointing at the monitor. Dr. Bodkin looked at the monitor and frowned, more annoyed than frightened.

"How did this happen?"

"Tara," Nora replied with hate. Even if it wasn't Tara, she needed a scapegoat until she found the true culprit.

"I told you! I told you that girl was up to something, but no, you had her under control," Joseph taunted. "Look at the situation we're in now!"

"Shut up and do something useful for once, Joseph." A small grin formed on Dr. Bodkin's face. He turned and started to leave the room.

"Where are you going?" Joseph demanded.

"It's finally time to run a field test."

Chapter 26

Dr. Heinrich Bodkin entered Katahdin's room with a worried expression when he didn't see him. He called out, "Katahdin." He opened the biodome door. "Katahdin." Moments later, Katahdin flew in front of him.

"What's the matter, father?" Katahdin asked, wondering why he was here and noticing his look of concern.

"My son, my son, please come inside." Dr. Bodkin sat on a chair. "Sit down." Katahdin sat on his bed. He was worried he knew Tara had been coming to see him and he was about to tell him they couldn't do that anymore. Dr. Bodkin looked Katahdin right in the eye and said, "My son, remember when I told you we were the only people left on earth?" Katahdin shook his head.

"Yes, father. I can tell something's wrong. What is it?"

Dr. Bodkin's face grew more concerned. "I was wrong. A group of people appeared outside." A look of surprise formed on Katahdin's face.

"How?" he asked, stunned, thinking these must be the people Tara had been talking about.

"I honestly cannot give you an answer. All I know is these are not good people."

"How do you know?" Katahdin questioned. Dr. Bodkin's expression became saddened.

"They have already killed several of our people, some of my friends." Dr. Bodkin could tell rage was building inside Katahdin. "They're going to kill everyone and take everything we have unless we stop them." He pointed towards the biodome. "Your forest will be burned to the ground."

Katahdin quickly stood up. "We have to stop them! What can I do?"

"My son, always willing to help others. I have to admit currently we don't have the strength to fight them." Dr. Bodkin looked like he was about to say something painful. "This is so difficult for me to ask, but I need you to ambush them ahead of our men. That might be enough to stop them."

"Of course I'll help defend our home." Bones in Katahdin's face started to crack. Soon his face took on a more demonic bat-like appearance. His spinous process started to enlarge, emerging from his back like sharp knives. Simultaneously bones emerged from his elbows and arms. Skin membranes started to form between his arm and rib cage. "What about my illness?" Katahdin remembered.

Dr. Bodkin handed him a sugar pill.

"This should keep the illness at bay for several hours."

Katahdin took it. "Show me where to go."

I knew I could count on you. My foolish creature, Dr. Bodkin thought.

Nora, Joseph, and Dimitri watched the SWAT team spreading out.

"Perhaps we can escape while the men distract them," Nora suggested.

"That seems to be our best option," Dimitri agreed. Joseph did not reply. He was too upset to and frightened about going to jail.

"Here is the solution to our problem," Dr. Bodkin said. Nora and Dimitri both gasped at the sight of the monster walking behind Dr. Bodkin.

"Don't say anything to him," Joseph quietly warned. Katahdin waved.

"Hi, Mr. Joseph. Nice to see you again." He looked at Nora and Dimitri. "I've never seen the two of you before."

"My name's Nora Peters," she replied. Joseph stomped his foot in annoyance. "And this is my assistant Dimitri."

"Nice to meet you," Katahdin said, offering his hand. Nora shook it. The skin had a slight leathery feeling to it.

"Nice to meet you, though I wish it were under better circumstances," Nora said, moving her eyes toward the window.

"Don't worry, I won't let these people hurt you or take our home from us," Katahdin assured. He looked around. "Is Tara around?"

"She's resting," Dr. Bodkin said.

"Katahdin, how do you know Tara?" Nora questioned.

"I've seen her before," Katahdin replied.

Before Nora could speak, Dr. Bodkin opened the window. "It's time to go." He placed a hand on his shoulder. "Some of our fighting troops will support you. The people wearing blue armor are the enemy. They have guns, so be careful." Dr. Bodkin pointed to the wall surrounding the estate. "Do you see the wall? Don't fly above it or you will be killed by the radiation."

"I understand," Katahdin replied. "I'll do my best to stop them." He gracefully leaped on the window, he changed color to mimic his surroundings, then flew off.

"Where did you find that thing?" Nora asked.

"Do us a favor and shut up for once," Joseph answered. Before an argument could start, Ivan, flanked by Miguel and Peter, approached.

"We're ready to attack," Ivan said. Dr. Bodkin was the first to speak.

"Wait for Katahdin to begin, then attack. The shock of his existence should give us the upper hand."

"You let Katahdin loose?" Ivan asked, shocked.

"Yes, I did," Dr. Bodkin answered. He stared at the camera screen like he was about to witness an historic event. Ivan turned around.

"Get everyone together. I need to explain something."

"Dimitri, bring me Tara. I'm going to ring that bitch's neck!" Nora added.

"No, leave her where she is," Dr. Bodkin ordered. "If Katahdin returns, she could cause unwanted problems."

Flying low to the ground, Katahdin circled the van. He could see at least twenty-five people making their way from the van to the estate. He landed in a tree near the vans, planning his next move. He could feel his heart pounding, never thinking in his life he would be in a situation like this. He had never seen a gun, but he knew what they were and how dangerous they could be. He closed his eyes and began going over the different battle scenes he had read about. He remembered in several stories the armies would have hidden people called snipers behind the main force. Right away he spotted a woman lying on top of the SWAT van. He scanned the trees. He saw a man sitting in one several yards from him, using a pair of binoculars to observe the building. *I'll need to take them out first.* Katahdin looked down at his hand, and for the first time he noticed a layer of bone covered his skin. He looked his body over. The new layer of bone covered all of it. *Hope this is enough,* he thought. Not wanting to make noise, Katahdin flew towards the tree the sniper was in. He landed several branches above him. Focused on the house, the man didn't notice the slight rustling.

"I've spotted several armed men exiting the front of the house," he said.

"I confirm the sighting," a women's voice came over the radio. While she spoke, Katahdin rammed the pieces of bone coming from his palm into the scout's neck. He let out a slight cry, then fell from the tree. Katahdin saw the path between him and the van was clear. His first idea was to grab the women while flying. *No, that would make too much noise. Need to do this quietly.* All the officers were spread out in front of the van. Moving slowly, Katahdin climbed onto the SWAT van. Allyson lay prone, one eye focused on the scope. Katahdin took a step forward. He heard the roof make a thud. Inside the van, Romy looked up.

"What was that?" she asked.

"Our sniper moving, most likely," Owen Adams answered. Allyson turned around. Katahdin froze, worried he had been spotted. He breathed in relief when her head moved back to the scope. He got down on all fours and moved slowly towards her. He quickly moved his hand over her mouth. Allyson started to struggle in surprise, squeezing the rifle's trigger before Katahdin stabbed her through the neck. *Damn it,* Katahdin cursed, knowing he'd lost the element of surprise.

"It's started," Romy said softly, feeling her body tense up.

"I heard a shot!" Peter said, dropping for cover.

"They're not shooting at us," Ivan commented. He pointed to Miguel and five other troops. "Loop around, we'll hit them on two sides. Stay out of sight. Don't fire until I do."

"Allyson, why did you fire?" Ryan asked in confusion. "Allyson?"

"What da hell! She's dead!"

"What!" Ryan asked, alarmed. Katahdin reached down, grabbing the man near him, ramming his palm bone into his chest.

"They have snipers, take cover," Commander Banner shouted. "Get down."

"Someone check on Perez." Two SWAT officers rushed over to their fallen comrade.

"Hollerger's dead too," an officer added.

"Anyone hear the shots?" another officer asked. Panicked chatter began to fill the radios.

◆ ◆ ◆

From her room, Tara could see officers frantically moving, looking in every direction. *What's going on?* she wondered. *I only heard one gunshot. Why would trained SWAT officers be that flustered over a single gunshot?* Tara saw an officer thrown against a tree, and the one next to him fall. *No!*

They let him out! Tara thought, realizing what was going on. This was one possibility she hadn't thought of. In her excitement she'd forgotten these people had a trump card. *Why didn't you tell them about Katahdin?* Tara asked, cursing herself for making the critical mistake. Tara closed her eyes, trying to think of the outcome with the added Katahdin factor. *Katahdin's probably going to die. Once he loses the element of surprise, he's dead. It sucks, but that's what's going to happen. There's no way he can take out two SWAT teams. Right? Right?* As much as she tried to confirm it, her mind only focused on the impossible things she'd already seen Katahdin do. She saw another officer go down.

"Katahdin, you idiot!" Her breathing increased as the possibility that her rescuers might lose became more and more likely. She could see the Omnipotent troops were beginning to advance and surround the SWAT team. Out of desperation, Tara grabbed her fan and slammed it into the window. She put her face up to the chain link and started screaming Katahdin's name, begging him to stop.

Across the facility, Dr. Heinrich Bodkin sat in front of the security monitors with a satisfied grin. Nora Peters had a similar grin, her thoughts focused on how Tara must be feeling, seeing her rescuers get killed one by one. Joseph Jackson had a concerned look, wondering how they could stop Katahdin if Dr. Bodkin lost control of him.

◆ ◆ ◆

Ryan examined one of the dead officers. Instead of the expected bullet wound, he had a deep cut in his throat. *What are we fighting?* he wondered. He could hear Romy's voice in his earpiece begging to know what was going on. Her voice along with the shouting of other confused officers made him want to call the operation off. To flee while they still could. He fought through the panic this unknown enemy brought with it.

"Fall back and create a circle around the SWAT vans," Ryan yelled into his radio. Three SWAT officers were back to back. Breathing heavily, they looked for their attacker.

"Lieutenant Cymric says to fall back to the SWAT van," Private Miller said.

"What does Commander Banner or Vice Commander Richardson say?" Private McCrary asked.

"I thought I heard Commander Richardson is dead," Private Doyle added.

"Who told you that?" Private McCrary demanded. The three heard the flapping of wings like a large bird was near them. Miller started screaming when he felt talons pierce his shoulders. His feet abruptly left the ground. Doyle and McCrary stood stunned, seeing their comrade lifted in the air by an invisible force. Miller started firing wildly, several shots accidentally hitting McCrary, instantly killing him. Doyle cursed.

With Doyle distracted by his fallen comrade. Katahdin flung Miller onto Doyle, then lifted his elbows and dove down, sending the blades of bone through their bodies.

Ryan, who was approaching the scene, saw a slight distortion in the air revealed by the small spatters of blood on it. *I'm I looking at a ghost?* Ryan wondered. He fired at it, not knowing what his next move would be if the bullets went through the specter in front of him. Katahdin cried out in pain as bullets impacted his bone armor. Ryan froze, stunned, as a bat-like demon materialized over the fallen SWAT members' bodies. Commander Banner shouted orders into his radio, trying to figure out how many people were left. Miguel lined his scope up, crosshairs on Commander Banner's head.

"Adios, bigshot." He pulled the trigger. Miguel snickered, watching his body hit the ground. Ivan slammed his fist, wanting to get in better position before they attacked. The other Omnipotent troops started unloading automatic fire.

Ryan's eyes were locked with Katahdin's. He barely flinched when the gunshots started erupting around him or when someone yelled Commander Banner had been killed. Ryan squeezed the trigger, unloading more bullets into Katahdin.

Katahdin leaped at him, letting out cries of pain as the bone on his chest began to break. Ryan's gun stopped firing. He reached for another magazine. Before he could load it, Katahdin slashed his chest, then leaped onto him. Ryan fell over, his gun landing in a brush pile next to him. Katahdin raised his arm, but before he could finish Ryan off, Donald Sorenson slashed his knife across Katahdin's right wing membrane. Again Katahdin howled in pain. That gave Sorenson the courage to keep attacking—he was hurting this creature. He thrust his knife into Katahdin's chest. Katahdin fell onto his stomach.

Overwhelmed by the pain, Katahdin didn't know what to do. *Is this how I die?* he thought. Sorenson pulled the knife out. Again, he rammed it into Katahdin's chest. Katahdin felt his bone armor break, and he felt the knife entering his skin. Katahdin managed to cover his heart with a layer of bone, but he knew it would not hold against the pressure Sorenson was putting on the knife. Suddenly Sorenson's head exploded. Blood and skin fragments covered Katahdin.

"No!" Ryan screamed in rage. He tried to get up but the pain from his chest wound was too great. Katahdin jumped up, trying to get the gore off him.

"Damn it. Thought he was dead," Miguel said, seeing Katahdin moving through his rifle scope. Ryan got to one knee. He looked around… the demon was nowhere in sight, and neither were any living SWAT members. *How could this have happened?* he thought right before he felt a bullet enter his back. Ivan got ready to finish him off when the man next to him hit the ground. Ivan cursed and turned his attention towards the attacking SWAT members. Ryan's vision was becoming hazy. He wanted to fall down and go to sleep.

"No, I can't die yet," he said, determined. "I need to get Romy to safety. I need to see Krista and Ryan Jr again. I need to come back for Tara." He started limping his way towards the SWAT van. Katahdin sat in a tree, letting his shock from the attack recover. He was in more pain than he thought he would ever experience.

"I should go home, sit near the pond." He looked down to see three of the intruders using a fallen log for cover. "No, I can't quite yet. My home is still in danger, people still need me." Katahdin focused. He moved some of the tissue from his back to repair his damaged wing, then flew into the air. When he was above the three men, he raised both elbows, lining two of them up with his bone swords. He dropped down, impaling two of them through the back. Before the remaining SWAT member knew what was happening, Katahdin raised his foot, wrapping his talons around his face and squeezed. "Eww," Katahdin said, feeling the man's head explode under his foot.

◆　◆　◆

Inside the SWAT van, Romy was trembling. The radio had nearly gone silent. *Was Ryan still alive? Was anyone still alive?* she wondered. Next to her, Owen Adams held a submachine gun tightly. Never being in combat himself, he was as nervous as she was.

"What—" Romy swallowed. "What do we do if everyone's dead?"

"I don't know… We try to drive out of here, I guess." Adams stomped his foot on the ground. "This is not supposed to happen."

"Can we call for help?" Romy suggested. Owen Adams grunted in frustration, angered he had not thought of it. He reached for the radio when the back doors swung opened.

"Ryan!" Romy cried, seeing her brother trying to climb inside.

"Stay there!" Adams ordered, rushing over to help Ryan inside.

"Look out!" Romy cried. Before Adams could react, Katahdin grabbed him, his talons pulling him from the van.

Knowing her brother needed help, Romy pulled her pistol out and dashed for the doors, slamming them shut. Romy knelt down next to him. She gasped when she saw the gash on his chest. "Ryan, hold on, I'll get you to a hospital." Fortunately she had asked where the medical kits were earlier. She opened one and started putting gauze on the wound. Ryan weakly grunted in pain. "Please don't die. Please, please don't die." Romy heard the door swing open. She screamed and fell to the ground when Katahdin landed in back of them, separating them from the driver's seat. Romy raised her pistol, screeching in horror. Ryan pulled it down.

"Romy, run! Get to the other van!" Ryan grabbed his pistol. Before he aimed it, Katahdin stepped on his hand, trapping it on the ground.

"Wait, your name's Romy? Are you Tara's sister?" Katahdin asked in a pleasant voice.

Romy froze, too scared to move. *Did this creature just talk?* In a frightened, muffled voice, she asked, "Where's Tara?" Romy flinched when she heard a crackling sound coming from Katahdin. To her surprise, the demonic bat face started to become human. Katahdin gave a gentle smile.

"She's inside. We're friends, she told me all about you." He looked down at Ryan. "Do you know this guy?"

"Yes, he's my brother, please don't hurt him anymore," Romy begged. Katahdin released his hold. This time Romy was the one who stopped the pistol being raised. "Now's not the time," she whispered to Ryan. Romy shot Katahdin an untrusting glance as he handed her more gauze and bandages from the kit.

"Sorry about the cut. You were shooting at me." Ryan grimaced in pain. "If it makes you feel better, I'm hurting too. Don't worry, Dr. Bodkin will heal us both. By the way, why were you two with the people attacking our home?" Romy didn't know what to say. She couldn't understand this creature's behavior. He had killed the entire SWAT team, and now he was acting like he wanted to be friends. Romy cautiously wrapped bandages around Ryan's wounds, not taking her eye off Katahdin, who appeared to be in deep thought.

"I get it," he yelled. Romy gasped in surprise. "Tara told me she got separated from her family. The bad people locked you in the truck so your brother dressed up as one of them to rescue you."

"Where's Tara?" Ryan asked through clenched teeth, trying to deal with the pain.

"She's inside. She's a little funny in the head, but I'm sure you knew that."

"What did you do to her?" Romy asked, fearing what he meant by Tara was funny in the head.

"Gave her snacks, took her to the top of a tree, hung out with my forest friends. You can join us next time. Tara will be thrilled to see you." Now Romy knew he was lying. Tara would never be friends with his inhuman monster. *Had these people given her to him as a toy?* Romy worried, trying not to picture all the horrible things he could have done to her.

"Katahdin? What do you have in here?" Ivan said, standing outside the van.

"Tara's siblings. I guess they got captured by the bad people." Katahdin jumped outside. A look of sadness formed on his face when he said, "I mistook her brother for the enemy and hurt him pretty bad. Have Dr. Bodkin look at him."

Ivan slapped him on the shoulder. "We'll take him there right away. Nice job." He whistled. "Miguel, Peter, help me take these two inside. I'll radio Mr. Jackson what we have." When Miguel and Peter came over, Ivan said, "Peter, watch the girl. Miguel and I will carry the injured man." His voice turned to a whisper as his eyes moved towards Katahdin. "Play nice."

"Come on out," Miguel ordered, extending his hand to Romy. Knowing she had no choice, her trembling hand took his. "Make a sound and you're dead," he whispered. He gently pushed Romy toward Peter.

Ivan pulled Ryan up by the arm.

"Cause any trouble and I'll kill both your sisters in front of you."

Too weak to resist, Ryan complied. Miguel and Ivan placed his arms over their shoulders and walked towards the estate. Abruptly, the sound of gunfire filled the air. Two Omnipotent troops fell to the ground.

"Go! I'll handle this," Katahdin ordered.

◆　◆　◆

On her knees, Tara saw the ground littered with dead SWAT members. Omnipotent troops strutted around, hands raised in victory, some firing guns into the air. She turned away from the window. *This can't be happening,* she thought, bursting into tears, and let her body sink to the ground. They had won. It was impossible, but it happened: the rescue team was dead. She knew more police would arrive eventually, but by then it would be too late, and she would be long gone. *Way to go, Tara, this is your fault. You should have warned them about Katahdin. You should have warned them.* She closed her eyes. *Think of your next move… Think of…* "Oh, what's the use. It's over. Way to go, Tara. Thanks to you, Ryan's dead," she said as her tears fell uncontrollably.

Chapter 27

Katahdin pulled his palm bone from the dead officer's chest. He scanned the area for anyone wearing the blue armor. *That seems to be the last of them.* The bones protruding from his body slowly worked their way back inside. *Wonder why they came here? Wonder what they wanted?* He started to head back home when a chirping sound caught his ear. He looked up to see a male cardinal flying overhead.

"No!" he said out loud, watching the little bird headed for the wall. *One of them must have gotten to the biodome.* Dr. Bodkins's warning about the radiation left his mind. Katahdin took off in a desperate attempt to save the little bird. As the bird landed on the wall, he reached out for it. His focus soon turned to what was behind the bird. The cardinal flew off as he landed on the wall and felt paralyzed by what he saw. Beyond the wall, green grass grew everywhere, and in the distance he saw hundreds of trees. Butterflies flew in the meadow, and other birds were starting to return to the area. He noticed a squirrel nibbled on an acorn in a tree a few yards from him. Tara's words about the world outside his home started to fill his head, and for the first time in his life he found himself doubting everything his loving father Dr. Bodkin had told him. *No, there must be an explanation for this,* he thought as his fists clenched.

◆　◆　◆

Miguel and Peter, followed by three Omnipotent troops, led Ryan and Romy to the pleasure room. Despite the bandages, Ryan's wound was still bleeding profoundly. Romy was breathing heavily, frightened out of her mind.

When they arrived, Nora Peters sat in the velvet chair, cockily smoking a cigarette, acting like she had just won a great battle. Brandon Aiden and Dimitri calmly sat on the couch next to her. Dimitri held a pistol firmly in sight. Joseph Jackson nervously stood by the couch, knowing there would be serious consequences for what had happened. Romy locked eyes with Nora. Nora returned a look to her that said *yes I tricked you, your sister's kidnapper was right in front of you*. Romy's attention turned to the smug, grinning Brandon.

"Traitor," Romy said in a fright-filled voice.

"Who's on the winning side?" Brandon asked cockily.

Ryan grunted, trying to lunge at him. In his weakened state he got less than a step before falling to the floor.

"Ryan!" Romy yelled, bending down to help him up.

"What do you plan to do with them?" Joseph asked.

"We'll get started in a moment," Nora replied. "We're still waiting on the guest of honor." Nora looked at Romy. "You are as stunning as your sister." She motioned to the chair across from her. "Please have a seat." Romy looked at Ryan, wondering what to do. Nora leaned towards her. "Your sister learned what happens when you cross me. Learn from her mistakes."

"Do what she says," Ryan said weakly.

"How are we going to get out of this?" Romy asked, desperate for an answer. Ryan gave her a look that said he didn't know. Romy nervously walked over to the seat and sat down. Dimitri positioned himself behind her.

"I wish we would have captured you from the start. You appear much easier to control than Tara. Perhaps you can replace her," Nora said to Romy, looking at her trembling hand.

"Speaking of," Peter added. At that moment Justin came in, holding Tara's arm. He tossed her towards Nora.

"Tara!" Romy said, happily getting to her feet.

"Remain seated!" Nora glared, which caused Romy to freeze.

"Ryan, Romy!" Tara said, equally pleased to see them. "Ryan, you're alive!" she said as she hugged him. He let of a cry of pain, which caused Tara to release him. She saw his chest wound. *Damn you, Katahdin.* Looking him in the eye, she said, "I'm sorry, thank you for coming for me."

Ryan placed a hand on her shoulder. "Anything thing for you, little sis."

Tara looked over at Romy and smiled. All three had tears in their eyes. The snapping of Nora's fingers caught Tara's attention.

"Isn't it an amazing coincidence both your siblings survived the…" Nora thought for a moment. "Massacre?" She gained a proud victorious look when she said, "Tara, you played your final card. Somehow you got the police here." She relaxed back in her chair. "And I still won."

"I've had enough of this! Do you really think this is over?" Joseph cut in. "It's not. The police know the operation those SWAT vans were a part of. When they don't come back, they'll send more here!"

"And we will be long gone by then," Nora countered. She looked at Romy, then Ryan. "I'm sorry my associate is an idiot."

"No, I'm a realist!" Joseph snapped back. "The cleanup costs alone are going to be enormous." Ignoring Joseph's words, Nora turned her attention back to Tara. "So, Tara, do you have anything you wish to tell us?"

Tara looked at Brandon and said angrily, "I told you this wouldn't work. Now look at the mess we're in."

"What?" Brandon asked, confused.

Tara stood and looked Nora in the eye.

"As you said, you already won, so I might as well spit it out." Her eyes shifted to Brandon. "He set this up from the start."

"Don't listen to her; she's lying," Brandon countered.

"Tara, what are you taking about?" Romy asked, giving Tara a confused look.

Tara ignored it and continued, "Baby, we both knew the risk. Sorry, but I'm looking out for myself. Now be quiet and let me finish."

Brandon quickly got up with a raised fist. "You lying…"

A gunshot above his head made him stop dead in his tracks. Romy let out a frightened scream.

"Sit down, Mr. Aiden," Dimitri ordered.

"Nora, may I continue?" Tara asked. Nora motioned it was okay. "Brandon got himself into a large gambling debt. We needed money, so he came up with the idea to sell me to you. I'd perform for a month, then he'd arrive with the police behind him, then we'd become rich off interviews, TV appearances, and reward money for your capture."

"That's a lie, all of it!" Brandon countered.

"An interesting story," Dimitri complimented. "Is this why you wanted to move to Florida, Mr. Aiden?"

"We were going to be rich. Florida equals parties, beaches, and booze," Tara replied, acting cocky. Dimitri looked at Brandon, then looked at Tara.

"That sounds convincing. If it were true." Dimitri gave Tara a look showing he saw through her lie. "Except Mr. Aiden is moving to California to work as a business manager for us." Despite her best efforts, Tara showed signs of panic. "Tell me why would a man want to bring down a business he expressed interest in working for?"

Brandon got up, standing next to Dimitri.

What do I do now? What do I do? Tara rapidly thought.

Growing weaker from the blood loss, Ryan fell on his side.

"Ryan," Tara and Romy said nearly simultaneously. Tara got on her knees, using an arm as a makeshift pillow. When Romy started to get up, Dimitri pointed the gun at her.

"Remain seated."

"Romy, they're not messing around. Do what he says," Tara insisted. She looked at Joseph. "We both know he's more valuable to you alive than dead. Have someone treat his wound."

"Tara, how would holding a police officer hostage help at all when an entire SWAT team is dead?" Dimitri asked. Before Tara could respond, he handed Brandon his gun and gave a slight nod towards Ryan.

"Mr. Aiden, here is your orientation." Tara gasped when both her arms were gripped from behind. Miguel lifted her off the ground.

"No!" Tara screamed, knowing what was about to happen. Romy started pleading with Brandon. He smiled at Tara, then fired the gun into Ryan's head. Romy let out a scream of sorrow and fear. Tara put her head in her hands and started crying. She couldn't scream. *That didn't just happen, did it?* she asked herself. Suddenly, Romy's screams turned to gasps for air. Tara looked up to see Dimitri had wrapped his tie around Romy's throat, creating a makeshift garrote.

"Noo!" Tara tearfully screamed. She tried, but despite her struggles and rage, she could not break Miguel's iron grip.

"Enough, Tara," Nora said, getting up and staring at Tara with a look of pure rage. "You will tell us how the police found this place. Tell the truth and I stop Dimitri, lie and we watch your sister strangulate."

"I called them," Tara admitted, knowing she had no choice.

"How?" Nora asked. Tara looked over at Romy. Her eyes were closed as she fought to loosen the garrote around her neck. Tara looked down and tried to tune out the gagging and choking sounds. *Come on, Romy, hang in there, please. I can't lose another sibling.*

"Last night when Devin was drunk, I memorized his cell phone password. I seduced him into taking me to his room. I got him to pass out, took the phone, and made the call."

"How did you tell them where to go? Our phones are prepaid, making them untraceable," Joseph asked. Tara once again glanced at Romy. She was still fighting but her eyes were becoming glazed, her outstretched tongue gaining a blue tint as she struggled for air. Tara gave Nora a pleading look, a look Nora didn't respond to.

"I tricked clients into giving me information, nearby towns, events, and street names. You said you had spies in the police station so I tipped my brother off," Tara said quickly. "Now please let my sister go." Nora waved her hand and Dimitri released his grip. Romy let out a loud gasp and started coughing.

Nora began pacing the room, Joseph looked stunned, not believing Tara was able to pull that off.

"So you admit to knowingly breaking company policy? The consequences of which force us to relocate a major base of operations." Tara didn't know what to say so she shook her head yes. "Tara, you know you must be punished for such behavior. Dimitri, continue." Dimitri retightened his garrote.

"Wait! What are you doing?" Tara cried in horror. "You said!"

"If you told the truth, I would release her, which I did. This is punishment," Nora calmly replied. Tara desperately tried to break away from Miguel, but he was holding on too tight. She tried to think of a plan but knew there was nothing she could do. She watched helplessly as Romy clawed, doing everything she could to get a breath, tears starting to fall uncontrollably as she screamed and begged. Romy's body started to go limp. Her tongue came out of her mouth, moving back and forth a few times, then her arms slowly fell to her sides.

"Nice neck tie, Dimitri," Peter said, trying to make a joke.

"Shut up," Miguel said, knowing Joseph was right about their situation. Through the haze of tears, Tara saw both her siblings' lifeless bodies. Inside she felt her feelings of sorrow becoming uncontrollable anger. *I'm going to kill all of you,* Tara thought as pure rage burned inside her. She could feel Miguel had loosened his grip, which allowed her to move her right arm freely. She made a peace sign and slammed both fingers into his eyes. He screamed in pain, losing his grip on her.

Tara got to her feet and charged Nora. Before anyone could comprehend what was going on, Tara tackled her to the ground. She was expecting to feel a gunshot go off any moment, but she didn't care... death would be a mercy. Fueled by sorrow and rage, Tara put all her strength into a punch that connected with Nora's face. She pulled it back and struck again and again.

"Hey, the attack is over, we're..." Katahdin paused, looking puzzled at the scene in front of him.

"What the hell is that?" Brandon asked. Every Omnipotent member froze, quickly exchanging worried glances as they scrambled to think about what to say. Nora let out a moan of pain.

Tara, still sitting on top of a bloody and bruised Nora Peters, locked eyes with Katahdin. *You bastard!* she thought bitterly before saying in an angry teary voice, "You! Do you realize what you've done! You just signed my death warrant! You caused my brother and sister to die!"

"Tara, what happened to them?" Katahdin replied, wanting to know what was going on. Dimitri gently grabbed Tara, attempting to get her off Nora. She let out a crazed scream and went after him. Once again, Miguel restrained

Tara. "Tara, what's wrong?" Katahdin asked, looking at Nora's bloody face. "Why are you hitting people?" Joseph sighed in relief when he saw Dr. Bodkin coming.

"My son. My son," Dr. Bodkin said as he entered the room. He placed an arm around Katahdin. "I'm so glad you managed to survive. Come, you must rest."

Katahdin lightly pushed his arm off.

"What's wrong with Tara? What happened to her brother and sister?" Katahdin asked, confused.

"They killed them!" Tara shouted.

"The one in the uniform went crazy and killed that poor girl in the chair. Tara was nearly killed herself and is very shaken up," Dr. Bodkin said calmly. Nora got up, bleeding heavily, and her left eye was beginning to blacken.

"You were right, Dr. Bodkin, Tara is out of her mind."

Tara lunged for her again.

"Katahdin, Tara needs to be retrained and sedated. You don't need to see it." Dr. Bodkin motioned for Katahdin to follow him.

"Katahdin, don't leave," Tara yelled. Despite being angry with him, deep down she knew his actions were not his fault. He was merely a puppet on a string. Reluctantly, Katahdin followed Dr. Bodkin out of the room.

"Thank God," Joseph said the moment the door shut. *This is how it ends,* Tara thought, knowing there was nothing she could do. *Romy, Ryan, I'll see you soon.*

Nora went up to a restrained Tara and spit on her, then hit her a few times. Tara felt her own nose starting to bleed. She shrugged them off, giving Nora the look of a crazed animal. If she was going to die, she was not going to give them the satisfaction of hearing her beg.

"You're more trouble than you're worth." Nora snapped her fingers. "Miguel, you and the boys may have your way with her. Take as long as you like, then kill her." Peter slammed his rifle butt into Tara's stomach. Miguel released his hold on her. She cried in pain, falling to her knees. *Get up, Tara, you need to fight,* her mind pleaded. As much as she wanted to, her body didn't have the strength.

"I have a better idea. Let's cut off her limbs. We can use a blow torch to cauterize the wounds," Miguel suggested. Before Nora could reply, the door opened.

◆　◆　◆

"Tara, are you okay?" Katahdin asked, quickly followed by Dr. Bodkin asking him to come with him. "I want to make sure Tara and Nora are okay first," Katahdin replied.

"I'm fine," Nora said as sweetly. "Tara's very upset and shaken from the experience. She also needs to rest. Miguel, would you please take her to her room?"

"Of course," Miguel said, also playing the innocent act. "Come on, Tara, off to your room." He kept his back to Katahdin to avoid him seeing the hand covering Tara's mouth. Tara saw both her siblings' bodies. *I'm not done yet; these people need to pay!* Tara bit down hard on Miguel's hand. The sudden pain caught him off guard.

"Katahdin!" Tara screamed, managing to get her body in a position so she could see him. "They did this, you're not sick, they're all lying to you! Just jump on the wall and look for yourself. The outside is nothing like they told you."

I already have, Katahdin thought.

"Come, Tara, I know you're upset," Miguel said as he moved Tara towards her room, Peter following close behind. Katahdin remind motionless, not knowing what to think. *Tara, why are you acting like this? Did these people really do what you said?*

"They're going to kill me!" Tara yelled before Peter closed the door.

"Katahdin, let's go to my office. I will get you some medication and take you to your room," Dr. Bodkin offered.

"Dispose of these bodies," Nora ordered. Joseph nearly shouted because she said it right as Katahdin was leaving. The three Omnipotent troops waited for Joseph to confirm the order.

"Hold on, I need to grab this," Dimitri said, removing the tie from Romy's neck. *Dispose of the bodies... why not bury them?* Katahdin wondered as he and Dr. Bodkin started walking down the hall.

"Father, why did those people attack our home? Why didn't they find their own?" Katahdin asked.

"Like I have told you, my son, the outside word is a barren wasteland."

"Have you ever seen what's outside the walls?" Katahdin asked, wanting to believe he would say no or give an explanation for what he saw.

Without any hesitation, Dr. Bodkin replied, "Yes, it's a barren wasteland." *No, it isn't,* Katahdin felt like saying, but was too confused to confront Dr. Bodkin, who opened the door to Katahdin's room. "Bones from dead animals and people litter the ground. Nothing is left from the old civilization but wreckage." Dr. Bodkin did not see the glare Katahdin shot him. *Why are you lying to me... was Tara telling the truth?* Dr. Bodkin removed two pills from his pocket. "Here, these two new pills should help with any effects from the radiation exposure you probably experienced while being outside."

After Dr. Bodkin closed the door, Katahdin put on some clothes, then broke a pill in his hand. He licked the white powder. He recognized the taste of sugar. *This isn't medicine! Were all the pills like this?* Katahdin wondering, sitting down. Confusion and anger coarsed through him. He found himself doubting everything he had believed for years. *Who is telling the truth? Who is lying to me? Why is Tara suddenly acting violent? Had she really lost her mind or was everything Dr. Bodkin told me a lie?* Both possibilities hurt Katahdin. His thoughts went back to Tara. If she had lost her mind, she must be suffering, and the most merciful thing he could do for his friend would be to put her down himself.

Chapter 28

Miguel burst into Tara's room, holding her around the waist with one arm. He threw Tara to the ground. Tara spit some blood onto the floor. *Tara, you know what's coming. Get up! Get away!* Acting on instinct, she crawled towards the closet. *I have to get to Katahdin,* she thought. *It's my only chance of surviving.* Like predators watching wounded prey, Miguel and Peter let Tara crawl, not wanting the game to end. As she crawled, she felt empty and devoid of life. *I don't even know why I'm fighting to live. Everyone I cared about was taken from me.* Images of Ryan, Romy, and Brandon's betrayal entered her mind. *No, I can't die yet. I need to make these people pay for what they've done.* Tara reached the closet and kicked the section of wall in. Before she could crawl inside, Miguel grabbed her by the hair.

"What is this?" Miguel asked, looking at the hole in the wall. "You sneaky little rat." Miguel slammed Tara's head into the wall and everything went black.

Tara woke up in an all too familiar spot: Peter's knees were on her arms, Miguel was behind her. She tried to fight, but she had no strength left. Her head was pounding, she felt tired, her vision was blurred. *No, don't give up, these people need to pay for what they did to you, you need to make them pay,* her inner voice begged. *I can't fight anymore,* Tara explained. *I only want to go to sleep.*

The sound of Miguel's zipper coming down reminded Tara what was going on. With what little strength she had left, she started kicking at him, anything to get him away. Miguel brought his fist down on her back twice. The pain seemed to zap what fight she had left. She turned her head. She saw Miguel unbuckling his pants. Tara turned and looked up at Peter.

"You really think you'll get away with this? You just killed an entire SWAT team. People are going to notice and come for me."

Peter smacked her on the head. "Keep hoping. We'll be long gone by then." Peter smacked her again. "You're going to be our play toy for a looong time."

"I will keep hoping," Tara shot back. "If they don't get you, Katahdin will. He'll learn the truth, he'll learn you've been lying to him about everything."

"What do you know about that freak?" Peter flicked her on the forehead with his finger. "Ivan said Katahdin's a stupid creature that believes whatever Dr. Bodkin tells him, and the only reason he keeps him around is to make money." Tara felt Miguel pulling at her pants.

"You're not going to rape me anymore." She kicked him in the stomach.

Unfazed, he cursed at Tara, shoving her head into the mattress.

"Keep still or I'll break your back, bitch!" Miguel yelled. When Miguel released her head, she again looked up at Peter not with a look of defeat or pleading but a victorious, wide smile. She moved her head and eyes towards the closet and started laughing hysterically. Not knowing what to make of it, Peter looked up.

"Miguel," he said in a worried tone. Miguel did not answer, too focused on Tara. "Miguel!" Peter screamed. He got up and freed Tara's arms.

"What!" Miguel demanded. Peter was backing up against the wall. Miguel saw Peter pointing behind him. He turned around and quickly got off Tara. Both men stared at Katahdin standing in the closet doorway. Neither knew what to do. Dr. Bodkin was not around and there was no time to get him.

"Katahdin," Miguel said, surprised. "Tara." He tried to quickly come up with a story. "Tara was acting crazy, we were trying to hold her down so we could give her medication."

"Ya, that's it!" Peter agreed. Miguel eyed his rifle leaning against the wall, but what good would it do against this thing?

"I heard what you said," Katahdin replied, coming closer.

"If you were giving me medicine, where is it?" Tara added.

Out of habit Peter yelled, "Shut up!" He readied his leg for a kick but caught himself in time.

"Katahdin, Tara needs a lot of rest. Her mind's really messed up," Miguel calmly said.

"Tara, please calm down, you're not well," Peter added, gently touching her on the shoulder. Tara elbowed him in the stomach and rushed for the rifle. Peter tripped her, then, enraged, he jumped on top of her. He raised his first, ready to smash her teeth in.

"Get off her!" Katahdin warned. Once again his face had taken on the bat-like shape. Sharpened bones emerged from his hand. Miguel pulled his pistol from the holster and hid it behind his back.

"Peter, get off Tara. That was not nice." Miguel looked at Katahdin. "Katahdin, remember Tara's mentally sick, she needs to rest. Why don't you go back to your room and let us handle her?"

"Katahdin, he's lying, don't listen to him!" Tara shouted. Not wanting Tara to rush for it again, Peter picked up the rifle. Katahdin looked at Tara, then at Miguel.

"See the blood coming from her nose. It's a sign of brain trauma. She's suffering greatly. I fear her brain damage may even be beyond help," Miguel said in a saddened voice.

"Katahdin, my nose is bleeding because they hit me!" she said frantically, fearing Katahdin was buying the story. He paid no attention to her.

"Can Dr. Bodkin heal her?" Miguel shrugged his shoulders. *No, Katahdin, don't believe him,* Tara thought, trying to get to her feet.

"I honestly don't know. Why don't we go see your father and ask him?" Miguel suggested. Katahdin walked past him.

"There's no point. Tara's my friend. If she's suffering, I'll end it myself." *What, no!* Tara thought fearfully. Tara shook her head no in genuine fright.

"Katahdin, stop! I'm not sick!" Peter and Miguel gave each other a look of relief.

"Sorry, Tara, I need to end your suffering. This is for your own good." Katahdin grabbed the sports bra's right shoulder strap. Tara felt her feet lift off the ground as Katahdin effortlessly lifted her. She looked at Katahdin with frightened, desperate eyes as he walked her towards the closet. *No, I can't die yet, not with these people still around,* Tara thought.

"Katahdin, please help me," Tara begged in a soft desperate voice. Katahdin pulled his hand back. A feeling of betrayal came over Tara. *It wasn't supposed to end like this. I was supposed to get away and live happy ever after.* Knowing she had lost, Tara closed her eyes, preparing for death. In a way Katahdin was showing her mercy; soon her nightmare would be over, and soon she would enter into a dream. A dream where she would be with Ryan and Romy and they would live happily ever after.

"They both have guns, didn't want you to get shot," Katahdin whispered. *Wait, what?* Tara thought, opening her eyes. Before she knew it, Katahdin dropped her. He spun around, planting the bones protruding from his hand into Miguel's stomach. The pistol fell from Miguel's hand, and he let out a yell of pain as he tried to pull Katahdin's hand away. Peter let out a frightened scream. He fired several shots from the rifle, hitting Katahdin in the shoulder. The shots cracked the newly forming bone armor but didn't reach skin.

In an instant, Tara leaped onto the pistol. Peter dropped the rifle and ran for the door. Tara fired at him. Her first two shots missed. The third one hit Peter in the leg. He cried in pain, limping through the doorway. Tara pulled the trigger a fourth time, the gun made a clicking noise. Miguel hit the ground.

Katahdin was ready to strike the killing blow when Tara yelled, "Katahdin stop! I need to be the one who finishes him." Katahdin acknowledged her request and went after Peter. Tara grabbed her knife from its hiding spot. Now the one too injured to move, Miguel looked up at her with a hate-filled glare. Tara let out a primal yell as she kicked Miguel. Thinking about and paying him back for all the mental and physical abuse he had caused her, she brought the knife down again and again. Miguel screamed, spitting up blood, then the screams stopped and his body went limp. "Burn in hell," Tara said, giving his lifeless body an extra kick.

Peter limped as fast as he could, using the wall as support, moaning in pain with every step. He turned to see Katahdin walking towards him, quickly gaining. He screamed for help, and, falling over, he turned to see Katahdin looming over him. Hearing his screams, two Omnipotent guards arrived. With Katahdin's back to them, they raised their assault rifles, getting ready to fire.

Before either man could pull the trigger, rifle shots struck them in the back. Katahdin turned his head, wrapping his clawed foot around wailing Peter's good leg. Tara smirked and nodded, standing over the Omnipotent guards' dead bodies. Katahdin used his leg to lift Peter. As Katahdin cut his throat, Tara lifted the rifle at Katahdin's head. For a moment she thought about pulling the trigger, but she then lowered the gun. It wasn't his fault

Romy and Ryan died; he was tricked into attacking the SWAT team. "We need to destroy the armory before they can regroup," Tara emphasized.

"I'm going to deal with Dr. Bodkin," Katahdin replied.

"Okay, kill anyone you see along the way, but leave Nora Peters and the guy in the blue button down shirt for me," Tara ordered.

"I understand," Katahdin acknowledged. Tara dropped the rifle, picked up the full automatic assault rifle, then ran towards the armory. *Everyone's most likely outside cleaning up the SWAT team mess. It should take them a few minutes to realize what's going on and several more minutes to get to the armory.* Tara briefly stopped at the entrance to the recreation room. Seeing no one, she cautiously sprinted to the living area.

"Tara, what's going on?" Devin asked, coming out of his room. Tara said nothing, only pointed the gun at him. Devin let out a single gasp before she fired, striking him several times in the chest. When Tara got to the loading dock door, she knocked rapidly.

"It's unlocked, asshole," a man inside yelled. Tara kept knocking until the door was jerked open. Like Devin, he only managed to gasp before the rifle cracked. Tara made her way to the gun room, holding her shoulder from the rifle's recoil. To her delight, the gate was unlocked. She used the rifle butt to smack the ammo locker. It opened on the first strike. Tara rolled her eyes, realizing it was unlocked. She laid the rifle down—it had too much kick for her liking. She grabbed a pair of pistols off the rack and two clips for each. She had fired pistols in the past and could aim pretty well with them. Tara looked out at the rows of cars and equipment in the garage area. *Now's my chance to escape,* she thought, looking at the garage door. *Or...* A new idea entered her mind, one she liked much better.

Chapter 29

Joseph Jackson dropped his office phone, his face turning ghost white.

"What is it?" Dimitri asked.

"Tara and Katahdin have escaped!" Joseph yelled. "Katahdin has already killed at least five of our men!"

"Where are Miguel and Peter?" Nora asked.

"Where's Tara?" Brandon added, not believing the mess he was now in.

"How should I know!" Joseph yelled back. "All I know is Ivan reported Katahdin's heading this way!"

"He's coming for Dr. Bodkin," Dimitri stated, as Joseph locked and tried to barricade the door.

"That will not keep Katahdin out. Only trap us," Dimitri said.

"I'm not trying to stop Katahdin from getting in! You said it yourself, Dr. Bodkin will be Katahdin's target! If he wants him, he can have him!"

◆ ◆ ◆

Ivan, followed by seven Omnipotent members, burst into the loading dock.

"Arm up. Five minutes. Hallow points, and armor piercing rounds," Ivan shouted, hoping that would be enough to bring down Katahdin. Everyone crowded into the gun room, grabbing guns, and several boxes of ammo were accidentally spilled. The man with the ghetto accent accidentally grabbed a box of shotgun shells. The box felt wet. He put it up to his nose, sniffing it.

"Yo, man, this smells like gas!" Several other people started to sniff, smelling the same thing. Everyone looked towards the gate when they heard it latch shut and a lock click in place. Tara stood next to it. She held up a lighter and smiled.

"Tara, don't!" Ivan yelled, desperately trying to load the shotgun he was holding. There was the click of the flint striking as Tara waved goodbye. Ivan and several others raised their guns as Tara dropped the lighter and ran. The flame hit the gas, and in an instant flames filled the room. Tara heard the screams of pain, and the smell of cooking flesh. The sickening sound of men and women burning was in a way music to her ears. *They deserve every bit of it,* she told herself, quenching any feeling of remorse she had. The screams were soon followed by heated bullets going off. In minutes, the screams ended. Tara went in view of the camera and shot two middle fingers at it, then blew a kiss. She then tossed gasoline on the cars and lit it. She didn't see Brandon's car. *He must have been parked out front,* which is where she was going.

◆　◆　◆

The computer in Joseph Jackson's office started beeping, signaling an alert.

"What's going on now?" Nora asked.

"There's a fire!" Joseph said in his now seemingly panicked voice. He viewed the camera feed inside the garage. Spotting flames, he zoomed in on the gun locker. Everyone gasped. Dead burnt bodies filled the room.

"Shit!" Joseph yelled, turning to Nora. "I warned you something like this was going to happen! We have a dead SWAT team, Tara and Katahdin are running around killing everyone! You sure had Tara under control the entire time!"

"Shut up," Nora screamed. She hissed when she saw Tara on the screen.

"Very mature," Dimitri commented, watching Tara give the middle finger. Brandon wheeled back in terror when she blew the kiss, knowing what it meant. She would always do that to him before one of them left the house.

"That's it, I'm out of here!" Brandon yelled, knowing his car was right out front. Joseph reached into his drawer, pulling out a pistol.

"No, the three of you are staying right here."

"What's the meaning of this?" Nora demanded. He pointed the gun at Brandon.

"You sold Tara to us." He moved the gun to Nora and Dimitri. "The two of you killed Tara's siblings. I had nothing to do with either of those things."

"What is your point?" Dimitri asked.

"I'm using you as trade bait. I hand the three of you over to Tara and Katahdin. In exchange for my life, I'll stop Omnipotent from hunting either of them down."

"Like hell I'm staying here!" Brandon said nervously. Joseph turned the gun on him. "Look, Mr. Jackson, my car is right outside. We can all escape. Live now, get revenge later."

Abruptly the sound of a gunshot filled the air. Joseph Jackson fell to the ground. Dimitri stood behind him, a light stream of smoke coming from his pistol. Nora spit on his body. "Like I said, I'm leaving!" Brandon ran out of the room. Nora started to follow him when Dimitri stepped in her path.

"Dimitri, what are you doing? We have to get out of here!"

"We're not going with him," he said, remaining where he was.

"Why not!" Nora demanded.

"Because Tara Cyrmic is waiting near Brandon's car," Dimitri said confidently. "Tara destroys our weapons and vehicles, leaving the cars out front our only route of escape. She wants Brandon dead so undoubtedly, she will be heading there."

Understanding his reasoning, Nora asked, "What do we do?"

◆　◆　◆

After killing Peter, Katahdin headed for the biodome. He locked the door, fearing someone would want to kill his animals in retaliation. He'd return to them when the battle was over. As he was about to leave, he heard approaching voices. He flew to the ceiling, pushing both talons into it and grabbing on to the support beam, his body flipped upside down. Suddenly a stream of bullets started coming through the door. Katahdin grunted in annoyance when he saw his room getting shot up. Bullet holes littered the walls, as many of his few possessions were being destroyed. Moments later the door was kicked in. Three Omnipotent troops, two men and a woman, entered the destroyed room.

"See anything, Steve?" Cody asked as he knocked over what was left of Katahdin's books.

"No, Cody. I don't think he's in here."

"Steve, he's above you!" Cody yelled in terror. Katahdin leaped over him. Flipping over, he moved both his elbow blades forward, slicing Cody and the woman's throats. Steven turned his gun. Katahdin jumped backwards, impaling Steve to the wall with his back spines. There was a squishing sound as Katahdin retracted his back spines. He sniffed the air, smelling smoke, and alarms started to go off around the facility. *Looks like Tara did what she wanted. I'll regroup with her later,* he thought as he exited the room. Now it was time to have a word with Dr. Bodkin.

Moments later, he was staring at Dr. Bodkin's office door. Black smoke was coming down the halls. Katahdin could feel the faint hint of heat from the approaching fire. As he reached for the handle, he heard:

"I hear guns don't have much effect on you." Katahdin turned to see Justin approach him, holding a fire ax. "Let's see how you fare against this."

Justin raised the ax, ready to attack. He and Katahdin circled for a moment. Justin brought the ax down, aiming for Katahdin's head. Katahdin side-stepped the strike. Off balance, Justin stumbled forward. Katahdin raised his elbow, sending his blade through Justin's shoulder. Justin fought through the pain and used his good arm to strike Katahdin with the ax. The first blow cracked the bone armor on his back, the second broke. Blood began spilling from the wound.

Not enough calcium left to heal, Katahdin thought, knowing he was nearing his limit. He retaliated with four strikes to Justin's ribs and chest. Blood flowed out of the many puncture wounds. Justin grunted and yelled in defiance as he slowly fell to the ground. On his knees he tried to swing the ax a final time. Before he could swing, Katahdin rammed the bone on his palm into his skull. With his final adversary dead, Katahdin kicked down Dr. Bodkin's office door to find him calmly sitting down.

"My son, have you come to stay goodbye?" he calmly asked. Katahdin found himself confused by Dr. Bodkin's clam demeanor. *Did he not know what was going on?*

"All my life, everything you ever told me was a lie!" Katahdin said with rage.

"Not everything," Dr. Bodkin replied. "The world I told you about has not yet come to pass." Dr. Bodkin looked forward like he was seeing something beyond both of them. He then looked at Katahdin and said, "I'm disappointed, you were meant for great things, and now I'm afraid, like the girl, you will have to be disposed of."

"You're not touching either of us! I want the truth! Why have you been lying to me? Keeping me locked in that room? To make money? Why?" Katahdin needed to know the truth. He needed to know why the man he respected and admired had betrayed him. Dr. Bodkin slowly rose.

"Katahdin, you want the truth?" Katahdin nodded his head, keeping a close eye on the good doctor. "You were to be a solider that was meant to help bring the current world to an end, and then bring a new world into existence." Dr. Bodkin's face took on a more menacing tone. "That is what I command." Katahdin continued his malicious stare. Dr. Bodkin rippled open the medical cabinet door and pointed to the statue. "That is what he commands!" Katahdin looked at the grotesque statue, wondering what he meant. By this time the rapidly spreading fire had reached their section of the building. Falling debris started falling from the ceiling, creating a barrier between the two. Dr. Bodkin's face slowly disappeared behind a wall and smoke and burning wood. "We will meet again," Dr. Bodkin said with assurance in his voice. A sound that sounded like the cry of wailing wind began filling the room. Before Katahdin could get to him, the entire celling collapsed.

Chapter 30

After safely exiting the building, Brandon rushed towards the driveway. His silver luxury car was one of three parked in it. He turned to see flames rising, and spreading across other parts of the facility. He pulled out his keys, rapidly clicking the unlocked button. He was about to place his hand on the door handle when a bullet struck the window, shattering it. Brandon screamed in alarm, stumbling down. In the gravel, a shadow appeared. He turned his head to see Tara standing several yards from him.

"Hey, baby!" she said with wide, exaggerated, happy eyes and a wide, cheerful smile. Her expression changed to a cold, bitter stare. "Do you have any idea what I've been through?" Brandon opened his mouth to speak. "Do you have any idea?" Tara again asked, this time in a loud, crazed scream. Brandon could not believe the girl standing in front of him was Tara. Her happy, carefree steps were replaced by a slow menacing walk. A cold, hateful stare replaced her warm bubbly eyes, her angelic smile replaced with a crazed look of malice.

"Tara, please..." Tara fired her pistol, hitting the car door.

"Shut up. Just shut up," Tara said in a crazed voice. "On my first day here, Nora told me you were behind this, but I didn't believe her. I spent each night dreaming about being held by you, comforted by you. Turns out she was telling the truth. I want to know why you did this to me!" Tara fired another shot near him. "Now!"

"Tara, I had no choice, okay!" Brandon quickly added, "Dimitri contacted me. He told me I could either take the money or he'd kill both of us and our families." *No, you're lying,* Tara thought.

"Liar!" Tara screamed.

"Why do you think I came here? When we were alone, I was going to tell you everything, then we could escape through the window." The crazed look on Tara's face turned to a look of uncertainty. *Is he telling the truth?* Tara thought, wanting to believe it.

"Ryan and Romy are both…" She tried but could not finish. Brandon stood up.

"I never intended for them to die. I'm so sorry you had to go through that, through all of this, but you made it, you survived." He reached out his hand for Tara to take. Tara backed up, pointing the gun at him. Brandon pulled his hand back in surrender. "If you shoot me, what family will you have left?" Brandon asked. Tara's face began to show some emotion.

"I don't have anyone left," Tara said, lowering the gun and sadly kicking some gravel.

"You have me and I love you," Brandon said passionately. Tara slowly looked up.

"How can I trust you, after what you did?" Tara asked, moving a few steps closer to him.

"Times heals all wounds. Right now you need to make a choice: do you live alone and in fear or do you work with me to take down these people?" Tara put her head down again, her body slightly moving side to side as she thought. Finally she looked up at Brandon and extended her hand.

"Take me home," she said softly. Brandon happily reached out for her hand. Right before they touched, Tara fired the gun, the bullet striking Brandon in the knee. He hit the ground screaming in pain.

"You…you bitch," he cried.

"You really think I'd fall for your fake caring act?" Tara asked, her look of malice returning. "No. You knew exactly what you were doing." Brandon tried to grab Tara, or knock her over with his legs. She effortlessly avoided the attempts. "Now what to do with you. Earlier your friends wanted to cut my limbs off and leave me alive." She playfully snapped her finger. "I think that would be perfect for you." Tara watched as Brandon broke into a panic with fright and pain seemingly clouding his judgment. Brandon started to crawl under his car, trying to create a barrier between them. Tara waited until his head and upper body were under it, then fired a shot into the back tire. Brandon start screaming and begging for help. The weight of the car trapped him. Tara sat down.

"Tara, please!" he cried.

"Baby, I need to confess I'm so glad we get to spend your final moment together." She slammed her knife into the front tire and slowly started letting the air out. Brandon's screaming increased, his arms frantically trying to lift the car off him. "Did you say something? I really can't understand you?" Tara taunted. Brandon continued to scream until a loud crunching sound occurred. Brandon's screams halted, his arms fell to his sides, his legs occasionally twitching. A steady stream of red started flowing from under the car.

Tara brushed her hands together and got up, giving Brandon's body one last kick for good measure. Suddenly a sharp pain filled Tara's shoulder, followed shortly by the crackle of a gun. She spun around to see a car coming towards her. She recognized Dimitri and Nora Peters in the front seats. Dimitri had his pistol pointed at her. She dropped to the ground right before he fired again. She aimed her own pistol and returned fire, the bullets hitting the front of the car. She aimed higher and fired again, and this time the bullet struck the windshield, creating a small hole webbing pattern. She tried to fire another shot but the gun only made a click. Tara cursed in frustration, throwing the empty gun at the passing car. Tara jumped on the hood of Brandon's car.

"I'll hunt you down wherever you go!" she screamed. She watched the car disappear from view, her clenched teeth making a hissing sound. Two of the three people that had destroyed her life had gotten away. In a way she was glad. Once Nora was dead, she had planned on ending it, joining Ryan and Romy in death. Now she had a new purpose in life, a new driving force inside her. When the depression and sorrow of her siblings' death hit her, she could use that purpose as a reason to keep on living. She looked towards the heavens. "Romy, Ryan, I'll avenge you, I promise. I'll kill both of them. I don't care how long it takes me, I'll burn Omnipotent to the ground! I won't leave a single person involved with them alive." She looked towards the burning mansion; that hell that used to be her prison was collapsing. She smiled a sinister smile when a bat-like creature flew from the wreckage and started heading towards her.

Epilogue

"That's my story. That's how I survived a nightmare," Tara said, standing in front of a good-sized audience at Buffalo State College. Some of the audience members believed her, others didn't know what to think of her fascinating story. Since her escape a month ago, her story had gotten international attention. The event organizers had asked her several times to share her story. She finally accepted under the condition she could wear a mask and her identity was kept secret. Tara sat down and the event organizer Tommy Birchwater took the stand.

"Thank you, Ms. Jane. Does anyone have a question for Ms. Jane?"

A young man stood up and said, "First off, I'm very sorry you had to experience all that tragedy and pain. My question is, what happened to that, um, creature. Katahdin?"

"I don't know," Tara replied. "I couldn't forgive him for my siblings' death so we went our separate ways. What's important is this group Omnipotent is still out there. Abducting people like me every day. Despite the danger to my own life, I'm never going to stop speaking about this until I bring the organization down."

Tara took a few more questions, then got into a cab. After driving several miles, the cab stopped.

"Are you sure this is the place?" the cab driver asked. The only building in sight was an abandoned warehouse with a rusty fence surrounding it.

"Yes, my family's renovating his place. I keep my car here to avoid city traffic." Tara paid him and got out. Once the taxi left, another car parked in its place. Two large men got out. Tara noticed them and nervously watched them as she walked towards the gate. The two men started to walk towards her. "What do you want?" Tara asked nervously. "I don't have any money, so there no point robbing me."

"We don't want money. Omnipotent pays us well enough to silence loose ends." Tara screamed for help, rushing inside the warehouse. The two assassins entered, thinking they were in for a short game of cat and mouse. When they entered the warehouse, to their surprise Tara was standing calmly in the middle of the room.

"Pretty convenient place. It's quiet, no one can hear someone screaming." She calmly placed a stick of gum in her mouth and asked, "How stupid can you guys be? Thought it would take a lot more effort to lure you here. Nora Peters must really want me dead." Before either man could react, a bone burst through one of the assassin's throats. "Worked like a charm!" Tara said, walking over to Katahdin, who had his palm bone dug into the surviving assassin's shoulder. She walked around them. "Do you like my new hair color?" she asked, waving her dark blue hair around. She pulled her hand through her bangs, which were dyed red, light blue, and yellow. Tara pulled a knife from her belt. "Want to know why my hair is colored like this?" she asked as she ripped the shirt off the dead assassin. The man spit and cursed at her. "I'll take that as a yes," Tara replied, sinking the knife into the dead man back. "Yellow and red were my brother and sister's favorite colors. The same brother and sister that Omnipotent murdered. Light blue was my favorite color; it reminds me of my old life. A life Omnipotent destroyed." Tara carved a star symbol into the dead man's back, then she stood over her captive. Her bubbly expression turned serious. "I was once forced to obey you, but now you're going to tell me everything I want to know."

Author Note

Thank you for reading *How I Survived A Nightmare*. If you enjoyed the book, please consider leaving a review on your favorite online book purchasing site.

About the Author

Vance Albright has been writing in some form or another since he was five. Throughout high school he wrote several book drafts but always fell into the trap of never finishing them. During college, he temporarily gave up on fiction writing to focus on his studies. After graduating, he renewed his love for writing and started working on Depths of Paradise and published it in 2019. After completing Depths of Paradise, Vance started Light and Dark Novelizations to begin creating his own universe of characters. Vance believes compelling storylines and believable characters that capture the reader's interest are the keys to a good novel. Vance is currently working on the Children of Fate series in which Depths of Paradise and How I Survived A Nightmare are a part of. The series is a shared contemporary fantasy universe with action/adventure and horror elements to each story.

Vance graduated from high school in 2008, and in 2016 he earned a B.S. in Environmental Science and minored in Biology. He is currently working in the environmental technician and horticulturalist fields.

Vance always has been an animal lover. He currently has two cats, Luna and Nova, three parakeets, and a tropical and brackish fish tank.

Vance's hobbies other than writing are watching football (Steelers and Packers are my favorite teams), martial arts, hiking, video gaming, collecting Godzilla figures, and 90s toys.